OVERNIGHT!

It was only a matter of hours. And the fate of the nation was in the hands of a relatively unknown young man named Mike Winston. The White House and its top echelons was paralyzed with fear and indecision. Several cabinet members and opinion leaders had already been killed.

The atmosphere was tense and ugly. The explosiveness pervading the capital needed only a spark. . . .

Two power structures were at loggerheads. The whites had controlled things for too long. The blacks were anxious to even things up a bit . . . and now they had the manpower and weaponry to force the issue.

The cooler heads on both sides were at an impasse as hotblooded factions cried for a showdown.

Into this chaos stepped Mike Winston. His destiny roared shudderingly to a halt—and wavered precariously—as he grabbed the hot-line telephone and made the decision that he hoped would prevent a national disaster.

CIVIL WAR II

by Don Pendleton

PINNACLE BOOKS • NEW YORK CITY

CIVIL WAR II

Copyright © 1971 by Pinnacle Books, Inc.

An original Pinnacle Books edition, first published under the author's pseudonym, Dan Britain, and based upon his original story, *Revolt!*

ISBN: 0-523-00758-2

First printing, October 1971
Second printing, January 1972
Third printing, November 1975

Cover photograph by Cosimo Scianna

Printed in the United States of America

PINNACLE BOOKS, INC.
275 Madison Avenue
New York, N.Y. 10016

CIVIL WAR II

FOREWORD

The time is late 20th century, the place is America, and the circumstances are . . . ominous. Three decades of upheaval and redirection have produced a new rural nation . . . almost. Metropolitan centers of commerce have been replaced by gleaming strip-cities, linear communities geared to the housing and servicing of the citizens of an agricultural economy. A small number of favored great cities of the past have been carefully preserved and virtually enshrined as cultural centers; a large number have crumbled into great ghastly hulks, incredible ghettoes utterly abandoned by most Americans but grimly clung to as the final refuge of a despairing and poverty-ridden minority of some twenty million citizens. These giant ghettoes, once proud cities, are now generally referred to as, simply, "the Towns."

As a contrast to the national gloom and depression of the seventies and early eighties, when the nation lost its prominence in the world markets, America has turned her technological genius into the perfection of agricultural techniques and has become the grocer of a world slowly falling into piecemeal starvation. International tensions now revolve chiefly about the food problem and other ecological considerations; the former "nuclear powers" have been defanged by the obviously suicidal nature of their arsenals—no wars are fought today which could endanger man's precarious balance with his environment.

The lifestyle of the average American has undergone vast changes—economically, politically, philosophically. The focus of government has altered radically since the series of constitutional amendments which began in the early 80's. With one important exception, the new look in the economy has produced, on the surface at least, a truly classless society in which the general preoccupation is with more and better ways to produce and package foodstuffs for the world market. The national philosophy has been altered accordingly. Problems involving domestic economy have been neatly resolved through automation, and the Automated Monetary System—a computerized complex evolved from the old credit card schemes and now wholly federally controlled—has completely replaced the archaic currency method of monetary exchange. Some would even say that AMS has replaced the archaic forms of American government.

That one exception to the classless society, mentioned above, rests with the people whom America has tried to forget. These have been split into three principal classes:

the residents of the nation's towns;

low-echelon federal civil service employees;

and the armed forces.

The first and largest of these three sub-classes are generally referred to as, simply, *town niggers*; the second and third collectively as *government niggers*. Within these classifications exist all of black America, but for another negligible exception, that small number who live and work in the white society—the *Uncle Toms*.

There has been no "racial problem" in America for most of two decades. Indeed, there have been few apparent problems of any nature during the past few years of this nation's history. Deep within the nation, however. . . .

BOOK I

OMEGA PROJECT

CHAPTER 1

Michael Winston left the pedestrian tube at the heliport atop the San Francisco Hilton and went directly to the Avis hovercar ramp. The powerfully built figure was impressively garbed in a conservatively-tailored knit suit of the new *sheenthetics*, a glossy black double-breasted affair with built-in climatizer. He stood impatiently shifting his weight from one leg to the other as the attendant brought the hovercar down, then he turned briefly to inspect his image in the window of the rental office. Handsome in a square-jawed, rugged manner, the National Commissioner of Urban Affairs was athletically trim and even a little mean-looking when he wanted to be. At the moment, he had caught the reflecting glint of premature silver at his temples and was suddenly struck with the realization that he was getting old.

"Thirty-six," he murmured half aloud. "Forget it, Pops, breathe twice and you'll be forty-six."

The Avis attendant had just stepped out of the hovercar. He gave Winston a curious glance and asked, "Sir?"

"Talking to myself," Winston told him, smiling. "Sure sign of old age, they say."

"Yes sir. Uh, this is the new twenty-one-hundred model, sir. The air jets are automatically programmed for—"

Winston said, "Yes, I know." He turned over his AMS

11

Creditor to the youth and watched disinterestedly as the boy slipped the plasticized card through an aperture in a small box worn at his waist. There was a barely perceptible click and the card popped out the other end of the box.

The attendant returned the creditor and commented, "F-VIP. And it's about expired, sir."

"What's that?" Winston asked absently, his mind elsewhere.

"Your monetary card. It's about to expire."

"Oh yes. Thanks."

Winston climbed into the little one-seater and stowed his briefcase, then went through the formalities of the pre-flight checklist and cranked the engine. A smooth hum told him that the powerplant was perfectly meshed, and a moment later he was airborne and slipping gently toward San Francisco Bay.

The grand old city, one of the few remaining cultural centers for whites, gleamed at him in the morning sun. No problems down there, he was thinking. No Winston-type problems, anyway. Cities like San Francisco were meticulously cared for—practically enshrined—by a nation gone back to the land but highly conscious of the value of cultural centers such as these. The *towns*, now—the *towns* were a different matter altogether, and all twenty of them together constituted a massive headache for men like Winston who worried about such things. Not that there were many men in that category—but of course he was being paid to worry.

A tone sounded on the console in front of him, announcing his incursion into the automated airflow control zones. He punched a button and announced, "Hover-Ford, Four-Five-Nine-Alpha. Enroute San Francisco Hilton to Oakland Town Central. Request uncontrolled transit."

An automated voice whirled back from a speaker in the ceiling to inform him that the request could not be granted, due to "congestion." Winston sighed and sat back with arms folded across his chest as the hovercar's controls were taken over by the electronic traffic flow-er. He did not mind being talked to by a computer, nor even ordered around by one. He did resent being shunted around a fifty mile course to cover an eight mile journey.

The automated flowlane would carry him across the Golden Gate and then over the upper bay for a southerly approach to his goal. Winston lit a cigarette and tried to think of something other than the unpleasant business awaiting him in Oakland. The electric cal-chron on the dashboard was indicating 08:39AM-09MAR-1999. Below him at the moment were the lush fields and terraced hillsides of the Marin headlands. A few years back, he was thinking, there had been nothing down there but rugged wastelands and sprawling subdivisions.

Now, thanks to the breakthrough into agricultural technology, there was field after lovely field of lettuce and cabbage and tomatoes and cauliflower—once plunging mountainsides were now beautifully terraced with avocado and grapes and Lord knew what else—and off in the distance the gleaming plastics of the new Marin Strip City reaching all the way to San Rafael in a quarter-mile-wide swath through the fields, where the workers lived and worked and played and laughed and loved. Yes, back to nature, that was the ticket—but Michael Winston was headed back to the ghetto, and that was a ticket of a different color.

Some minutes later he hit the Oakland approach lane and heard the controls cycling over to manual. Directly below was Berkeley and what had once been the campus of the largest university in the land. It, too, had passed—removed from the proximate danger of Oakland and consolidated at the Los Angeles campus, where nice white kids would not daily face the danger of eyeball confrontation with the black rabble of "town."

Winston shook his head over the memories of things passed, and dropped into the five hundred-foot corridor for town central. Not much traffic here, for sure. What damn fool would wish to drop in on a million town niggers?

The car settled into the pad with a gentle sigh. As Winston threw the door open and stepped into the town, he felt like an alien visitor from another planet. A couple of hundred blacks had moved into a semi-circle about the pad

13

and were standing there gawking at him.

"It's Uncle Mose," declared an anonymous voice.

Sure, Winston had heard that one before too. The cynical tag was meant to infer the exact opposite of an Uncle Tom. Winston was not impressed by tags. He grabbed his briefcase, set his shoulders, and marched straight at the crowd. A wide avenue opened for him and he passed through and onto the steps of town hall. A little boy of about four toddled down to meet him, eyes aglow with curiosity and ivory gleaming from ear to ear. *He's never seen a white man.* Winston thought to himself. A breathless mother appeared from somewhere and whisked the child away. Never fear, mother dear, Uncle Mose won't *eat your child.*

The news of his arrival had preceded him, and Mayor John Harvey was standing there in the doorway to greet him. A rotund black man of about fifty, Harvey always managed to greet his visitors at the front door of town hall. Winston could not decide whether it was some sort of a safe-passage guarantee or simply a status symbol to be seen with the money-man from Washington. And somehow there always seemed to be a crowd of people standing around outside town hall and roaming the corridors inside for what possible motive Winston could not fathom. Not just here in Oakland but in all the towns everywhere.

He shrugged away the feeling of desperate depression and stuck a smile on his face as he wrung the big black hand of Mayor Harvey. They walked arm in arm along the corridor and passed startled and curious black faces which seemed never to tire of gazing into a white one. When they reached the Mayor's office, both men stopped smiling and began fiddling with material objects—Harvey at his desk and Winston in his briefcase.

Sure, Uncle Mose from Mars—and now what do these two aliens say to each other to crash the communications barrier?

Harvey was first. He cleared his throat noisily and said, "We expected you last week, Commissioner."

"I got hung up at Cleveland," Winston explained.

He made a face and added, "You think *you* have

14

problems. Cleveland has three miles of clogged sewers and a polio epidemic. Can you imagine *polio* in 1999?"

"Sure, I can imagine it," Harvey replied quietly. "We had it here in '97—why not Cleveland in '99?"

"No sense to it, John. You know that." Winston withdrew a sheaf of papers from his briefcase and dropped them on the Mayor's desk, then he stepped to the window to gaze onto the grimy ghetto streets.

"Why are there always so many people on the streets?" he asked in a cool tone. "They never seem to be doing anything in particular. They're just *there*."

"I guess they just want to prove they're alive or something," the Mayor replied, sighing. He was flipping through the tabulated sheets from Washington.

Winston said, "Put them to work, John."

"You know I can't do that."

"Why not? Pass out waste baskets, if nothing else. Let them pick the crud up off the—"

"What is this shit?" Harvey cried, suddenly slapping the desk with the stack of papers.

Without turning away from the window, Winston told him, "You're getting cut again, John. That's what it is."

"Hell I can see that! But I can't believe it! How can they *cut* me? Dammit, Commissioner, I requested an eight percent *increase*! I can't live with a cut. I *won't* live with it."

Winston sighed and left the window to drop into a chair facing the desk. "I warned you last time about those work refusals, John."

He raised his hands and dropped them. "You're not operating at maximum employment potential, and you know it."

His eyes wavered from the harsh gaze of the black man and shifted to the stack of papers. "It's all in the tab run, and you can't argue with a computer."

"Screw your goddam whitey computer," Harvey muttered. "I don't want arguments, I want *credits*." He sighed heavily and asked, "All right, how much of a cut?"

Winston lit a cigarette and exhaled noisily toward the ceiling. "I warned you last time . . . I told you what would happen. Four and a half percent, John."

"Dirty bastards! The dirty rotten whitey bastards! Okay, what is it? It's not the work refusals, is it? So what is it? That little bit of noise on the Bay Bridge last month? The excursion to Castro Valley? Listen, we disciplined those kids. And that's all it was, *kid* stuff, regardless of what you damned honky newspapers had to say about it. We don't need to be slapped with a four and a half percent cut to stay in line."

Winston smoked quietly for a moment. The guy needed to save face, and Winston could stand a bit of abuse. Presently he said, "You know I can't do anything about the cut this time, John. Pull up your performance during this quarter and we'll try to restore it. You know the routine as well as I."

"Some routine," Harvey replied, snorting with repressed rage. "Listen, *you* listen. Those work refusals. You know what they were. Ten credits a day, in the Vallejo cabbage fields. *Ten credits.* The work is twelve hours long, the transportation day is four more hours. Sixteen damn hours a day, Commissioner, for ten lousy credits. White men in the very next field are getting *twenty five*, and they work eight hours, and their transportation day is ten minutes long. *Work* refusal!" He snorted some more, then muttered, "It's *slavery* refusal, Commissioner."

Winston returned his attention to the man at the desk and told him, "It's not the fields that are hurting you. It's your Uncle Tom quotas that are killing you."

"Oh, hell—*that* again," Harvey growled.

"Sure. You carried something better than a thousand unfilled requisitions this past quarter. That's a hell of a lot of jobs going begging, and permanent jobs at that."

"Permanent is right!" the Mayor yelled. "You call those *jobs*? That's worse slavery than the fields. It's twenty-four hours a day and it's total isolation in an alien world. I can't force my people out there to live with the whiteys!"

"What's so bad about it?" Winston wanted to know.

"You really don't know, do you."

"Frankly, no. I'd like it if I was a *light*—a fractional Negro. I'd get to live in a natural environment instead of in

16

this stinking cement ghetto. Instead of working fields in the hot sun or swinging back and forth on the factory shuttles or barely existing on a government handout, I could chauffeur some rich guy around, or take care of his garden—maybe even service his wife or daughter when nobody was looking. What's so damn tough about Uncle Tomming?"

"You really don't know."

Winston shook his head. "No, dammit, I don't."

"The black man has his pride, Winston. Even a *fractional* black man. He's not going out there and serve Ol' Massa, not for all the material comfort in the world. And living like that is grinding to a man's soul. You can't expect a man to live totally isolated from his own kind."

"A lot of 'em are doing it," Winston pointed out.

The Mayor shook his head adamantly. "Not *real* black men, Winston. Black is not in the color of skin, it's in the quality of soul. No black men are serving Ol' Massa. Uncle Toms, sure. But no black men."

Winston was certain that they had repeated this stale argument several thousand times. But he went on. "And the federal blacks? What of them? Four million of your people, John, serving Ol' Massa on the federal payroll, practically *running* Ol Massa's white establishment for him, and protecting him against foreign adventures to boot."

"Not *my* people," the Mayor insisted. "A government nigger is even worse than a Tom, and you know it. Those people live in a fool's dream. Some day they're going to wake up and feel those chains on their ankles."

Winston sighed and leaned across the desk to put out his cigarette. "Try to improve your performance figures this quarter, John," he suggested. "You do and I'll get that four and a half percent back for you."

"And in the meantime what do we do?" Harvey asked dismally. "This town is bankrupt, as of the minute you walked in that door. I wanted that eight percent raise for street repair. As bad as the streets are, we needed the jobs even worse. Instead, you're taking away. We have no tax base now. What good does it do us to send out Uncle

Toms? A few bucks off the dole roll, sure, and that's a drop of sweat in the bay. What we need is—"

"Get that performance curve climbing," Winston interrupted with a heavy sigh. "You know that's the only thing that counts."

"*People* count."

"Not to a computer, John." Winston picked up his briefcase and went to the door.

The black man remained dejectedly at his desk, eyes studying the palms of his hands.

Some of the starch went out of the Commissioner of Urban Affairs and he muttered, "Dammit, I feel as bad about this as you do, John." He went on through the outer office, showed the pretty receptionist a sober smile, and made his way through the heavy traffic of the corridor, stonily avoiding the stares being directed his way. Then, on an impulse, he spun about and retraced his steps to the mayor's office.

The receptionist was disappearing through the doorway to the private office. Winston crossed quickly, followed her to the threshold, and pushed his shoulders through for a quick word.

The girl had turned about and was regarding him with obvious confusion and indecision, frozen in her tracks halfway across the big room. Harvey was standing behind his desk and grinning at two other black men who were entering from an adjacent office. His grin also froze as he became aware of Winston's presence.

The two men in the opposite doorway halted momentarily, and it appeared for an instant that they were going to turn and leave. Then the one in the lead smiled at Winston and came on in.

Winston's gaze flashed across to the dismayed face of Mayor Harvey, and he told him, "I just wanted to say, John, that I am not a computer. I'll delay the funding for a week. Give me at least an indication of a promising curve characteristic and I'll override the machine's decision."

Harvey showed him a glassy smile and replied, "Thanks, Commissioner. I appreciate that."

Winston nodded at the other two, pulled the door shut,

18

and returned without further dalliance to the hovercar. He rose quickly to the transit altitude, then used his F-VIP code to request an immediate uncontrolled transit to San Francisco International Airport. The airflow computer responded without hesitation to the F-VIP override and cleared him for direct flight.

With a bit of scrambling he could make the nine-thirty commuter to Washington. It had suddenly become very urgent that he do so. He wanted to determine if General Jackson T. Bogan, Army Chief of Combat Forces and the country's highest ranking Negro officer, had a spitting-image double. If not, then he wanted to know if the nation's top government nigger made a practice of donning civilian clothes and visiting towns in the company of Abraham Lincoln Williams, lord high potentate and soul daddy of all town niggers everywhere—and why they should be so upset over the discovery of their visit to Oakland Town by a lowly Commissioner of Urban Affairs.

Not that anything had made much sense in the Negro world for the past few years—but there were some things that even a second-echelon bureaucrat could not swallow. Mike Winston could not swallow Bogan and Williams tiptoeing about the back rooms of the Oakland town hall, even if he could accept the mere fact of them being together.

And somehow he knew, the entire scene with John Harvey had been some sort of silly game. The guy hadn't been really concerned about the budget cuts, and even less impressed with Winston's second-thought offer to personally intervene in the funding settlement.

So what *was* he concerned about? And Bogan, and Williams. What the hell were *they* so concerned about?

Mike Winston did not know. But he for damn sure was going to find out.

CHAPTER 2

It had once been the home stadium for a national champion football team, and there had been times when eighty thousand and more fans had lifted roaring approval to the heavens over the legal mayhem being committed across the artificial turf of the playing field. Cheers and chants had long since disappeared and the tiers of seats lifting in all directions toward the skies were showing the evidence of years of crumbling neglect. Still, the stadium had become the hope, the dream, and the rallying point for the million black townsmen of Oakland—and was regarded as the unofficial soul-quarters of some twenty million others.

Now, tall, muscular young men practiced games of another sort here. They were games of survival and death. Here they learned the games of war and the machines of war. They learned to shoot, unemotionally and accurately, and they learned how it felt to be shot at. And here they dreamed of war and plotted for war and prayed for war. This place was called *The Warhole*, because that's what it was—a hole in space, a place of stealth for men who plotted for dignity and freedom.

Abraham Lincoln Williams paced up and down the former locker room, now operations central for the

Western Division of the Black Militia, impatiently awaiting the arrival of Norman Ritter, Chief of Militia Intelligence and also, officially, Special Intelligence Aide to the U.S. Army Chief of Staff.

The others were already present—General Bogan, in charge of all black military operations, legal and otherwise; Mayor Harvey, senior civil authority for the western region; and Major General Hawley Matthews, Commanding Officer of the U.S. Air Force Tactical Air Command.

Williams stepped to the open doorway and gazed out. Norman Ritter—a thick and powerfully built man of indeterminate age, soft red hair and freckled skin—was moving briskly along the ramp.

Williams moved back inside as Ritter hit the outer door and all but exploded into the operation center. The man's every movement seemed to be accompanied by an explosive release of stored energy; he moved quickly and bouncily whether the task be climbing a stairway or lighting a cigarette. He passed in front of Williams, showed him an upraised fist, and plowed into a chair with a backward fling that would have rendered some men unconscious.

Williams got to the point immediately. "They're onto us," he declared simply, his eyes on Ritter.

The intelligence chief shrugged. "Had to happen sooner or later," he said mildly. "Who got smart?"

"Who else? Our esteemed Uncle Mose from the Urban Bureau. Our old buddy-buddy Mike Winston, the white man with a conscience."

"What exactly does he know?" Ritter asked, smiling grimly.

Williams dropped into a chair at the head of the small conference table. "I don't know," he replied. "But enough to make him suspicious and wondering, I know that much. That guy is danger, with a capital *D*. There was a time when he was one of the most awesome men in Washington."

"In the Urban Bureau?" the air force general asked humorously.

21

"Hell no, before that," Ritter put in. "He was one of the first federal cops when the FBI was revamped. Got into some kind of trouble. But don't think he's not just as dangerous. I've been uneasy as hell, frankly, ever since they transferred that guy into Urban."

"You think maybe it was a cover transfer?" Williams asked. "And you're just now mentioning it?"

"All you had to do was ask *me*," General Bogan said. "I've known about Winston all along. His trouble was genuine, nothing put up about it. He got busted, pure and simple. And I can tell you why. He wouldn't go along with their programmed suppression of the blacks. It's as easy as that. So old Arlington thought he was being cute by transferring an Uncle Mose into Urban. An act of mercy, he called it at the time. Mercy!"

The general laughed, a gentle wheezing. "By presidential direction, Mike Winston was transferred to the Urban Bureau instead of being drummed out of federal service. And after all these years, it probably turns out to be the smartest move old Arlington ever made."

"All right," said Williams, "let's forget about Winston's troubles and talk about our own. When that guy starts digging, what's he going to find?"

Ritter shuffled his feet nervously but said nothing.

Mayor Harvey spoke up, almost apologetically. "I imagine he'll start by looking at the Toms."

"Why that?" Ritter, the intelligence man, asked quickly.

Harvey shrugged the massive shoulders. "Because I think he's already starting to wonder about that. You've been gobbling them up too fast, Norm. Faster than we can shove in replacements. Yeah. That's next. He'll start wondering why so many Tom requisitions these past few years."

"Well, then, that will really cut it," Williams declared angrily. "I warned you to be discreet about that business, Norm."

"Oh bullshit!" Ritter railed back. "Where else am I going to get operatives who can move about freely?"

"Norm's right, of course," General Bogan put in quietly. "Let's not fall into what-if's and what-might-have-been's.

Let's talk about the current problem."

"Is there any way to head Winston off at the pass?" General Matthews inquired.

"I'm looking into that," Ritter growled. "I got a position report on him just before I came over .He hopped the commuter to Washington—" The intelligence chief glanced at his watch and frowned. "—just about twenty minutes ago. Don't worry, he'll be picked up on the other end and we'll be on his every move."

"Why not just discreetly dispose of him?" Matthews mildly suggested.

"Not until we know for sure how deep he's gone," Ritter shot back. "We want no loose ends flapping about."

"Norm's right, of course," Williams said. "So okay. Assume that Winston is definitely onto the Omega Project. What will he do? What *can* he do?"

"He'll have to present his case to Arlington, of course," Bogan murmured.

"Clear to the top, immediately?" Williams asked.

The General nodded his head and replied, "Wouldn't you? Besides, he's gone back up the ladder rather quickly in Urban. There's no one between him and the President but the bureau chief. And that guy is a total zero. Yes, that's where I'd go with it. Directly to the top. Where else can he go?" Bogan smiled. "Not to the military, that's for sure. And the federal police . . . well . . ." The old soldier shrugged his shoulders. "I imagine he wouldn't feel too comfortable there."

"I don't know," Mayor Harvey put in. "Winston is gutsy. He'd go to the FBI if he thought he had a case."

"Just what I was thinking," Abe Williams agreed. "That's exactly where Arlington would go, too. He'd have to. He would be moving for a quick and quiet bust, no fanfare, no panic, no loss of face to the administration. The federal cops would be swarming us like hornets in no time at all, and we'd all just quietly disappear." He smiled grimly. "Never to be seen or heard again in the world of living things."

"That wouldn't stop anything," Ritter pointed out.

"No, but Arlington would probably think it might. He's

smart enough to know how long it takes to set up a thing like this. He'd have no way of knowing how far it has gone."

"Any move they make now will simply cause wider bloodshed," Bogan observed. "If they get to us first . . ."

"Right," Williams said. "The boys would run wild. Okay. We have to stop Winston. We have to stop him dead."

"And advance our timetable," Ritter declared.

"Will that be necessary?" Williams murmured.

Bogan sighed and said, "Yes. We have everything to lose and absolutely nothing to gain by idling along now."

A silence of some thirty seconds followed Bogan's declaration. It was Abe Williams who broke in. He cleared his throat noisily and said, "All right. Let's advance the timetable. Let's move tonight."

Another brief silence, then Harvey said, "Can we do it?"

Williams was watching the military chief. Bogan scratched his head and turned his gaze to his military aide. "What do you think, Norm?"

Ritter jerked his head in a quick nod. "My boys have been up and ready for over a month now. From my end, yeah. Go."

The Air Force Chief said, "Naturally, TAC is always ready. Just give me an hour's notice."

Bogan sighed and turned his gaze to Mayor Harvey. "Well, my adjutant just completed a nationwide inspection of the militia. They seem ready, but I'm still a bit concerned about the discipline. They're eager and they've been penned up all their lives. I just hope we don't have a blood orgy."

Harvey blinked his eyes rapidly and said, "You don't have to worry about the Oakland units."

"I'll vouch for the readiness of the militia," Abe Williams said quickly. "They're ready. I guess the only loose ends we have are political. But we can work out the politics by ear."

"Okay," Bogan said, sighing heavily. "But just remember that the militia will be carrying the brunt. The regular army forces are largely specialists in the quick-reaction philosophy—brushfire teams." He glanced at Abe Williams. "I see no reason for a change in the battle order, do you?"

Williams shook his head. "None at all. Do you want me to contact Admiral Parks, or will you,"

"I'll get with him," Bogan replied. "I'm going to be busier than a cat covering up crap, though, so you'll have to work the readyline with the other units."

"I'll get them in," Williams solemnly assured the general.

"Then I guess that's it," Bogan said. "We hit tonight."

Ritter leapt to his feet and did a little dance alongside the conference table. "Hot damn, hot damn," he cried. "I can't hardly believe it. Tonight's the night, and oh what a night! Burn, baby, burn—and watch my fucking smoke. We're gonna jerk old whitey apart at the seams. Wait'll you see the chaos in the skies when I blow the whistle on automated airflow. And the gas mains, the power stations, communications—man, I got the whole world in my hand. I got the water systems, the fuel lines, the—"

"Don't forget your assassins," Harvey put in icily.

"Hell yes, I got death in my hand, too—and why're you all sitting around so gloomy? This is the day we've been awaiting for twenty years! Why the hell are you all looking so gloomy?"

Abe Williams smiled faintly and said, "The day of the black cat."

"Yeah," Ritter cried happily. "The day of the big black cat."

"Let's just leave ourselves someplace to live," Williams said. "Remember that. We have to live more than one day. So knock off the Sambo act, Norm. And I don't want any kill orgies. Understand? We stick precisely to the battle order."

Ritter's big moment was not to be dampened by censure from the chief. He laughed loudly and told Williams, "Sure, Abe, sure. You mad at me? Hell, I'm not mad at anybody. Hey, Jackson, I want one final review with you. I don't want our boys getting in each other's way. For God's sake, Jack, do you know what this means? Do you know

25

what day this really is? God, I don't believe it, I just can't believe it. Tonight's the night, and we're going to tear old whitey apart at the seams!"

"You'd first better be doing something about Mike Winston," Bogan pointed out.

"I'll do that. He'll be the first to come apart. First man out, Jackson, good old Uncle Mose Winston. And then just watch my fucking smoke!"

CHAPTER 3

Winston stepped from the moving sidewalk into the vestibule of the commuter, walked over to a battery of plastic boxes, selected the proper one, fed in his AMS card, then stepped over to the escalator gate. His card popped out of a rectangular tube and the gate opened to admit him. He shoved the card into a pocket and moved on to the upper deck of the giant aircraft. There, another plastic box awaited. He inserted his monetary card through a slot at the bottom of the box. An instant later it clicked out on top, bringing with it a thin rectangle of cardboard.

Winston returned the AMS card to his pocket and glanced at his berthing assignment, printed on the cardboard. He grunted with satisfaction, noting that he had drawn a forward dayroom, which meant more head-space for one thing. He decided, once again that there were compensations for the F-VIP coding on his AMS card. The "F"—indicating Federal—qualification to the VIP rating had usually managed to work against him, but the airlines must have known who was buttering their bread. And this was one time when Winston was prepared to appreciate it. He was unnerved, excited, his thoughts jumbled—and he needed that hour and a half of flight time to collect himself and try to pull together several years of casual observations

27

of goings-on in Black America. Not one thing, standing alone, meant a damn thing. But . . . put it all together and . . . it was enough to worry a guy.

He located his room, a six by ten cubicle, closed the accordion-type plastic door and immediately undressed. He AMS'd his suit through the tube to the valet shop even before the big craft left the ground and as soon as the safety light extinguished, indicating that they were airborne, he stepped into the shower stall and refreshed himself.

He could have been in a hotel room, for all the sensation of flight or even movement a guy got from these new supersonics. Had to hand it to the French—those people knew how to build flying machines. As Winston soaped down, he thought vaguely of the old lumbering airplanes of the eighties, the terribly inept, uncomfortable and dangerous cracker-boxes of the seventies and he was glad it was 1999. Imagine wasting half a day just getting from one coast to the other. He recalled his first air trip back in '70 or '71. He'd been about six. He smiled, remembering the excitement of that adventure. Some adventure! Two hours to get a thousand miles! Still, he had to admit, there'd been a vitality to that age. A vitality. Where had all the vitality gone? Had technological smoothness and monetary order sucked the guts out of the world?

Winston hadn't experienced thoughts such as these for years. They bothered him. What was it Abraham Lincoln Williams had said to him on that chance meeting in New Orleans a few months earlier? Williams was supposed to be an urban lobbyist, and that was something that had never rung quite true for Winston. What was the sense in lobbying? Nobody on Capitol Hill gave a damn for black problems anymore. Williams would be the first man to recognize that fact. The blacks had screwed themselves completely out of the national political picture when they all went to town. The way the country was apportioned now, they couldn't even get a seat in the House of Representatives.

Oh yeah, he remembered now what Williams had said to him. "There was a time," he told him in that quietly

28

troubled voice he managed so well, "when the black man thought he had a friend in you, Mr. Winston."

Well, shit! Winston hadn't turned the Negro's world over, they'd done it themselves. What the hell could they logically ask of anybody now? What was a guy supposed to do? Get up on a soap box and start preaching? And wind up with his ass nailed to a willow tree?

Thanks, Abe, no thanks, you quietly troubled black bastard. The world has seen enough crucifixions, they're not getting Winston's ass too. They almost did once. Once, Abraham Lincoln Williams, you people damned near got Winston's ass. And for what? Screw you, Black Abe, and your Buck Rogers' ghettoes, too. You asked for them, buddy, and you got just what you asked for. Call *me* an Uncle Mose, eh?

Winston turned off the shower, caught a glimpse of his snarling face in the revolving mirror, and laughed outright at the fierce countenance. But he still felt nettled as he stepped into the cabin—he could not get rid of it all simply by laughing. He went over to the table, lit a cigarette, studied the service box, decided he didn't want anything, then took his cigarette to the recliner and made himself comfortable. Windows! That's one thing he remembered and missed on these modern jobs. Windows! Once there were windows on airplanes. You could sit there at the window and look down to the earth, far below. Well, what the hell . . . never could see anything anyhow. You sure couldn't sit around bare-ass on one of those old crates. You couldn't get your suit pressed, or take a shower, or take a stewardess to bed. Hell, he didn't miss the damn windows.

He lay there in a quietly troubled reverie and finished the cigarette, then dropped the butt into the tube, puffed the pillows beneath his head and began trying to put the pieces back together in his head. His door opened and a pretty young woman stepped in. She wore the familiar sky-blue shortie smock of the Accomodations Stewardess. She smiled and moved to the table, picked up his AMS card and ran it through the service box, then shrugged out of the smock and posed for his inspection.

Accustomed as he was to female nudity, Winston gawked nevertheless. She was a tall girl, maybe five-nine or ten, her body flowingly arranged in rose-tinted hues of soft hills and vales and swinging planes. Her hair was some odd shade between black and red, the eyes wide-spaced—almost oriental—glowing with lights. A red gem, probably synthetic, adorned the deep dimple of her belly button.

"Acceptable?" she asked quietly, turning to give Winston the side view.

"I guess I got the wrong section," he growled.

She studied his face briefly, then said, "This is the accommodations suite. Didn't you want sexual accommodation?"

He shook his head, a bit uncertainly, and told her, "Not especially."

"Then you programmed the wrong box when you boarded," she said. "But as long as you're here . . ."

"Well, let's not, and just say we did," Winston murmured. "Nothing personal, tigress. I just . . . uh . . . want to lie here and think."

The girl moved on to the recliner nevertheless and perched on the edge, a warm hip pressing against him. "I already ran your card through," she pointed out. "You may as well get your ten minutes' worth. If you don't want sexplay, how about a little massage?" Her hands were already kneading the flesh of his arms, the delightful aroma of her creating a delicate atmosphere between the polarized bodies.

His hands merged with the soft warmth of her body. "Don't any girls of this generation ever wear hair?" he asked casually.

The girl wrinkled her nose at the remark and languidly wriggled her midsection in recognition of Winston's presence there. "Girls today don't have that kinkup," she told him. "Anyway, who needs hair *there*? The skin's the thing, isn't it?" She eased down and kissed him softly on the lips, bringing the rose-tipped breasts to rest on his chest. She found him with a free hand, giggled softly into his mouth, and playfully manipulated his torrid zone.

30

"What do you want massaged first?" she asked tauntingly.

Winston gently slapped her hip and said, "You win," and pulled her down beside him, his hands tracing the outline of smooth flanks and flawless femininity.

The girl laughed and pulled free, reasserting her command of the situation. "You sure don't need an energizer, do you," she commented.

"In my day, an exciting woman was all the energizer a guy needed."

"Here it comes," she said, sighing.

"Here what comes?"

"The lecture I get a dozen times a week. On the modern generation and chemical sex."

"I'm no lecturer," Winston told her, and showed her.

"Wait a minute!" the girl cried. She struggled to her feet and went to the service table, returning with two small plastic packets. She tore them open and shoved a wafer-thin tablet toward him. "Have a hype," she suggested.

"I'm hyped enough already," he assured her.

"You'll have to take it," she insisted. "It's a proph and a sterilizer too. Sorry, rules."

Winston knew all the damn rules. He accepted the wafer and popped it in his mouth.

The girl chewed hers, gave Winston a measuring look, then popped in another. "Okay," she said, sighing. "On your back, Flame."

"*I'm* on top," he informed her.

She sighed again, then smiled engagingly and moved onto the recliner, twisting onto her back and raising her arms for Winston's embrace. "The customer's always right," she murmured, the lovely face suddenly taking on an entirely new and hungered expression. She lurched against him and caught her breath in a sharp intake. "See how fast it works?" she gasped.

Sure, Winston knew how fast it worked. Artificial vitality, another technological breakthrough for a world quickly going flat and sterile. Another artificial abundance, a hype for the masses, a joyride into biological oblivion. Hell, he didn't care. This was an animal thing beneath him, an explosive and joyous animal released from the primeval jungle by 20th century chemical magic. Snarl, baby, snarl—and he'd ride her clear to hell and back if that's what it took to subdue the beast—and he knew very well that it would.

Sluggishly she said, "Your ten minutes are up, sir."

"Drop another nickel in."

"What?"

"Go run the card through again."

"I—I'm sorry. I don't think I could go again right now."

"Haven't you ever heard of after-play? Don't you find anything rewarding about just lying here, all shot to hell and breathing on each other, listening to each other's heartbeats, enjoying the—"

"I knew I'd get that lecture sooner or later."

"Forget it. If you want to leave, then leave. If you want to rest awhile between assignments, then go run the damn card through again. Suit yourself."

"Well . . . I could use a breather. This *is* nice."

"Sure it is."

"I'll run the card through on my way out. Okay?"

"Sure. Uh, how old are you, honey?"

"Old enough. I'll be graduating next month."

"From what?"

"From the accomodations section."

"Oh? I never knew it worked that way. What do you go to from here?"

"Flight service. You know—coffee, tea, or chemicals?"

"That's a graduation?"

"Well—the credits are better. And it's more fun—you know—you get to mingle more, move around more."

"See what you mean."

"Uh—I noticed you're an F-VIP. What bureau?"

"Urban."

"Urban what? What does that mean?"

"You've never heard of the Bureau of Urban Affairs?"

"Oh, that. Do you like blacks?"

"They're just people."

"I mean the *town* blacks."

"Yeah, I meant that too."

32

"I don't believe I ever saw one. Except pictures."

"Oh, sure. You've seen some, I know. You just didn't know it. They look just like the government blacks."

"But do you have to actually go *inside* those towns?"

Winston chuckled. "Yes, I do."

The girl shivered. "President Arlington says they live like animals."

He sighed, and told her in a conspiratorial whisper, "That could be because they're *treated* like animals." He pinched her thigh and added, "But no, they're just people. They get by the best they can."

"Well . . . what do they live like?"

"Are you really interested?"

"I guess so."

Winston pushed to an elbow and reached for a cigarette, lit it, and watched the girl through narrowed eyes. Presently he told her, "No, I doubt that I could ever make you understand. It's something you have to see for yourself."

The girl's eyes were speculating on him. She said, "I had a teacher once who talked like that. We used to have these rap sessions. He, uh, got fired. I always liked him. I guess he just had too many radical ideas."

"Yeah, well, don't look at *me* like that," Winston told her. "We can't afford radical idealists in this society. When one pops up, we all get together and tear him apart and nail what's left to a willow tree. Hey, this isn't afterplay talk. Give me your lips. Kiss me."

She smiled and melted against him, then wriggled suggestively and said, "You guys are just different."

"What guys?"

"You older guys. You're . . . romantic, I guess. Even about sex."

"Yeah. That's pretty terrible, isn't it."

"Oh . . . I don't know. Sometimes I get to thinking . . . like now. I feel funny."

"And without chemicals?"

She giggled and rooted against him. "It seems that you have enough for both of us."

Winston grinned and moved his hand onto a pulsing

33

breast. Odd, he thought, how public opinion shaped the bodies of every generation of women. He could remember a time when heavy bosoms and sleek legs were the focal point of a woman's sexual attractiveness. Somehow the women managed to shape themselves around those focal points. Now it was all in the curves of the rear . . . pulchritude of the posterior. He fanned his palm around, cupping a breast in a loving caress, then he pushed the girl's legs apart and. . . .

"Oh, yeah, great," she sighed. "But you're ruining me. I think I'm getting to like it better lying here looking up at you."

The overdeveloped muscles of her midsection rippled and grabbed for him as he lowered himself into moistly heated welcome. The girl gasped and rolled her eyes toward her forehead, wrapping her arms about his neck with a stifled little moan. Odd too, Winston reflected, how this undereducated and over-sexed young Amazon made him think of another girl, another place, and another long, long, time ago.

The girl ran his card through twice on her way out. She hesitated in the doorway, turned him a wan smile, and said, "See you around, Papa,"—and disappeared into the aisleway.

Winston watched the vacated doorway for a moment, then fell back to the pillows. Something was chugging around in his think chamber. He was tired, tired —exhausted was the word—and something, some deep something connected to the exhaustion was clamoring for attention.

Then it surfaced. Winston experienced the giddiness of illumination. *That's where our vitality has gone,* he realized. He lunged toward his cigarettes, lit one, inhaled deeply, then swung his feet onto the floor. *It's gone right into those overdeveloped asses!* Something bothering you, citizen? Well, hell, go get accomodated, that'll make you feel better. In plain English, *go get laid!*—get screwed!—get lost.

That's what they mean! Don't get mad, just get screwed.

Don't get depressed, just get screwed. Don't think about those pathetic starving creatures in Asia and Africa, just get screwed. Don't think about twenty million Americans penned up in Buck Rogers ghettoes, *just get screwed*. Talk about a screwed-up society!

An almost forgotten emotion was beginning to well up inside Winston's rocking head. *Rage*. He felt *rage*! But at what? What was he enraged about? Was there something left to get mad about in this country? Wasn't everything provided?

He could live any way he wished to live, couldn't he, so long as it was compatible with the little squiggle-lined engravings on his AMS card? Need somewhere to live, Charlie? Hell, drop your card in the box and get a housing assignment. It's all paid for. Just pray to God you never get a *town* override on your card.

Want some booze, Charlie? Jam your card in the service box, old buddy. Want a woman? AMS her, Charlie. Want something to eat? Just find the right box, old buddy. And if something comes up, Lord forbid, that you *want* and there's no *box* for, then just shove something into one of those always quivering and overdeveloped asses!

The *Passport to Abundance,* they'd called those cards. Passport to Abundance. Shit! *Passport to Sterility*! That's what it was. Winston had no idea, no idea whatever, what his annual earnings were. It was all figured out for him, as a matter of credits and debits, by some monster computer in Washington. The entire domestic economy was programmed by that monster. *The Abundant Society*! BULLSHIT!

It would seem that Winston's insights into the American society, and particularly the Automated Monetary System, were entirely valid. The plan, introduced by then Senator J. Humphrey Arlington of Alabama in 1984, was officially inaugurated on January 1, 1986, after a bitter and futile battle by the nation's banking interests to have the law declared unconstitutional. Opponents of the measure had pointed out that the end effect of AMS would be a rigid control of the national economy by the federal government, and eventual direct control of the lives and fortunes of all Americans. They hinted strongly that a major thrust of the bill was toward the control of minority groups, specifically the blacks, and that this control could easily be extended to include every American citizen. It appeared that, by the year 1999, this end had indeed been accomplished—certainly, without doubt, as regarded the black Americans.

And, with regard to the blacks, Winston's other insights were directly on target. A patient plan of years had come to an abruptly unplanned maturity, and the programmed abuse of a race covering an era of centuries was about to be run head-on into the new reality. The *Omega Project,* a plan designed to end an era, had led the way to a day beyond expectation. At least from one pale point of view.

CHAPTER 4

Birdie Howard watched the broad back of her husband as he pulled on the khaki shirt. Impulsively she stepped forward and gripped his shoulders, laying her face against the great strength there between the shoulder-blades. "I'm scared, honey," she whispered.

"Don't be scared," Bill Howard said gruffly. "This is a time for singing, not crying." He went on buttoning the shirtfront, opened the waist of his trousers, stuffed the shirt tails neatly inside. Then he turned to survey the cramped apartment, pulling his wife into his arms, squeezing her tightly to him.

"No more shadow living for these folks, Birdie," he reminded her. "No more crumbling buildings and nightmarey nights, no more eating powdered foods and fighting the rats. We're moving out into the sunshine, honey. We gonna bring our kids up in sight of God's heaven, and we gonna give 'em fields to play in, and a place to laugh and sing. Isn't that worth some risk?"

"If there's gonna be killing and bleeding, I'll stay here in town, Bill." She shivered violently. "I don't want no blood of yours trickling out on white folks' ground."

The black youth chuckled. "If my blood spills, maybe it'll look like the same color as theirs. Now look, we been

37

through this ten million times. Now something that ain't worth risking a little bit of blood for ain't worth wanting, is it? I'm not raising no kids in this town, Birdie. Not if all my kids wither up and die in my dead nuts. Now give me a smile and a kiss. I gotta go out there and get my weapons."

Birdie choked back a flood of tears, stretched to her toe tips, and gave her husband a soulful kiss.

"Hey," he said, grinning, "that's a let's-go-to-bed kiss."

"I don't know how to give go-on-off-and-get-killed kisses," she replied.

He laughed and slapped her bottom. Then he took one last long look about the tiny "efficiency" apartment, a place where his life had centered, as though looking at it for the last time. He gave her another quick peck, pushed her away, and Lt. Bill Howard of the Hattiesburg Town Militia went off to the wars.

Joe Johnson sat on the Hattiesburg Mayor's desk, swinging one leg idly back and forth, listening to the rapid exchange between Mayor Wayne Elliott and Intelligence Director Sam Hatfield. These two older men never failed to amuse the youthful military boss of Hattiesburg.

Elliot turned to him with a slight sneering tone and inquired, "Well, aren't you going to join in on this, Joe?"

"Hell, man, I'm joined," Johnson replied. "You two go on. I'm listening."

"Joe never liked to talk politics," Hatfield observed, smiling. "He just wants to be turned loose. Right, Joe?"

Johnson nodded curtly. "You can jaw about this all day long, and you'll just end up going along with Abe Williams anyway. So why talk it to death? I thought everything was settled."

"We never completely agreed with Abe in the political area," Elliot said impatiently. "Now we're just trying to explore the possibilities. That's all. And it wouldn't hurt for you to add your thinking to this. Even if you were a baby when all this started. Your thinking wouldn't hurt none."

"It seems pretty clear cut to me," Johnson said, sighing. "United we stand, divided we fall. Isn't it that simple?

38

Whitey is the enemy. Not Abe Williams. If he says take and hold, then we take and hold. Isn't it that simple?"

"Abe doesn't understand the southern psyche," the intelligence man put in. "Now we *know* we can't just take and hold. Not down here. Not in Mississippi, Joe. You don't remember that much, that's the trouble. We either take and kill, or we take and get killed. It's as simple as that."

"Speaking from the military standpoint, I say that's a lot of townshit," the younger man commented. "If the battle order holds up, and things go the way we figure them to, then whitey's going to be helpless. He can't move against us."

Hatfield was glumly shaking his head in an emphatic rebuttal. "You don't know some of these people down here, Joe. You been protected from them all your life. That's why we towned up, to get away from them. You don't know. You just don't know how hard they hate."

"We got some hate working for us too," Johnson shot back. "And we got more than that. We got outrage. Outrage. Now there's a strong weapon."

"I take it, then, that you're in favor of bowing to Abe Williams," Eliot said.

"It's not a matter of bowing," Johnson replied uncomfortably. "It's just common sense. Somebody has to call the shots for this thing. Abe's calling them. I say let 'im call them."

"I say I wish we'd had time to settle this matter," Elliot flashed back.

"Well we don't have the time," Hatfield told him. "So it looks like we better just go along. And play the thing by ear. We'll go along to whatever extent the situation allows. Then . . . if things start getting rough . . . then we do it our way."

"You see that as our only recourse?" the Mayor asked.

Hatfield nodded, a faint smile playing upon his face. "That's the way Atlanta sees it. They're going to play it as cool as possible. But if things start getting too mean, Georgia's going to think General Sherman came back."

Eliott said, "Well, I guess we should . . . uh, I hope

everybody appreciates the unique situation we have here in the south. There's a lot of old, painful memories down here, on both sides. We got a lot of boys in our militias who grew up without mommas and daddies, or without nuts, or without brothers and sisters—because of those wild men out there. And a lot of them are still out there."

Hatfield shrugged and said, "I told Norman Ritter he could count on my operatives to play it straight." He chuckled. "Course, he don't know about that list we got, but I guess we can make some disposition of those bastards when the time is right."

"You're speaking of the triple-k," the young soldier spoke up.

"Yeah. You wouldn't know much about that. Not first hand. But a lot of us do. A lot of us." He shivered. "That last big outbreak in '81 is gonna be remembered by a lot of us."

"We have unique problems here in the south," the Mayor repeated. He grunted and scratched his white-domed head. "I guess nobody ever has really understood that."

"I understand it," the troop commander said. "They terrorized us off the land, now we're going to terrorize our way back onto it. It's as simple as that."

"So, the south is gonna rise again, isn't it," Hatfield said, grinning.

"Yeah," Elliot growled. "It's going to rise about two feet. In blood."

CHAPTER 5

"Abe Williams ain't no Black Messiah!"

"Well, hell, I didn't say he was." Phil Smart, Mayor of Kansas City, stepped to the window and let his eyes follow the gently rolling terrain clear to the horizon. "But goddammit, give the man credit. When the rest of us were laying around moaning and licking our wounds, he's the guy got this Omega Project to turning. *He* set up the communications links, *he* made the contacts with the government niggers, *he* got the towns organized and pulling together toward the common goal. It's been his show from the very beginning. A bunch of whining Johnny-come-latelys aren't going to stand up now and start telling him how to run things."

The military commander, Warren Hutchings, rolled his eyes heavenward. "He still ain't no damn messiah! And I'm telling you a limited war never did work. Now I learned that in the mudholes of Vietnam. Where'd Abe learn his military stragegy? On what campus of what university in what protest demonstration? Huh?"

"He knows what he's doing," Smart muttered. "General Bogan is not exactly anybody's damn fool, you know. A man don't get to be boss of the whole damn armed—"

"I don't trust that son of a bitch either!" Hutchings said.

41

"He ought to know better. He fought in Vietnam, he fought in Laos, he fought in Thailand, he fought every damned limited war there ever was to fight. Once I'd like to hear about just *one un*-limited war he ever fought. I'm telling you, Phil, this plan is crazy. When an armed force seizes the initiative, then they've got to hang onto it. Hell, man, you don't break a charge in mid-stride!"

"Abraham Williams says Phase Two only, and Phase Two only it's going to be," the Mayor said doggedly. "Now are you going to lead the KC forces or aren't you?"

"I'm leading! I'm leading! But you mark my words, and you remember I said it three times, and I haven't even heard any cock crowing around here yet. Abe Williams ain't no Black Messiah!"

CHAPTER 6

The council of war was underway in the only Phase Three area of the nation. Present were Abraham Lincoln Williams, serving as unofficial Chief Executive of Black America, Army Chief of Combat and Commander of the Unified Town Militia; General Jackson T. Bogan, Tactical Air Command Chief; General Hawley Matthews, also representing the Military Airlift Command; Colonel Brownleaf, Troop Commander of the small army garrison at The Presidio in San Francisco and also special adjutant for the California State Guard; Norman Ritter, Intelligence Chief for the Omega Project; a Captain Toney, USN, Tactical Officer for the 12th Naval District; a Colonel Horace, Commanding Officer of the Special Reaction Group at Ford Ord; and a number of junior officers from the several services. Also present was Sam Danniger, a newly commissioned colonel in the black militia and in charge of the Oakland forces.

The meeting was being conducted in the special war room at Oakland's Warhole, and Abe Williams was presiding.

"Now listen, I want no goofs," he told the assembled brass. "When I say a *limited* Phase Three, that's exactly what I mean. How's our timetable, Jackson?"

43

"Looks good," the old soldier reported. "Colonel Horace sees no problem with the airlift. By the way, I've got Bob Donaldson manning the war room at the Pentagon. He's a sharp boy, and he's going to be right on top of the show throughout the night. We have the dummy wargames board up and running, with the press and all invited to observe. So far no takers, the nation lost interest in wargames several crises ago. But just in case something slips and someone gets the idea that a lot of troops are moving about . . . well, we've got the cover."

"Fine," Williams said. "Let's run through our timing once lightly. Forgive me if I'm belaboring, but this entire operation hinges on split second timing, complete discipline, and absolute intimacy with the battle order. Colonel Horace—if you will."

Horace was a man in his mid-fifties with the rock-jawed hardness of the career combat soldier. He stepped up to the chart and tapped a thick finger on the marker at Ford Ord. "In line with the dummy wargames, we're lifting off twenty-two troop copters at 2200 hours. I will be in the lead vehicle with a special reaction team to be placed at the disposal of Mr. Ritter. The other carriers will be lifting five rifle companies, a special weapons company and command vehicles. These will be dispersed to the Presidio, to the state guard facility near Sacramento, and to various other points in Northern California, where they will be joined by motorized units from Parks and Davis. I will remain at the Presidio, where I will join Colonel Brownleaf at Command, and where Mr. Ritter will take charge of the demolition team." The Colonel spread his hand across the northern area of California. "All these assignments have been carefully selected to completely neutralize any reaction capability the whiteys might try to throw up. Each of the twenty-two choppers will be released in sufficient time to rendezvous here at Warhole for the 2330 hours lift-off."

Williams smiled and said, "Thank you, Colonel. Swift and concise, that's how I like it, and that's the way I want it to go tonight."

"It will, sir," Horace assured him.

The militia commander, Danniger, was the next man up. Quite young, but all business and obviously very sure of himself, he picked up the battle order precisely where the other man had left it. "Colonel Horace's choppers will begin arriving here at Warhole at 2330 hours. Oakland Armor will be in embarkation order and we begin loading immediately. By 2330 all twenty-two choppers will be on the ground and receiving. At midnight on the dot and in consonance with command units out of Presidio, Able Company lifts off and proceeds directly to target. Succeeding departures are spaced at two-minute intervals, and the first wave will be clear of Warhole by 0045 hours. How much of this do you want, Mr. Williams?"

"Just take us through Able Company, Sam."

"Yes, sir. Able Company will arrive at the State Guard Central Motor Pool at the Southwest edge of San Francisco—in the beach area—and land inside the compound. This area will be secured no later than 0030 hours, and there is to be no gunfire whatsoever. The stationkeeping force of whiteys will be quickly and quietly subdued. They will then immediately begin servicing the vehicles which the Department of the Army has been systematically stacking there since 1997."

General Bogan chuckled and told Danniger, "Thank you, son, for that nice detour around the word 'stealing.' I just saw a communication last week from Governor Raleigh asking what in blazes did the State of California want with all these hundreds of war machines. I'll bet he won't be asking that tomorrow morning."

"Yes, sir." The young militiaman was not to be deterred from his report. Soberly he continued. "These minimally-mothballed transport and armored vehicles will be placed on the line with all speed, special priority going to 60 troop carriers, 42 weapons carriers, and four of the 87 jeeps. These specified vehicles must be serviced and on their way to the Warhole no later than 0200 hours. They will travel in traditional military convoy fashion, and they will proceed through the city of San Francisco and into Oakland via the prescribed route. Any civil authorities attempting to either aid or interfere with this convoy will be discreetly disposed of. The convoy must arrive at the Warhole no later than 0300 hours. Embarkation of the Oakland Rifles will then commence immediately. Meanwhile, the armor brigade will continue servicing the combat vehicles at San Francisco motor pool. This will include 32 of the M-60 tanks, and 57 of the lighter units, including also six armored scout cars for unit commands. All armor will be fully serviced and on the line at 0500 hours, at which time this armored column will depart for rendezvous with regular army elements from Presidio and Mission. Rendezvous point is at the head of Market Street, just below Twin Peaks."

"Very good, Colonel Danniger," Williams complimented the youth. "You keep it just that tight and we'll see a bright tomorrow. Colonel Brownleaf?"

The Presidio Commander stepped up to the chart and glared at the enlarged area of San Francisco for a moment, then cleared his throat and continued the recital. "We'll, uh, have our light armor moving down Lombard Street, and we'll have taken positions at Van Ness Avenue, at Geary, and in the Fisherman's Wharf area. Bayshore elements of the regulars will have entered the city via the Bayshore Freeway, and they'll be in position along lower Mission, lower Market, and along the Embarcadero." He glared at the intelligence chief. "Did I understand Mr. Ritter to say there will be over two hundred thousand tourists to contend with?"

Ritter jerked his head in a bounding nod and replied, "You did. That's a standard weekly count of whiteys flocking to their fabled city with the golden streets."

"I've seen them," Brownleaf said. "Well, so our timing will have to be perfect. We'll want to accomplish the deployment before the city awakens. They're going to find their sightseeing suddenly greatly enhanced by the dawn's early light. But we'll have road blocks at all critical points, just to assure non-interference from the early risers."

"So far, so good," Williams commented. "This moves us through Phase One, *seize the means*, and Phase Two, *seize the city*. Before we go into Phase Three, let's hear from Navy and Air Force.

The navy captain remained in his chair and mildly declared, "No naval problems. We will continue our normal convoy operations for the merchant fleets, outbound only and through noon tomorrow only. All inbound shipping will be turned back at the twelve mile limit, and we seal the bay as of 1200 hours tomorrow. We could catch a bit of guff from the whitey Coast Guard, but we're bigger and meaner, so I see no real problem from that direction."

General Matthews also remained seated for his report. "We'll have two squadrons of fighters alternating in the airspace above the Bay area from dawn until you call us down. We are also going on Continental Alert for the duration, just in case some of our hungry neighbors get sudden ideas to exploit this operation."

General Bogan added, "And of course, we are leaving Automated Defense Command in full operation. Our black brothers in Africa and the yellow ones of Asia are beginning to get frantic. Some idiot might try to capitalize on this internal dispute and try to join the act. Don't worry, they won't."

"Give us the Phase Three wrap-up, Jackson," Abe Williams suggested.

"Okay. Norm Ritter will have the demolition boys out at Golden Gate Bridge. Phase Three begins at precisely zero six hundred hours, when the old bridge will splash into the drink. I'll hate to see that, just between us brothers. But . . . everybody agrees that war is hell. So the bridge has got to go. It's a symbol, and that's what we have to go after. Anyway, the explosion will be heard all over the city. Hell, all over the Bay area. This will be the signal for all elements to commence the assault upon San Francisco. Element leaders, using the armored scout cars, will have to mix it up with the whiteys and stay down in there to reconnoiter potential trouble spots. Direct the armored units accordingly. Keep our foot soldiers out of trouble. You never can tell what half a million whiteys might decide to do. You have to respect those people, even if they don't respect us. But remember, this is a *limited* Phase Three. We're not going in there to kill. We just want to tear down

47

some of their beloved symbols, wake 'em up, let 'em see beautiful black faces behind weapons of destruction, let 'em know what we *could* be doing if we had a *mind* to.

"The civic center element will raise as much hell as possible in a thirty minute period. Other elements are primarily screens, except for the Embarcadero units, and they have a few walls to breech along Market. Does that about cover it, Abe?"

Williams replied, "I guess so. But I want to emphasize, and I want all your people to clearly understand, that the Phase Three mission is simply to *wake them up*. No more killing than absolutely necessary. We want to shock them. We want them to be frightened. But we *do not* want them all dead. We want them to be helpless, to be at our mercy, and to *know* that they are."

"Yes, I think that's pretty well understood," Bogan murmured.

"Okay. Uh, Colonel Danniger . . . would you care to give us a quick scan over the hinterland section."

"Yes, sir." The militiaman rose halfway out of his chair and turned about to address the junior officers. "As a quick scan . . . the first wave from Warhole covers Bay Area targets only. Then the copters return directly to Warhole and embark the hinterland elements. The second wave will place Oakland Rifles and Armor Brigades in a fan-shaped pattern from Redding to the north to Sacramento east. The third wave covers the coastal area between Eureka and Sausalito. Succeeding waves will blanket our part of the state from San Luis Obispo up."

"Thank you, Sam," Williams said. "That's it, gentlemen. Needless to say, every place that's worth it in California—and every other state on the mainland—will know what Phase Two means by early tomorrow morning. All eyes, of course, will be on us, here in California, because we have the only three Phase Three cities. So let's follow the battle order. And . . . for God's sake, let's watch it. We don't want to destroy this country. It's *our* country too, you know. And this is probably our very last chance, the final forlorn hope for tomorrow for the American Negro. We've tried everything else, and none of it worked.

We tried humility, and they walked on us. We tried passive resistance, and they terrorized us. We tried the courts, and they weaseled us. We tried economic power, and they cheated us. We tried local violence, and they crushed us. So now we have to try open warfare. We have to try it. We could fail, you know. Let's make it work. I consign our fate to your hands, gentlemen. God stand strong in your presence, my friends. God ride with you all the way."

Williams marched out of the room without a backward glance. The older ones would understand, but he did not want those young men to see the moisture in his eyes. To the young, leaders never cry.

Immersed in his thoughts, he went directly to the old press box, high atop the Warhole, bit off the end of a cigar, and looked out upon the grimy inheritance of Black America. "Not *my* people," he murmured. "*Thy* people, Father. Let this cup pass from my lips. Dear God, take away the cup." But he knew the cup would not budge. There was no place for it to go. Abe Williams was stuck with it. His eyes swept toward the bay. Yes, and San Francisco was stuck with it also.

CHAPTER 7

Winston had been to the Pentagon and to the Bureau of
National Labor Standards—and now, he was positive, he'd
picked up a couple of shadows somewhere along the way.
A picture had begun to definitely focus in his mind back
there at the Pentagon—nothing definitive exactly—but a
fuzzy image crawling with all sorts of wild possibilities and
insane conclusions. He had been trying like hell to shrug it
all away when he became aware of the tail. Two guys,
young, impeccably dressed, and doing their job with such
skill that only another pro would have spotted them. But
dammit they were there. And now Winston was wanting in
the worst way to know *why* they were there.

With his two shadows, he hopped the hover jitney to
Capitol Hill, knowing that congress was not in session but
hoping nevertheless to run into someone from the Senate
Armed Forces Committee. He found there nothing but an
army of white tourists being led around by black guides,
then he and his shadows took another jitney to the new
Senate Office Building in Takoma Park. Here he located a
senate aide who laughed nervously at every mention of
mothballed war machines but professed complete
ignorance of the subject.

After some ten minutes of parry-thrust learn-nothing

conversation, Winston stuck a cigarette between his lips and asked the aide for a light. When the guy brought the lighter up, Winston studied the hands and not the flame, and found there the telltale clues he sought. The fingernails and the palms told it all, as he exhaled the smoke from his lungs, Winston asked the senate aide, "Is Senator Marvin aware that he has a Tom working for him?"

The guy flushed and told Winston to go to hell. Instead, he tried some stunting from hovercar to surface taxi and back to airborne shuttle, and was satisfied at the third shift that he had lost the double shadow—then he proceeded directly to a downtown Washington hotel which, by tacit agreement between the races, catered to those of light skin and tender sensitivities.

He did not register, but went directly to a telephone turret in the lobby, closed the door and locked it, made himself comfortable on the lounge, and dropped his AMS card into the meter. A soft tone sounded and he placed the call in precise audibles, then sat back and folded his arms to await the connection.

A feminine voice filtered up from somewhere beyond the meter to announce, "Mr. Waring's office."

"This is Mike Winston. Is the Chief in?"

"Oh. Are you calling from California, Commissioner?"

"No. I'm in Washington, Becky. This is important. Put me through, eh?"

"I'm sorry, Mike," the warm contralto declared. "He's gone for the day. Will you be staying overnight?"

Winston recognized the tone accompanying that question. He let his own tone become more formal as he told her, "Maybe. Uh, look, this is pretty hot stuff. Can't you zot-spot him for me?"

"I'll try," she replied, a hint of frost settling into her voice. "Just a sec."

A barely audible click sounded and Winston was treated to a minute of soft music, then the contralto returned and the music vanished. "I found him," she reported. "He stopped off at CAC on his way home. Be there about another thirty minutes."

"He still living in Silver Spring?"

"Uh huh. But you could probably catch him at CAC."

"Which CAC is this?" he inquired.

"The Community Accomodation Center," she replied. "The *white* one, of course."

"Uh . . ."

The woman laughed through the connection. "Don't tell me you've never . . . It's at the Federal Center, Mike."

"Oh yeah. Okay, I'll try him there." His mind crawled, and he quickly added. "Do something for me first, Becky. Get me passkey codes for Central Computer, data retrieval on military weapons and munitions. Also demographic data on interurban and landflow characteristics."

"Are you calling from a turret?"

"Yes."

"All right. I'll code you through and patch you right now, if you'd like." .

"Yes, I'd like that."

"My pleasure." She hesitated a moment, then said, "By the way, I live at the same cube." She laughed with a trace of embarrassment and added, "I mean, if you decide to stay overnight."

He replied, "Okay, thanks. No promise though, Becky—I mean, don't sit up waiting for me. I told you I'm on something hot. But I'll let you know. Okay?"

"Okay. Here's your patch."

She was gone abruptly and the automated voice from central computers was making the standard announcement. Winston fed in the data request, using precise audibles, then poked a button on the turret panel to switch in the printer. Within seconds the machine was running rapid-fire tabulations and the paper was falling in perforated folds into a small box at Winston's knee. He scanned the information as it came through, jotting quick notes along the way, and he was ready with the cross-check interrogation by the time the initial data scan was completed.

Moments after he had programmed-in the interrogation, the data picture he had sought and feared began to take form on the perforated sheets as a data summary. Ten minutes after he entered the turret, he was fumbling his way into the lobby, hands shaking slightly with the knowledge of the dynamite packed into his briefcase. He ran outside and hailed a hovering air-taxi, and within another few minutes was feeding his AMS card into the plastic box at the entrance to the national capital's most exclusive federally-subsidized sex club.

The dining room was an endless sea of tables and chatter and drifting smoke from a thousand burning cigarettes, all superimposed into the unvarying hum of the electronic waiter service. Winston stepped up to the automated maitre d', punched a button, and spoke into the machine. "Zot-spot Urban Bureau Chief Charles Waring. Commissioner Mike Winston requesting."

There was a brief pause, then a buzzing which was swiftly replaced by a rasping voice announcing, "Waring here."

"Mike Winston, Chief. Hot stuff. Where can I find you?"

"Where are you now, Mike?" came the cool reply.

"I'm right here in the dining room."

"Oh." A pause, then: "Okay. Come on over. A-22."

"Be right there," Winston assured him. He made his way across the numbered aisleways to the *A* for Availability section, and quickly located his target.

Waring sat there alone, a large hulk with white hair and a perpetually distressed face. These were eyes which Winston had always found it difficult to gaze into . . . there was too much misery there, too much betrayal—self-betrayal, perhaps—and entirely too much bitterness for any one human being to contain. He pulled out a chair and silently sat down, fished the summary sheet from his briefcase, glanced at his boss, then lay the sheet face up on the table.

"I'm sober," Waring said, without preliminaries, "If that's what you're wondering."

Winston doubted that. But he replied, "I wasn't wondering anything of the kind." He glanced at the tray alongside Waring's chair, noted the level mark of the

53

bourbon bottle, smiled, and tapped the tab summary with a finger. "Something here I want you to look at," he said.

"You eat yet?" Waring wanted to know.

Winston shook his head. "It can wait. Just look at these figures, Chuck."

The nation's head nigger-tender, as he liked to call himself, sighed and reached for the paper. His eyes traveled about in a random inspection. Then he speared Winston with a puzzled glance. "What's all this computed yuck about?" he asked unemotionally.

"It's a demographic read-out on landflow and urban shift, keyed specifically to the Tom count. And a cross-read on the status of retired military surplus arms, the mothball arsenal. Look at the flow of the past three years."

Waring grunted and said, "So what?"

"So there's some damned significant stuff there. Something is brewing in Black America."

Waring sighed heavily and returned once again to the sheet of data. Presently he said, "Well it still looks like a lot of computed yuck to me."

"Cross-relate, Chuck," Winston urged. "The picture is downright scarey. Most of the Toms are fractos, many of them could easily pass for white if you don't look at them too closely. And look at their flow. God, they're clustering in an entirely new trend of their own, moving in on all the vital spots of the nation. State capitals, major economic centers, mothballed military installations, the whole shmear."

"How'd you get this stuff?"

"AMS demographics. I've been wondering for several months now over the towns' inability to keep up with the demand for Toms."

"Some hot stuff," Waring said disgustedly. "You track me down here to talk about labor problems?"

A cold feeling was traveling slowly up Winston's backbone. He told his boss, "Demographics is only a part of it. Department of Army has been suspiciously busy for several years also. Those guys are planning an uprising—I'll stake my job on it—and the government

54

niggers are backing them up. Listen, I saw Bogan and Abe Williams together this morning. And, of all places, in a back room of Oakland Town Hall."

Waring emitted a dry cackle. He reached for the bourbon, poured a hefty slug into his glass, squirted in some seltzer, and said, "You don't drink, do you."

Winston shook his head. "But I might learn to."

"At your age, Winston, it's hopeless. You have to get an early start if you want to practice this art with total dedication.

"Aren't you going to discuss this situation with me, Chuck?" Winston asked stiffly.

"Nothing to discuss. You can't wait 'til middle-age to start drinking and expect to get anything out of it."

"You know what I'm talking about. Now Chuck, I'm disturbed as hell over this data. Let's—"

"Then go be disturbed someplace else," Waring growled. "This isn't the place for it. I can tell you where you went wrong, Winston."

"For God's sake, Chuck, this is—"

"Shut up! I was just looking at your dossier the other day. There's a lot of dangerous stuff in there, Michael my boy. A lot of it. How come you're not in prison?"

Winston sighed and retrieved the print-out. "Well, I'd better go find somebody sober to talk this over with."

"You talk to nobody!" Waring rasped. He finished the drink, wiped his lips on the back of his hand, and hunched his shoulders into an aggressive posturing. "Every word you say, you hang your ass a little higher. Now I'm not going to answer for your sophomoric flag waving. *No sir*. You talk to nobody but *me*. Understand?"

"Chuck, there are something like fifty thousand Toms in this country who are almost certainly organized into some wild sort of espionage ring—God, maybe even trained assassins and saboteurs. There are tons upon uncountable tons of war munitions and heavy weapons of every description being stockpiled about the country in either direct control of black army forces or minimally protected by skeleton crews of white state-guardsmen."

Waring poured himself another drink. "Do tell. Who gives a shit?"

"The Toms are into everything. I talked to one awhile ago who is an *aide* to the Chairman of the Senate Armed Forces Committee, such as it is. And two of them were tailing me all over Washington today."

Waring chuckled. "And they may be servicing the President's niece. You gotta learn to mind your own business in this city, Mike. That's something you still have to learn."

"Oh, hell," Winston commented miserably. "You haven't the merest grasp of what I'm telling you, do you?"

"Watch it, sonny. Just watch it. This is the *head* niggertender who's doing all the talking. Don't forget that. Don't ever forget that. Baby sitters to a bunch of damn town niggers. God damn! Lot of useless effort if I ever heard it!"

"Don't drink any more, Chuck. Let's go get some air. The air in here is enough to—we simply *have* to talk about this."

"I'll tell you where you went wrong, Winston. You're too ambitious. You think too much. You're always pushing, making waves, always running around waving a flag over somebody's head. You fucking-near got your ass hung back there at UC. It's in the dossier. Hell, it's all in there. Did you know the Attorney General backtracked you through five generations?" Waring laughed raucously. "You didn't know it! They thought sure as hell they'd bought themselves a fracto for the country's top cop. Scared the abundant society right out of them. You never knew that, huh?"

"I'll be going," Winston said. He scraped back his chair, but did not quite get out of it.

Waring lunged across the table and captured him with a heavy hand, roaring, "You'll go when I tell you to!" He gazed about to see if anyone was noticing the ruckus, then showed Winston a crafty smile. "You think you're bucking for my job, don't you? Even got my personal secretary making googy eyes at you. You wanta be head niggertender, don't you? Listen, sonny boy, forget it. Arlington would never have it. Never. It satisfies his weird sense of justice to let you sweat your ass off over nigger problems, but he'll never see you in a bureau chief's spot. Never."

"I don't want your job, Chuck," Winston wearily replied.

"Then why're you running around making waves all the time, huh? A youth center for Detroit Heights! A new hospital for Cleveland! Housing developments for this place and that, town roads, higher relief credits, better work offers! Where do you come off with all this dream stuff, boy? You know the old man hasn't bought a thing for a nigger in all the years he's been here! And now look at you! A *conspiracy*, for God's sake, an *uprising*."

The bureau chief threw back his head and howled. "Those dumb shits can't hardly keep themselves *alive* even. And you sitting here all wild eyed and calling *me* drunk. You're the guy that's drunk, Winston. Drunk with *ambition*! You're the drunkest bastard I ever knew, Winston, and you ain't even smelled the cork. You wanta know why they ran your ass outta the Justice Department?"

"Not particularly," Winston replied, gritting his teeth in a growing rage.

Waring underwent a sudden change of mood. Tears sprang to his eyes. He released his subordinate and gently patted his shoulder. "Mike, don't listen to this shit. Don't listen to it. You're right, and I'm drunk. I got no right raving at you like this. Listen, little buddy. You and me. Right? We got the stinkingest job in government today."

Winston was beginning to see a new glimmer of hope. He said, "Chuck, let's get out of here. The air's bad and the whiskey is worse. Let's go find—"

"Well now, wait a minute, Mike, wait a minute. Let me tell you this." Waring stopped talking, his attention diverted by the approach of a woman. She looked about thirty, medium height, rather pretty in an overtly suggestive manner. The hair was blonde, she wore a nice smile and one of the new knit fabrics styled into a peek-a-boo shrug-dress, so called because the entire thing was of wide mesh

57

and fell away with a shrug of the shoulders.

"Hi, honey," Waring said thickly. "You looking for me?"

"I was just wondering," she said in a high-pitched voice.

"What were you wondering, honey?" Waring asked, winking at Winston.

"Well . . . if the boys were enjoying each other's company. I mean, if you're satisfied with each other or if you'd like some feminine presence."

"Oh we like feminine presence," Waring assured her. "Don't we, Mike?"

Winston grunted and looked around for a way out.

The woman stood with one hand on the back of an empty chair, her eyes moving uncertainly from Waring to Winston.

"Which one of us you like the most, honey?" Waring asked, winking once again at his companion.

"Well . . . I already reserved a cube upstairs. Anything wrong with all three of us going up?"

Waring reached across the table to slap Winston on the shoulder. "Hey, that sounds like just the ticket for a couple of old nigger-tenders, huh Mike?"

"I guess not," Winston said. "I have a lot to do, Chuck. We *both* do."

"Hell, it don't take no credits, sonny. It's a social club, you know, just for the convenience of us Washington slaves. He laughed boisterously. "Seriously now. Don't you want to make friends with this little lady?"

Winston looked at the woman and felt miserable for her. He smiled uncertainly and mouthed the words to her, "He is drunk."

She returned the smile and told him, "That's okay. I, uh, I don't *have* to come here, you know. I mean, there are other places to go. But he's right. It is nice to make new friends. Isn't it?"

"Two at a time?" Winston asked quietly.

"It could be interesting," she replied. "I mean, three doesn't *have* to be a crowd. If you know what I mean."

"By God that sounds great, just great," Waring declared loudly. "What d'ya say, Michael son? You want to share a bed with your boss?" He broke up completely, pounding the table with a hammy fist, and choking over his laughter.

Winston was already halfway to the door, and nobody heard his angered, rasping reply but the automated maitre d'.

Winston stood in agony before the door to the office of the Chief, Federal Police Bureau. He'd rather talk to almost any man in Washington, but . . . to hell with personalities. So the guy had knifed him once and he would undoubtedly do so again if a similar profit-motive should arise. So maybe the guy had grown a little. Winston squared his shoulders and pushed on into the reception room.

It hadn't changed much. Same pictures on the walls, same mottled carpeting. New girl, though, and a beaut. He presented his identification and stated his business.

She examined him from beneath partly-lowered lashes and eyes that told him she'd heard of him, oh yes, I've heard of *you*, Mike Winston. "The Chief cannot be disturbed right now, Commissioner," she told him. "If you'd like to have a seat, I'll see if I can get you in shortly."

Get him *in*? Winston was not *that* far down the Washington totem. He told her, "You announce me right now, young lady, and let Fairchild make that decision."

She wasn't to be bullied. The pretty lips hardened and she told him, "The Chief cannot be disturbed at this moment, Commissioner."

Winston said, "The hell he can't." He vaulted the railing and pushed into the FBI Chief's inner sanctum with a grimly struggling secretary hanging on one arm.

A handsomely graying man with surprised eyes rose hastily from his desk and turned off a tape deck. He sized up the situation in a single glance, waved the girl out of the office, and walked toward Winston with outstretched hand. "Damn, it's good to see you again, Mike," he said amiably. "How long has it been . . . three years? Four?"

"About halfway between the two," Winston replied, smiling tightly. "This isn't a personal call, Tom. I have urgent business."

Fairchild waved him to a chair and stepped over to a sideboard bar. "Name your poison," he suggested.

Winston said, "Uncle Tom."

The police chief chuckled, somewhat nervously and said, "No, I meant liquid poison. Oh hell I forgot, you don't. Or have you started?"

"Not yet, but I'm getting closer to it every day. No, nothing for me Tom, thanks."

The Chief swirled some liquids into a glass and took it to his desk to perch there on the corner and inspect his one-time friend with a measuring gaze. "You haven't changed much," he decided. "Bit of silver at the ears, there." He laughed. "I guess it's catching up to all of us, eh. The years, I mean."

Winston nodded. "Maybe more so than we realize. That's what I want to talk about. I guess old cops never die, nor even fade away. I've stumbled onto something, Tom. My boss is in the cups again, and it's like talking to the roaring surf. I'd like to get your opinion."

Fairchild grinned and replied, "If it's cop business, I'm all ears. You know that."

"Try the eyes," Winston replied. He leaned forward and thrust the cross-check summary into the policeman's hand. "I won't talk. You draw your own conclusions."

Fairchild studied the paper for several minutes, pausing occasionally to sip at his drink, sloshing the liquid now and then, clinking the ice against the side of the glass. As he read, his face hardened. Lines of amiability vanished. The brows began forming peaks above the eyes and the eyes themselves became murky, almost seeming to change color and to recede somewhat into the head. Winston knew the look and knew it well. Once he had even thought it a sign of the whirring cogs of an acutely tuned police mind. He had learned, though, that it was a sign of other mental activities as well.

Without looking at his visitor, Fairchild pushed a button on his desk. A door opened and a pretty young woman came in. Her glance took in Winston and flashed quickly to Fairchild. He handed her Winston's paper and told her, "Get me a copy of that, doll."

She nodded, showed Winston another curious look, and went back the way she'd come.

"Nice," Winston softly commented.

"Very," Fairchild agreed. "Well—that's a nice piece of work there, Mike. For an urban commissioner. Thanks very much for your interest. You can pick up your original in the outer office, if you want it."

Winston growled, "What the hell are you saying?"

The cop finished his drink and went around behind the desk and sat down. "I said it. Thanks. Good seeing you again, Mike. I'm busy as hell. You understand that, I'm sure. Drop in again when you have more time."

In a voice working very hard at remaining level, Winston asked him, "What will you do with that intelligence, Tom?"

"We'll investigate, of course."

"Routinely."

"Naturally. You know the channels. We, uh, have the same access to classified data banks as you." He emphasized the *classified* in a voice becoming clearly antagonistic.

What the hell, Winston told himself. The guys thinks I'm trying to set up a competitive shop. He said, "Look, all I want to hear is that you're as upset over this thing as I am. Then I'll bow out. I stopped playing cop a long time ago. The only reason I came here was to—"

"Look, Mike, get the hell out, will you? I've got to clear up some stuff and blow this joint myself. Dinner date, big one. Get on the hell out of my hair, eh?"

"This is one hell of an urgent matter, Tom. Just tell me that you understand that."

62

He'd said the wrong thing and he knew it immediately. Fairchild's eyes blazed and he said, "I don't have to tell you a goddamned thing, Commissioner." He got to his feet, looked at the door, and told Winston goodbye.

"I'm not budging," Winston said adamantly. "This is a very serious matter, and—"

"So is mine, Commissioner. That dinner engagement is at the White House."

He said it rather proudly, Winston thought. *Get off my back, nigger-tender, you're talking to a guy who dines with the President.* Yeah, Winston thought, and I'm talking to a guy who undermined *me* out of that very spot.

Winston told him, "Great. Take me with you, and we'll discuss the matter with the man."

"I don't invite people to the White House. You're smart enough to know *that*, Winston."

Sure, but not smart enough to look out for a knife from a friend. "I'm smart enough," he said aloud, "to know that there are going to be twenty million howling niggers pouring out of those towns with blood in their eyes. A military coup is underfoot, I know it now and *you* should have a long time ago. Now you pick up that telephone and clear it with the man, and then let's go to dinner."

Fairchild showed him a twisted grin and asked, "Are you feeling all right, Mr. Winston?"

"No, I'm feeling like hell. But I can stand it if you can. Pick up the phone, Tom."

The police chief sighed, dropped his eyes to the desk, then raised them slowly to the still figure in the visitor's chair. "I guess I'd better detain you, Commissioner Winston," he said thoughtfully.

"In a pig's ass," Winston replied calmly.

Fairchild smiled. "You understand. A security hold, just until we've had time to check out this, uh, threat. You shouldn't be running around making threats like that, Commissioner. It's against the law."

"Knock it off, Tom. You know exactly why I am here, and that I am not dashing about alarming the populace." Winston stood up. "Now let's end the game. Make the call or I will."

"In all seriousness," Fairchild said smoothly, "I am placing you in security hold. You're trying to mix yourself into something that is way beyond you, and that's all I'm going to say about it. You'll just have to understand."

Winston simply could not understand. He let go from the hip, falling over across the desk-top with an arcing hook that removed the set smile from the cop's face. Fairchild toppled over behind the desk, spinning to hands and knees, and Winston was over the desk with both feet before the cop had completely touched down.

A small nickle-plated revolver clattered to the floor. Winston scooped it up, leaned back against the edge of the desk, and said, "Okay, Tom, come up carefully."

"You're nuts . . . totally insane!" the police chief panted.

"Not nuts enough to let you lock me up at a time like this. Now you get on that telephone. You set it up for us to talk to the old man. And you set it up clean. Or else I am going to set you down very dirty, and I have never been more serious in my life."

Fairchild obviously believed him. His eyes receded even farther into the skull and he grunted, "Don't be melodramatic, Mike. You don't think I'd turn a lunatic loose on the old man."

"And you know I'm no lunatic. Something is happening in blackville, and it could be happening at this very moment, the *big* happening. You set it up for the White House, Tom. Set it up right now."

Fairchild glared at him through a half-minute of silence. Then he gave a heavy sigh and rubbed the contusion on his chin. "All right. But you'll have to turn over the gun. You're not going to dinner at the White House with a gun in your hand."

"Of course not."

"You're a throwback, Winston."

"I'm a what?"

"You were born several hundred years too late. You belong in King Arthur's court."

"Right now I'll settle for King Arlington's," Winston told him. "The phone, Tom. Pick up the damn phone."

CHAPTER 9

Mike Winston was not often awed by the mere presence of another man. Right now he was trying to decide whether the awe was inspired by the man or the office. Perhaps it was a combination of both, he decided. After all, J. Humphrey Arlington had become an American institution, a "servant of the republic" for more than forty years and nearly eight of those years as President. And this was Winston's first intimate contact with the man.

The old boy was still a handsome and commanding figure, even at this septegenarian stage of life. The mind seemed as sharp and the eyes as penetrating as any young man Winston knew. Right now the presidential gaze was fastened securely onto one Mike Winston, and the object of that gaze was finding the entire thing entirely uncomfortable. He was even now beginning to wonder what sort of fool it is who demands, at gunpoint, an audience with the President of the United States. It was no coincidence that Arlington had just expressed that same question.

"There seemed to be no other way, sir," Winston explained. "I simply felt that this intelligence should be placed at your disposal at the earliest possible moment."

The fierce old eyes probed the depths of his brandy snifter, then he swirled the liquid in a gentle motion and commented, "So you think the Negruhs are planning an uprising."

65

He looked back into the presidential gaze and replied, "Yes, Mr. President, that is precisely what I think."

"And you say this in your official capacity as National Commissioner of Urban Affairs?"

Winston's eyes flickered. What was the old lion getting to? "Yes, sir, I do."

"You realize, then, that you are expressing an official view of the United States Government?"

"I am expressing a subordinate view to my Chief Executive," he replied curtly. "I would be remiss not to do so, sir."

"Have you ever considered expressing such views through the regular chain of command?"

The interview was taking on a dreamlike quality for Winston. Or nightmarish. He explained, "I felt this situation lay beyond official courtesies and protocol, sir. My bureau chief is—at the moment . . . personally indisposed."

"Your bureau chief, sir, is drunk," the President said quietly.

Winston blinked. What the hell was going on? Surely, for God's sake, the *President* couldn't be with the *blacks*. The idea was almost laughable. He said, "I neglected to tell you, sir. The incident that turned me onto this investigation was . . . well, I'm certain that I saw General Bogan this morning, in company with Abraham Lincoln Williams. He was in civilian clothes. I came across them in the Oakland Town Hall, and you'd have thought I was the truant officer and they were a couple of kids cutting classes. I—"

"General Bogan has a right to a personal life. Has he not?"

"It's totally out of character, sir. The town niggers supposedly hate the government niggers as much as they hate whitey. I just can't see the two of them—"

"It has been common knowledge for some time, both in the Pentagon and at the White House, that Jackson Bogan is interested in a rapprochement with his less favored brothers. Is there something immoral in that, Commissioner?"

The old bastard. Why was he doing this? *He knew*

better. Winston told the President of the United States, "Talking to you, sir, is as frustrating as talking to Tom Fairchild and Charlie Waring. No, sir, doubly as frustrating. I feel ashamed, sir, deeply ashamed."

Winston was halfway out of his chair when the President cackled and said, "Sit down, Commissioner. You've not been dismissed, nor will you be on such a note as that."

"My apologies, sir," Winston muttered. "You have no idea how difficult it is to command any attention in this city. Paul Revere would have never made it in the twentieth century."

The President smiled. "We have our Paul Reveres, Commissioner." He turned to Fairchild. "Well, Tom?"

Fairchild smiled and spread his hands. "I thanked Mike for his alert assistance, sir. I gave him every assurance that the matter would be dealt with." He smiled. "That's when he pulled the gun on me. I thought it best to let you be the judge of the . . . uh . . . urgency of his intelligence."

The President chuckled. "I suppose I would feel the same way, with a gun at my head. I understand, Tom, that it was your own gun he pulled on you."

Fairchild flushed. "I didn't expect a Washington bureaucrat to come on like a television melodrama, Mr. President."

The President was still chuckling when he turned back to the urban commissioner. "Don't you like your job, Mr. Winston?" he asked. "I mean, aren't you satisfied with it, ministering to the needs of the black community? Do you find yourself continually pulled back into the intrigue of police work?"

Winston was getting a deeper taste of rage. President or no, he'd had a cup full. "What sort of game are you two playing with me?" he asked quietly. His hands were beginning to shake. He clamped them firmly onto his knees and leaned forward tensely in his chair. "Who the hell do you think you're talking to?"

"Here here, sir!" the President cried, in a tone used to scold undisciplined children.

Winston ignored the call to order. "I came here to present facts—*facts*, not vague ideas—which appear highly critical to the national security. I believe I made an impressive case. And your only reaction is to try to make me feel like an idiot. I am not an idiot, Mr. President."

The old boy had come to a boil, and the eyes were blazing with outrage. "If the President says you're an idiot, sir, then you are an idiot," he intoned haughtily. "And believe me, sir, you *are* an idiot!"

Well, Winston thought, so this is what it's like. This is what it's like for an Abe Williams or a John Harvey, trying to act like a man in the presence of pompous foolishness. His eyes blurred. He wondered if he were going mad. He wanted to get up and hit that old man, knock his goddamn leering old head off. Yes, he must be going mad. His fingers dug into his knees. He took a deep breath, let half of it out, and aaid, "Mr. President, our nation is in peril. You *must* understand that."

"This nation is forever in peril!" Arlington thundered. "When the President places his head upon the pillow at the end of day, the nation is in peril. When the President rises from his bed at end of night, the nation is in peril! Your President has lived for half a century with the daily knowledge of his nation in peril. From within and from without. Does an administrative junior stroll into the White House, fresh from a once-in-a-lifetime self-important game of intrigue, and presume to tell his President that the national is in peril? You, sir, are a *total* idiot!"

The old man had used a lot of wind for that emotional speech, but Winston was too far gone to tread water now. He dived into the uncertain depths with a flaring, "You, sir, are a pompous ass!"

Yeah, he'd gone insane. Arlington's face was white death. The lips were moving without sound. Winston had broken through; he had joined that exclusive inner circle of political suicides. But the Presidential gaze was, at least, of a different quality now. He wasn't toying with Winston any longer.

"I apologize for my outburst, Commissioner," the President said, sucking hard for air.

"And I for mine, sir," Winston replied.

Arlington stared with glassy eyes at an unlit cigar. Tom

Fairchild was trying hard not to smirk and not quite succeeding. Presently the President sighed and said, "Tom, would you be so kind as to bring some more brandy."

Winston's was untouched. He waved Fairchild away, fidgeted, and watched his President attempting to pull the mantle of dignity back. The police chief completed his chore and resumed his watch in the chair. The silence ticked on. Presently Arlington sighed heavily and told Winston, "I must apologize to you, sir. I have treated you badly."

"Thank you," Winston said.

"And you have treated me badly."

"Yes sir. And I also apologize."

"Good. Now we have that rot out of the way. We have made a terrible mistake in this nation, Mr. Winston."

"Yes sir."

"Yes. A terrible mistake. We turned the military over to the blacks—lock, stock and artillery. And now we are at their damn mercy, sir. Do you understand that? We are at their mercy."

"It may not be too late to—"

"Of course it's not too late! That's the whole idea. It is *not* too late."

"I, uh . . . I've lost you, sir."

"You've never had me, Commissioner." The tired old eyes slid over to inspect Fairchild. "We are going to have to tell him, Tom."

"I agree, Mr. President."

"And you understand what this will mean."

"Yes, sir. I understand."

Winston did not particularly like the looks exchanged between the two. He watched Arlington, and waited, wondering what sort of game was starting now.

The President lit his cigar, coughed, then leaned forward in his chair to impale Winston with a faint echo of the earlier hard glare. "You are not in the midst of fools, Commissioner. Did you imagine that you are the only man in government who is aware of the treachery developing in this republic? We have been watching them. We know who they are, and we have suspected for some time what they are up to. I must candidly confess, however, that your intelligence was a bit of a shock. We were not aware of the arms stockpiles. And we were not aware of General Bogan's treachery. Others in the military establishment, yes. We mean to know *all* of them, and we mean to learn precisely what it is they are planning. And you, Commissioner, must guard your information with your very life. You must keep it to yourself, and you must make no further moves, or you will upset our intelligence effort. Do you understand?"

"I believe they already know of my suspicions, sir. I had a tail earlier today. I am being watched."

"All the more reason, then, for you to go about your activities as though you are completely innocent. Go back to your job, your job of administering the Negruh's needs. Speak no word to any man regarding this matter. And let your government handle the matter."

"Forgive me, sir," Winston said hesitantly, "but I feel in my very bones that the situation has gone beyond the help of an intelligence effort. I believe that you should move immediately, forcefully, tonight. Every person known or suspected of treason should be rounded up and locked up. Every police department in the nation should be placed on federal activation, and each of those arms stockpiles should be seized and destroyed. Tonight."

Arlington sighed, stared at Winston for a moment, then turned to his chief cop. "Tom?"

Fairchild shook his head. "No, Mr. President. It's the wrong approach. Our intelligence indicates no need whatever for panic at this stage. And we could lose the heart of the entire thing if we move too hastily. Another ten days, I feel, and we'll be ready to move. But certainly no sooner."

The President nodded and said, "My feelings exactly. Thank you, Tom. Goodnight, Mr. Winston. Thank you for coming."

Winston's head was spinning. Only vaguely was he aware that he was leaving the President's study. He was moving woodenly at Fairchild's side, through the doorway and along the wide corridor, down the steps into the waiting automobile.

Fairchild started the engine, moved the car gently along the sweeping drive, through the gate and onto the avenue. Then he pulled to the curb, produced a set of plastic handcuffs and the nickle-plated revolver.

"You're under arrest, of course," he said quietly.

Winston did not immediately comprehend. His thoughts were tumbling, a sense of frustration and urgency plucking at the taut fibres of his nervous system. Fairchild snapped one end of the cuffs onto Winston's left wrist, closed the other end around a clip on the dashboard, then moved the car back into the thin traffic of early-evening Washington. It was just beginning to get dark in the nation's capital. Winston stared at the handcuffs, at the little gun resting between Fairchild's legs, at the cold face of his captor.

Then the taste of rage came sweet to his tongue. *So that's where Charlie first got fucked! By that old man back there, that pompous and empty-headed ass who sold the nation on a sleight-of-hand apartheid plan called AMS!*

The curtain rang full open in Winston's mind, and he saw it all then, the entire conspiracy of two decades, *a white conspiracy*, an entire nation bent to the will of one pompous and probably demented leader.

He reached across with his right hand, snared the steerling wheel, and lunged across it. His left foot found Fairchild's right, on the accelerator, and he stomped with everything he had. The cop was fighting him for the wheel, scrabbling desperately to disentangle his foot.

"You crazy bastard!" Fairchild screamed. Then the brick wall loomed up over the scrunching hood of the car and Winston felt the piercing bite of the plastic cuffs as he became a dislocated flying object.

I did it! he exulted, in that smashing amount of impact.

Not until some time later, however, was he to be entirely sure of just what it was he had done.

He had, in effect, become an integral part of the Omega Project.

BOOK II - GATEWAY TO TOMORROW

CHAPTER 1

Fairchild was unconscious, a white welt traversing his forehead and a bit of blood on one cheek, but he was breathing. Winston fumbled through his pockets, found the key to the handcuffs, and freed himself. He glared at the little revolver through a moment of indecision, then pocketed the weapon. Fairchild was beginning to stir. Winston backed out of the wrecked vehicle on all fours. Several other cars had halted and a crowd of curious pedestrians was forming.

"A man in there is hurt," Winston advised nobody in particular. Then he slipped through the crowd and walked rapidly down the avenue, turning off onto the first side street he came to.

There was an ache in his ankle and his head was beginning to spin. He saw a familiarly-shaped building, one of those modernistic atrocities they were calling religious architecture in the nineties, and the neat plaque set into the side with the two words almost apologetically whispering: AMERICAN CHURCH.

He merged in with the twenty or so people moving up the stone steps, fingering his AMS card and wondering whether he could risk using it. If there was a Zot-spot out on him . . . no, surely not so quickly.

Winston hadn't been inside a church for a long time, and he felt vaguely uncomfortable at the prospect. But he was not seeking an enlightenment of soul—merely a place to wait and rest and bring his whirling mind together.

The plastic box at the head of the stairs featured three slots. One was inscribed CHRISTIAN TRADITIONAL, another NON-CHRISTIAN, and the third NEW AGE. A small line of people waited to use the latter two. Christian Traditional was not making it too well and most of the cards feeding into that slot, Winston noted, belonged to the very aged.

The ankle was hurting and Winston followed the line of least resistance. He carded Christian Traditional and went on through the electron door, picking up his card on the other side. He dropped it into his pocket and shuffled along a narrow passageway with the old folks.

They came into a large vaulted chamber. A choir of heavenly voices was singing softly somewhere, recorded of course. A tremendous montage was playing on the back wall, semi-motion, depicting a group of robed figures baptizing one another in the rushing waters of a stream.

Winston took a seat in a far corner of the chamber, dropping his wearied frame onto an uncomfortable wooden benchlike affair. He AMS'd another inevitable plastic box affixed to the backrest of the seat just ahead, and this started a soundtrack near his right ear, just loud enough for personal listening. Sure, God still lived . . . via the AMS sermonette. Winston was not interested in the soundtrack, only in appearing inconspicuous.

He tried to shut out the soothing tones of the automated sermon and pulled his throbbing ankle onto the opposing knee and tried to rub the ache away, allowing his eyes to travel slowly about the big room.

He wished the droning voice in his right ear would shut up. "Christians have no guilt with the state of this world," the voice was assuring him. "To many scholars, the present world situation is Armageddon come to pass. (Bet your ass, buddy). It is the prelude to the millenium, and God's chosen have been gathered together here on this continent to receive the blessing of abundant life. We must share no sense of guilt for the famine and starvation loosed upon the abandoned peoples of Africa and Asia. Does mortal man question the wisdom and design of He Who Createth All? Rejoice, Christians. Christ has overcome the iniquities of a sinful world, and America we must rejoice over our God-given abundance. This is the end of this sermonette. Please re-program with your AMS passport to receive the next message, the text of which is . . ."

Winston abruptly stopped listening and jerked upright in the chair. Two young men had just entered the room and were now standing poised on the balls of their feet, hands clasped behind their backs like undertakers, looking the place over. They spotted Winston and began moving slowly in his direction.

He casually got to his feet, pivoted toward the exit, then beat it in a fast walk. He glanced over his shoulder as he cleared the doorway and saw that the men were now walking rapidly after him. He went through the exit vestibule, then doubled back to mix in with a thin crowd of churchgoers who were moving up the steps to the entrance.

Winston jostled and pushed his way to the head of the queue, flipped his card into the NEW AGE slot, and passed back inside. It seemed unlikely that his pursuers had been able to follow that quick reverse.

The New Age chamber featured a totally different atmosphere. It was semi-dark. The domed ceiling was a universe in slow motion—stars, moons, and distant galaxies all moving about some sublime center. There was a sweet smell to the air and a faint humming sound trailed down from the dome, the sound of spheres or molecules in motion, Winston presumed.

He dropped onto an overstuffed leather lounge, noting the inevitable plastic box buried in the armrest. A pretty girl sat to his right. He smiled at her but she offered no awareness of his presence. Winston supposed that she was meditating or something. He debated using the AMS card again, then decided again in favor of inconspicuity. He dropped the card through and immediately experienced a not-unpleasant electric shock where he sat. A little tray slid out of the armrest, offering the worshipper a plastic packet.

He picked up the offering and glared at it in the dim light. It contained some sort of fine powder. A trade name, stamped near the top of the packet, read merely EXPANDO.

Hallucinogen, Winston decided. He dropped the packet into his pocket along with the AMS card and wondered about the tingling in his butt. Something was getting energized down there. He felt himself getting an erection, and tried to mentally discourage it. He looked at the girl next to him. She was still in some other world. Then he noted the color wheel in a little box facing her. Psychedelics. He cautiously moved his head across the dividing arm, then quickly jerked it back. God, what sounds! An electronic insulator, he presumed, kept the noise confined to the personal dimension.

His curiosity aroused, Winston explored his own area and found another card slot just beneath the first one. He pondered a moment, then slipped the card in. Immediately Winston had a color wheel and sounds of his own—and it was too much, too much. He felt himself slipping into some sort of mindless abyss and quickly lurched to his feet. Thank God he had not taken the Expando!

He left the New Age of religion where he had found it and made a casual exit. The two men from Christian Traditional were nowhere in evidence. Winston had his own personal pipeline to that thing some people called God, and he quietly thanked it for a minor miracle neatly worked.

He moved cautiously around the building, hoping he'd just been *feeling* persecuted. His ankle still hurt. He leaned against the wall, pulled the ankle up into his hands, and rubbed it some more. His head came into contact with a harsh metallic object. He reared off and stared at it. AMERICAN CHURCH, it sneered at him.

Winston sneered right back. This must have been at least the second place where Charlie got screwed!

If God were truly dead, Winston decided, then this was the place where they buried him.

CHAPTER 2

Bettina Fairchild glanced anxiously toward the window of her Alexandria mansionette and tried to disentangle herself from the amorous grasp of her husband's young disciple, Jimmy Royal. "Listen," she warned him in a purring voice, "if he *is* coming home, this is about the time for it."

Royal chuckled and massaged her hip with a manicured hand. "I told you, Betts, he's supping with the old man tonight. Won't be along for hours yet." He lowered his mouth onto hers, sighed into the warm reception, and gyrated his midsection for her benefit. She gyrated back, whimpering and pressing close against him.

"Not out here," she moaned. "Take me to bed."

The young federal agent, easily ten years the woman's junior, grinned and told her, "Say, you're in high prime tonight."

"Don't talk that way, Jimmy," she gently chided him. "Don't talk period. Let's—"

A bright light swept across the windows, immediately followed by the screech of tires on the driveway. The woman flung herself out of the embrace of her paramour and gasped, "It's Tom!"

"Hell, take it easy," Royal growled. He smoothed his hair and inspected his face in the wall mirror, glanced at the woman, grinned, and walked toward the door.

He froze there in mid-stride as a glassy-eyed Tom Fairchild threw the door wide open and lurched inside. An angry welt seeped with congealed blood traversed the handsome forehead. Two men had come in on his heels and were standing quietly behind him as the FPB Chief swayed drunkenly just inside the doorway.

One of the men was quite young, younger than Royal, and he seemed to be holding something to the back of Fairchild's neck. The other was considerably older, heavily put together. The door closed as violently as it had opened, and the older man moved immediately to the windows. He drew the blinds, snapped his fingers toward the younger man, and walked rapidly toward the rear of the house.

Not a word had passed. Bettina Fairchild was staring at her husband's face, and she was obviously wondering if she should run to him or away from him. Jimmy Royal, an inane grin plastered stiffly to his face, was watching the disappearing back of the older stranger. The young man who had entered just behind Fairchild cleared his throat and pushed the swaying man forward, one hand remaining close to the back of his neck.

Fairchild staggered toward the center of the room. His wife raised a hand to her mouth and uttered a stifled little scream as the nation's chief cop lurched into a side view, revealing the snub-nosed pistol pressed firmly against the base of his skull.

A startled yelp crossed Jimmy Royal's lips. His right arm jerked across his chest—the man with the pistol growled "Uh-uh" and cruelly jammed the muzzle of the pistol into Fairchild's neck. Royal's arm dropped and hung loose, and he muttered, "What the hell is going on?"

The gunman quietly told him, "Shut up."

Mrs. Fairchild's legs were failing her. Royal made a move toward her but again the gunman warned, "Uh-uh."

Royal poised there and watched the older man return.

"It's clean," the man reported. He went over to Royal and relieved him of the revolver in his sideleather, then asked the other gunman, "This the guy you were talking about?"

"That's him," the younger man said.

"Okay, let's get going." The big man, obviously in charge, shoved Royal toward the narrow hallway leading to the rear of the house and snared Bettina Fairchild by an arm and propelled her along behind Royal. She whimpered and threw an agonized look over her shoulder, but went on without argument.

Fairchild and the gunbearer followed close behind. When he reached the bedroom, his wife was lying on the bed, one arm raised across her face, softly sobbing. Jimmy Royal stood against the wall, an uncomprehending mask twisting at his face.

"Okay, let's get undressed," the older man snapped.

Bettina jerked noticeably but otherwise remained motionless. Royal glared at the big man, unspoken questions in the look. "Yeah, I mean you," the man told him. "Get 'em off. Get everything off. I mean you too, lady." He grabbed Bettina's leg and dragged her onto the floor.

She came up breathing harshly, fear and guilt and resignation showing in the pretty face. She turned dully toward the young man with the gun at her husband's head and told him in a flat voice, "I know you. You worked with the gardener last summer. You're a Negruh."

"Yes ma'am," the youth replied, confirming the identification with a sniggering caricature of black docility. His eyes traveled meaningfully about the bedroom. "And I know this here place too, ma'am."

"Enough talk, lady," the big man growled. "Get your clothes off."

Bettina looked to her husband. He appeared to be a man in deep shock and hardly aware of his surroundings, but he nodded his head and told her in a barely audible voice, "Better do what they say, Betts." His head was craned to one side, as though cringing from the cold steel impressed there.

Bettina unfastened her dress and let it fall, stepped out of it, tripped, and fell onto the bed. The big man helped her upright, ran an appreciative hand along her hip, then stepped back. "You're doing fine," he told her. "Get the rest of it off."

She stared at him dully, dropped her eyes, unfastened the bra, and slowly drew it off. Heavy breasts jiggled in a sudden release. She stood there quietly, her eyes moving slowly about the room.

"*All* of it honey," the man commanded.

She stripped off the panties, fell again with the silken flimsy girding her ankles. The man helped her again, this time running both hands the full length of her legs and pausing to gently pinch the soft inner thighs. Then he flipped her onto the bed and stared down at her, the panties in his hand.

"See, I told you," the younger man commented. "No hair."

"That's the way whitey wears it now," the other man replied heavily. "Well . . ." He turned with a sigh, went over to Royal, and tossed the panties into his face. "I told you to get undressed," he said.

Royal's fair complexion turned even fairer. He fumbled with his tie. Giving that up as an impossible job, he tried to remove his shirt while still wearing the jacket and generally showed signs of total disorientation. The two invaders chuckled and watched him. Tom Fairchild was staring stonily at his wife's figure on the bed.

Royal finally got the clothing off and looked at the big man for further direction.

"Take off those socks," the man told him. "You don't get in a lady's bed with your damn socks on, do you?" He gave the naked man a shove, and Royal fell to the bed beside Bettina.

Then the big man turned to Tom Fairchild. "Okay, Chief," he said quietly. "Let's talk business."

Fairchild croaked, "I told you all I know."

"You told me *nothing*!" the man growled. "Why did you have Mike Winston in custody. Why did he make the break? Why did you two go to the White House? What did you talk about? What was said in there that put Winston in chains?"

"I don't know why the President wanted him arrested," Fairchild insisted in a dead voice. "I was not party to the

White House conversation. I merely escorted Winston there and back. He was already in custody when we went there. I don't know anything else."

"You keep saying the same tired old words!"

"It's all there is to say," Fairchild replied woodenly. "It's truth."

The man laughed nastily and said, "*White* man's truth!"

Fairchild's head raised quickly. He gazed closely at his tormentor. "You're a white man," he observed, the voice quivering.

"Not where it counts, cop. Inside, I'm just as black as any nigger you ever murdered."

"I've murdered no niggers," Fairchild replied dispiritedly.

The man raised a foot and kicked at Royal. "Fuck his wife!" he commanded.

Royal quivered. Fairchild's eyes flared. The younger gunman snickered and observed, "How? He's soft as a noodle."

"He damn sure better get it hard! You want me to shoot that thing off for you, boy?" The man laughed. "Hey, where've I heard *that* line before?"

"This isn't going to prove a thing," Fairchild muttered dismally.

"It'll prove he can do what he's done a hundred times already," the younger man put in. "These folks been sneaking around behind your back, Massa."

Fairchild shivered. The youth jammed the gun harder against him and said, "You be still."

The older man said, "Lady, you better give that boy some help. Don't disappoint us now. That's a nasty little weapon on your husband's head there. My friend gets disappointed, that weapon might splatter your husband's brains all over this pretty room. You wouldn't want that, not with all these pretty boys you got calling on you here. Now would you?"

Fairchild groaned and cried, "Bettina for God's sake. Do what they ask! They're crazy. If you've done it before you can do it again. God, I don't care!"

83

Her eyes rolled and she gurgled, "Please, Tom . . ."

"You think I haven't known?" he moaned. He turned his head and muttered, "Go ahead. Once more won't make any difference. Do what they say."

Bettina gave her husband one last, long, imploring gaze, then she turned to her bedmate, her hands deftly imploring that of him which could prove the salvation of the moment. The future would provide for itself, her actions seemed to be saying. She flung her legs about and wriggled against her husband's star fledgling cop, and lunged at his mouth with hers, and the actions seemed to go on interminably with no visible results.

"You better get with it, boy," the big man urged. "I don't have all night for you to get your manhood up."

Tom Fairchild's eyes were floorbound. The young man behind him sighed and said, "She keeps sexpills in the drawer of the nightstand."

The other man grunted and bent over the nightstand. He opened a plastic packet and dropped the wafers into Bettina Fairchild's hand. She willingly accepted them and pushed one into Royal's mouth.

"You take one, too," the man growled.

She did so. Moments later the sounds of labored, passionate breathing were filling the bedroom. Tom Fairchild clenched his fists as his eyes were magnetically drawn to the couple on the bed, and to the writhing, straining, and moaning scene being enacted there.

Bettina's face, distorted and reflecting some indefinable emotion, was visible at the top of Royal's shoulders. She gasped and curled her arms about her partner's neck, her hips rising to meet his rhythmic thrusts.

Royal tremored and a little yelp burst from Bettina's parted lips. At that instant, the big man extended Royal's police revolver toward the bed with his left hand and pulled the trigger four times in rapid succession, the explosions jerking Fairchild out of the near-trance he had seemed to be in.

"No!" he screamed. "No no no"—and catapulted forward across the room, falling to his knees beside the bed, the roar of the big revolver still resounding, and he tried to stop with bare hands the flow of blood which was welling up from two ugly holes in his wife's face.

The gunman stepped across him, placed the revolver to Fairchild's left temple, and squeezed the trigger once again. The FPB Chief's head toppled forward onto the bed, his blood mingling with that already spilled there.

The man quickly wiped the gun clean and placed it in Fairchild's dead left hand, squeezing hard to insure a good grip. Then, with pressure on the dead man's trigger finger, he squeezed off another shot into the mattress.

"For the paraffin test, see," he told the youth, as though explaining the sum of two plus two. "Also he's left-handed. Watch things like that."

He stepped back to survey the scene, grunted, and said, "Right to the end, he never thought we'd do it. Right to the end." He grunted again. "Now that's realism, kid. Always remember this. You set the scene with everyday realism. Nothing phony, see. He's in her, or he was 'fore I blew his brains out. And he was in his rocks. That'll show, if they want to lab it."

"Too bad it's not Winston," the youth commented.

"Well, he'll get his. That guy's a traveling plague and don't know it. Come on, let's get out of here. Ritter says we have to take out everybody this Winston talks to. It'll be a lot easier to just get to Winston."

"Who's got to get old man Arlington?"

"That's not for us to wonder about." The two men were headed toward the front door. "Anyway, I take it Winston didn't make much of an impression on the old man. This Fairchild guy had 'im under arrest."

"These whiteys are all crazy," the younger man commented.

"They're more dumb than crazy. Like Fairchild. He really thought we weren't going to do it. Right to the bitter end, he thought it."

They turned to their car and made a quiet departure.

"Think anyone heard the shots?" the youth inquired.

"Sure. They'll get around to looking into it. Air Patrol

should be showing up pretty soon. Just wish I could be there to see their faces when they find them."

"That woman was a common slut, George. She took on all comers."

"Well, that's a sickness, they say. We cured it for her."

"Yeah." The youth was staring at his hands. "They thought we were white. They really thought that."

The big man shivered. "Like I told you, Marty. Whitey has got a lot to learn."

CHAPTER 3

Becky McCoy stepped into her cube, shrugged off her spring coat and dropped it into a chair, and tossed her handbag into the vestibule depository. It had become dark out and the automatic lighting system was operating at about 30 per cent glow, producing a twilight effect in the small apartment. She went to the far wall and waved her hand across the opening of a small box emplaced in the wall. Stereophonic music immediately filled the room, coming from all four walls and quite loud. She swung back and once again raised her hand, palm open, in front of the same box and slowly closed the distance between her hand and the box. The volume lowered with the progression of the hand movement; when it reached her level of taste, she whisked the hand away and marched off toward the recess which served as a kitchen.

The lighting sensors were beginning to react to the heat of her body; wherever she moved, growing brilliance preceded her. She looked through the clear plastic of the refrigerator door, working a little control near the top to cause the shelves to revolve for inspection. Nothing she saw inspired her. She decided she'd better do something with that beef—she was nowhere near her consumption quota for the week. It would sit in there and rot and then the meat people would be on her butt. She sighed, wondering what she could do with the beef. Then she stepped across to the *Working Girl's Chef*, studied the beef dishes, sighed again, and finally selected beef stroganoff, ignoring the *servings* selector entirely. That selector control had not moved off the "1" digit for so long the thing would probably blow up if she disturbed it.

Becky wondered idly if she would forever dine alone.

The corner of her vision caught the motion inside the refrigerator as a cut of beef slowly disappeared into the Chef Tube. She guessed she'd never fully accept the damn thing. There was something eerie and almost immoral about automated food preparation. If she had a couple of healthy kids to plan for, she certainly wouldn't rely on a damn automated chef to . . .

She forced herself to stop. Becky McCoy would never have a couple of kids, or not even one kid, or not even one husband to plan for. At thirty-five a girl had to face the reality of her life and times. Becky was facing it. And it was a gruesome reality.

She went back into the social, humming along under her breath with the canned music. A cigarette ash was on the couch. She wrinkled her nose and made a mental note to remind Maintenance to check her AVS, the automated vaccum system. Then she sat down and thumbed through the Television Annual, turned to the Marth 9th programming, and intently studied the list. Her mind wandered through the fifty selections and she found herself wondering if Mike Winston had managed to intercept Charles Waring.

Her mind returned to the program list and she began making her selections for the evening. Damn the television!

She wondered why she stayed in Washington. It was the loneliest city in the country. For a girl especially. She smiled grimly. Who the hell did she think she was kidding? It was the same everywhere. And Becky McCoy was no girl. She was slipping rapidly toward forty, and the abundant life had somehow passed her by. Out of all those years, just a few moments, a few golden moments when she had really known that she was live, and a woman, and loved. Couldn't a person logically expect to receive more than just a few golden moments?

Becky had thought, once, that there had been a chance with Mike Winston. Once. Not anymore. She had given Mike up, even the idea. But that had been one mad weekend, hadn't it? Almost her total treasury of remembered moments, that weekend. She sighed, lost in retrospect, and when the little gong sounded she mistook it for the Chef's signal. She got up and started for the kitchen, then she heard his voice in the Announcer, and her heart lurched.

"Becky, it's Mike Winston. May I come up?"

Breathlessly she replied, "Yes, yes, of course—come on up, Mike." Then she made a dash for the dressing room to see what Mike would see when he came through the door.

He did not appear to see much of anything. He was limping painfully, and his eyes were registering an emotion she'd never seen there before. He gave her a wan smile, limped on past her with a brief look over his shoulder, and sank onto the couch. "There was an accident," he explained. "I think I sprained my ankle."

"Let me take a look," she said. She sat on the floor, removed his shoe and sock, and said, "I have just the thing for this."

She pushed him onto his back, peered anxiously into his eyes, and asked him, "It's more than the ankle, isn't it? What's happened?"

He told her, "The world turned over on me, Becky. Don't ask for details, eh?"

She nodded her head and ran off toward the bath. Winston lit a cigarette, took two deep drags, and then she was back, applying some cool jelly-like goop to the injured area. The throbbing immediately began to subside.

"Good stuff," he commented. "Mother McCoy, you're some good medicine."

She said, "Keep your dirty comments to yourself. And keep your leg in this position until the stuff dries. It will take away the swelling too."

"Thanks," he said, and lay weakly back, the cigarette forgotten. Becky removed it from his fingers and dropped it into the tube. Then she went back to the bath and returned the Spranepak to its place in the medical dispenser. When she returned Winston was sound asleep.

She dropped to the floor beside the couch and lay her head on his shoulder. Miracles, she decided, still happened. And here was another golden moment for the treasury.

Winston sat bolt upright and tried to make his eyes focus on his wristwatch. The couch had been cantilevered out into a circular bed; the ceiling television viewer was activated. Becky McCoy lay beside him, wearing a lace bedjacket and, he presumed, nothing else. She had obviously been watching the television. She rolled toward him on an elbow, smiling, and asked, "Do you always awaken like King Kong?"

He told her, "My watch is dead. What time is it?"

"Almost ten," she replied.

"I have to get out of here, Becky," he muttered.

"You've hardly arrived," she told him.

"A war game is scheduled to start on the West Coast at midnight. I have to get out there."

"I didn't know you played at war," she said cooly.

"Well this one may not be a play. I've got to . . . uh . . . say, the ankle's feeling fine. You're a good doctor."

"Awhile ago I was Mother McCoy," she reminded him.

He was up and hobbling about the small room, rounding up his things. He told her, "You know I appreciate the breather, Becky."

"Drop in any time," she said. "Any time you need first aid."

Something in her tone pierced his mental turmoil and turned him around. He looked at her through a long moment of silence, then grinned and told her, "I'm a hell of a guy. Becky, you're a woman in a million. Thanks. I mean it, thanks."

She said, "You're welcome, and I mean that. You're welcome to anything you can find around here, Mike Winston."

He said, "Becky . . . something wild is going on. I can't tell you about it, but believe me, it's wild. And it's about to eat me, maybe all of us. I have to get out to California. Will you give me a raincheck?"

"For what?" she asked quietly.

"For whatever I can find around here."

She dropped her eyes. "You've had one for three years. You know that."

He sighed. "Yes, I've known it. Becky . . . I really *must* get to California."

"The next commuter doesn't leave until midnight," she informed him.

"Is that right?"

"That's right."

He sat down and pulled his feet onto the bed. "Well, I can't think of a nicer place to wait for midnight."

Her eyes thanked him. She said, "I'm too old for pride, Mike. I'm dying of loneliness."

He told her, "You're too much woman for that. You're not built for solo."

She sighed and said, "Amen, and I am open to suggestions."

"I think I'd like a drink," he told her.

Her face brightened. "Me too." She flipped about to all fours and crawled to the wall-headboard, slid open a cabinet, and started punching buttons. "The last time we drank together," she reminded him, "you had whiskey, lemon, and water."

She pressed a frosted plastic tumbler into his hand and toasted him silently with her eyes. Winston tasted his drink, winked at her, and took a mansized pull at it. "You know, that stuff does help," he commented.

He stared at her for a thoughtful moment and allowed his eyes to roam the luxurious figure beneath the lace. Then he soberly asked her, "Do you feel in the mood for a bit of sexplay, Becky?"

A tear squeezed beyond control and rolled down the smooth plane of her cheek. She gave her head a dainty toss and admitted, "I'm half-dead for lack of some. But I don't want it as a gift, Michael."

He smiled soberly and told her, "It's the nicest gift one human can pass to another, Becky."

"I'm in love with you," she said.

He said, "Your drink is getting flat."

"Story of my life." She smiled brightly and swiped angrily at another tear. "I've been in love with you for three years."

He threw his glass across the room and swept her into his arms. The lace fell away, and one hell of a lot of woman came alive in his embrace. He whispered, "This is no gift, Becky."

"Yes, yes it is," she gasped. "It's the gift of life."

And he knew that it was—not for her, but for him. There were two ways of looking at the AMS society, he decided. Some people buried themselves in quivering flesh. Others, if they were very lucky, found themselves there. And, for awhile, Mike Winston gloried in the paradox of sexual love; and he lost himself to the problems of the world, and found himself in the problems of two very lonely people.

At eleven o'clock he told her, "My God!" with a longdrawn sigh.

Her head was nuzzled into his shoulder, her rhythmic breathing was traveling through his flesh in some strange osmosis of empathy. She stirred, traced the outline of his jaw with an exploring fingertip, moaned softly, and moved her face onto his chest.

"I'll take half of that any time," she murmured.

"Then I think we ought to get married," he announced lazily.

"Some things we just don't joke about, my love," she said languidly.

"I wasn't joking."

"You mean a real true-blue AMS card in the slot ceremony?"

"Yeah, even that," he said, sighing.

"Okay."

"Okay? Is that all? Okay?"

She giggled. "Okay, I'll marry you. But you'll have to give me time to prepare. At least ten minutes."

He rubbed a hand lightly across her hip and told her, "I'm serious, Becky."

She said, "Okay, serious, tell me about Leslie, your other love."

He sighed. "Leslie was a fracto. She died tragically at the uncomely age of twenty-two. And I've mourned her long enough."

She had raised up to peer into his eyes. "Did you say fracto?"

"Uh huh. That's what killed her. She didn't know it until the day before we were to be married. She jumped out of a window on the 20th floor of the Eisenhower Building." He sighed. "And I guess I've been leaping out that same window every day since."

The light mood between them had vanished. Becky moaned, "Oh Michael."

He said, "One of life's little cruelties. Didn't even get a newspaper mention. It was during the Arlington purge of '92. I was with the justice Department then, and she was an adorable little thing in the programming section." A muscle worked in his jaw and he added, "I told her it didn't matter to me. It did, of course. But not that much. It wasn't that she was any better looking than the average woman. You've got it all over her in the body-beautiful department. And, let's face it, you're probably twice the woman Leslie would have ever been. But there was . . . I don't know, something about the way she carried herself. The tilt of her head . . . a sort of vibrant something . . . a fire, I guess, an inner fire. She just stood out. In my vision, anyway. I loved her very deeply, I think. Think, hell. I loved her like the flowers love the sun."

"What did the purge of '92 have to do with it? I thought that was a subversives' purge."

He reached beyond her and snared a cigarette and lit it, then watched the smoke drift away and said, "Well, that was when the Asian panics began. And there was some sort of nutty fear about the Asian-African pact. All the blacks in government service were given the fine-sieve treatment, especially those in the military arms and in those civil branches regarded as quote sensitive unquote. Justice was regarded as one of those. I was on Harold Postum's staff then, that was in the days before FPB. They would not have checked Leslie so closely if it hadn't been known that she was engaged to marry me." He exhaled a long column of smoke. "They found a nigger in the woodpile, four generations back. They call that an *octoroon*. And they told me that the Attorney General's number one man could not be married to an octoroon. So I told the Attorney General what to do with his job. I begged them—I mean I *begged* them to not tell Leslie. But they had to. The AMS override, see. They had to classify her as an Aunty Tom. She fell apart. I tried to hold her together, and I thought I almost had it whipped. Then Postum called her in and told her what she was doing to my quote fine career unquote. And she went right out of his window. Head first."

"Oh God, Mike," Becky commented.

"Yeah, oh God. I think that's when I told him to get lost."

Horror and misery were evident in her voice as Becky said, "So that's how you happened to leave the Justice Department."

He smiled thinly and told her, "No, not quite that heroically. I was half crazy for a week or so, but they gave me time to collect myself. And when I did, I had my tail down and firmly captured between my legs. I rode it out, and tried to forget. I couldn't, of course. And . . ." He sighed and got rid of the cigarette. "And I started dragging my feet in one area and another. To put it bluntly, I hit the skids. I kept seeing Leslie in every black person and I filed some briefs in the courts on behalf of a number of them . . . and one thing led to another. In '95 I was being considered for the number two job in the new federal police force. And a buddy of mine wanted the job worse. He was the first one to call me an Uncle Mose. Then it all fell in. And that's when I came to Urban." He chuckled drily. "By presidential direction."

"I'll be proud to marry you, Mike," Becky quickly told him.

He kissed her, warmly and slowly, and then he rolled off the bed and got into his clothing. "Stay ready," he said. "Quit your job. Go some place quiet and far away from any Town. How about Connecticut? Your aunt still there?"

She showed him saucer eyes and nodded her head.

"Okay. Go to Connecticut. I'll contact you there. Take some good books and lose yourself until you hear from me. I have a job to do, or a job to at least *try* to do."

"Something is going on with the blacks, isn't it?" she observed in a frightened voice. "That's why you wanted the passkeys. It's why you came in here all banged up."

He nodded. "I think they might be getting ready to come out of the Towns. You stay clear, *way* clear. I don't want to lose love again to this insanity."

Her eyes watered and she said, "This may be inappropriate, but that's the nicest speech I've ever heard."

He smiled and told her, "No, I guess it's very appropriate."

"I'll be waiting for you in Connecticut. With my Mailer."

"With your what?"

"The collected works of Norman Mailer."

"Well there's a start," he said. "Mailer knew where it was at."

"Call it a whisper from yesterday, Becky. From an age of *guts*. Hey. Come on, help me find my stuff. There's a bucket waiting for me in California."

"A bucket of what?" she asked, the puzzlement growing.

"Guts," he said. "A bucket of guts."

CHAPTER 4

It was a large house, in the synthetic early colonial styling—mostly plastics—with huge white columns gleaming in the brilliance of floodlights. Winston set the Avis U-fly down on the oval of the circular drive, cut the engine, and consulted his watch. It was eleven-twenty, Mountain Time—so far he'd lost less than half an hour in this sudden inspiration to detour through Colorado; the side-flight from Stapleton Field to the Cherry Hills estate of Jason Tromanno should cost him another half-hour at most, all time considered.

His inspection took in the ornate sweep of grounds surrounding the mansion. Winston was glad that the old man had been able to preserve an acre or two through all his troubles. He walked rapidly along the flagstone footpath, ascended winding plastic steps, and pulled the pendant-type door bell. A little man in a domestic's white jacket responded immediately, a magnificent Doberman on a short leash at his side.

The visitor eyed the big dog uneasily and said, "I'm Winston."

"Identification, please," the other requested.

Winston produced his credentials. The man smiled, and said, "Step in, please. The man is waiting in the library."

The man. Yeah, he still deserved to be called *the man*.

The little guy in the white jacket was a Tom, not much doubt about that. They went across a foyer along a short hallway, and into the library. The first thing to catch Winston's eye was the nurse; he caught his breath and gazed at her closely, then smiled away the resemblance to Leslie. It wasn't so much the physical characteristics—it was something about the way she stood, the way her head angled a bit to the side as she looked at him.

She returned his smile and said, "Don't let the man overexert himself. He shouldn't even be up this late."

Winston nodded his reassurance and went on into the room. Tromanno occupied a huge overstuffed chair in front of the fireplace, and he seemed to be raptly studying the flames from the synthetic logs. Winston hoped his face did not reveal his sense of shock at the old fellow's appearance. Never a large man, the former U.S. President was now a delicate stack of bones encased in transparent skin.

The old man leaned forward, brushed a silvery wisp of hair from his forehead, and extended a bony hand. Winston took it, warmly and carefully, and mumbled, "It's good to see you again, sir."

"I'll just have to take your word for it that you're Mike Winston," Tromanno told him, in a surprisingly strong voice. He peered closely into Winston's eyes. "Everyone changes with age, of course. Even in the eyes. As I recall, you had very daring eyes."

"You once told me I had *your* eyes, sir," Winston reminded him.

The old man laughed, a deeply booming flood of pleasant music, then cut it off abruptly and placed a hand on his chest. "Every laugh takes another hour off my life, they tell me," he said. "People used to tell me I'd die laughing." He sniffed. "Better than dying crying, I suppose. Well . . . what've you been up to all these years, Michael? I hear you're a nigger tender now."

"That's why I'm here, sir. I need your counsel."

The old man leaned forward in the chair and peered around Winston's figure, his gaze taking in the nurse and the manservant who had remained nearby. The dog was watching Winston, head cocked to one side, ears standing stiffly.

Tromanno said, "Henry, you and Em go take a coffee break, or a brandy break, or whatever young people break with these days. I'll ring if I want you."

"Should I leave Rhinemaster, sir?" the manservant asked.

"Take the slavering beastie with you," the old man commanded. "He'd as soon eat me as anybody else. I've noticed him giving hungry looks at my legbone here lately."

The manservant laughed, sent the ex-president an affectionate twinkling of eyes and went out with the dog. The nurse paused in the doorway to give Winston a final critical appraisal, then she too vanished.

"They are a couple of your responsibilities," Tromanno told Winston. "Or I suppose you noticed, if you still have good eyes."

Winston said, "Yes sir. I've been noticing many things during the past few months. I'm afraid, sir, that the black volcano is rumbling again."

"That so?" Tromanno eyed his visitor thoughtfully, sank back into the cushions, and drummed his fingers on a bony knee. Presently he asked, "Would you like a smoke, Mike?"

Winston declined.

"I sure as hell would," the old man declared. "But I've had my three for the day. Well so what—it's almost midnight, isn't it?" He opened a pedestal type humidor, selected a cigar, lit it, coughed, glared at it, then quietly said, "It's about time."

"Sir?"

"It's about time for some rumbling. When do you figure the lava will start flowing?"

"I expect it most any time, sir. It may already be flowing."

"I see. Well . . . good! I hope I live to see it."

"It could get pretty brutal," Winston said soberly.

"More brutal than the seventies? Than the eighties?"

Tromanno puffed furiously at the cigar. "They say two wrongs never make a right. Baloney! I say it always *takes* the second wrong to restore right. So do you think the second wrong will be wronger than the first one?"

"Perhaps more damaging to the nation as a whole, sir," Winston replied.

"Damn the nation as a whole! The nation as a whole ceased to exist twenty years ago."

"In a sense, sir, I suppose I agree with you."

The old man smoked and coughed some more, then he asked, "Why'd you come up here tonight, Mike?"

"Grabbing at straws, I guess. I've come to a conclusion that a Negro uprising is imminent. I can't get anyone to listen to me. I suppose I—"

"What's happened to you, Michael?"

"Sir?"

"Why aren't you standing up and cheering them on?"

"Well, I . . . we're speaking of carnage, Mr. President. Destruction of an undreamt magnitude . . . civil war, that's what we're contemplating, sir."

"It started more than two hundred years ago."

"Sir?"

"This civil war you speak of. It began in the Eighteenth Century. It has never ceased. It *shall* never cease. It cannot. It must not. Can you understand that?"

"I'm not sure I do, sir."

"The problems between the governors and the governed are unremitting, especially in a so-called democracy."

"Yes sir, I accept that."

"But listen, Michael. There is no such thing as a pure democracy. We can make grand speeches about freedom and we can sneer at the totalitarians, but it's all one big ball game."

"I'm afraid I don't quite agree, sir."

"Some day you'll see it. Arlington saw it. To our everlasting damnation."

"I, uh, think I get your drift, sir."

"Drift, hell. Tell me something, Mike. What is the most horrible sort of tyranny? That of a despot? Or that of a democratic majority?"

99

"I, uh . . . That seems to be a paradoxical question, sir."

"Paradoxical hell. It's pure grim reality. When you've got one-man rule, everybody in the state is riding the same boat. The problem of the governed is a common one. Everybody's alike. But there is no more horrible form of despotism than to find yourself a part of a hated minority in a state run by majority rule. Then the despots are on every street corner, in every public place. They are your employers, your neighbors, your policeman, even your doctors and preachers and teachers. Oh, Michael . . . what terrible tyrants we free men are!"

Winston grinned. "This is like old times, sir. When I was a little boy, hiding in the dark in the next room, and listening to the arguments between you and my father."

"Yes and we argued about the same damn things, didn't we? Ah well, your father was a good man, Mike. Misguided here and there, but a good man who eventually saw the truth."

"Yes sir. He died for his convictions, sir."

"That he did. And what are your convictions, Michael?"

"I'm not sure." Winston took time to light a cigarette. He gazed at the old man and softly declared, "But I don't want to see a totally black America, I'm sure of that."

"Neither does anybody else. Not even the Negro, if he's honest with himself. Arlington niggered us, Mike. He niggered the whites and he even niggered the blacks. He got us all shook out and set apart from one another, just like one of those whirling machines they use in the laboratories to separate everything out. They called me a nigger lover, Mike. Hell, I'm not a nigger lover. Never have been. But I'm not a nigger hater, either. I'm an *America* lover, Mike. You know what a principle is, Mike?"

"I think so, sir."

"So what is the guiding principle of this country today?"

"I, uh, couldn't say, sir."

"That's because there are no guiding principles in this country today. A principle, Mike, is usually something you don't particularly like to do. While ago you said something about paradox. A principle is a paradox. We all want the other man to be principled, but we don't want to be

100

chained by that same method of personal conduct. So a principle is always something for the other man to observe. But you remember this—if you're going through life just being comfortable, just doing the things you like to do, or want to do, then you're unprincipled. And if you're unprincipled, then you have no character. Where is the character of America today, Michael?"

"I don't know, sir."

"Could it be stirring itself, do you think, in the Towns?"

Winston gave the old man a startled look.

"You can't answer the question. All right, don't answer it. But when you find the answer, just be sure you let yourself know. So, the niggers are coming out. Hip hip hooray. Who do you think their top people are?"

"Williams, for one. Bogan, I believe. Most of the town mayors."

Tromanno nodded thoughtfully and dropped his gaze to the fireplace. "Well, whoever they are, let's hope they're a blending—I mean a well-balanced blending of Eldridge Cleaver, Martin King, and Whitney Young. That'll give them fist, heart, and mind—and they're going to need all of it."

"These people here, sir, in the house. Can you count on their loyalty? To you, I mean?"

"Why not?" Tromanno snorted.

"I have reason to believe that many of the Toms are figuring prominently in the uprising. They have more freedom of movement, without appearing to be out of place. This would be vital to any intelligence operation. Also I wouldn't be surprised if many of them were trained assassins."

"You said Bogan is in it," Tromanno recalled. "If they have the army, what else do they need?"

"Our armed forces are pared to the bone, sir. Quick-reaction teams and hordes of technicians—that's most of the army. The navy is little more than a convoying force to protect our foodstuffs shipments from the desperate nations. Air Force is mostly mothballed except for a few fighter wings for continental defense. Automated Defense Command is the major fist of the nation; it could have no

101

role in a civil war. No sir, it's going to be an old fashioned method of warfare if any at all. It's going to be a people war and they've got the weapons."

"Where'd they get them?"

"Army has been secretly unwrapping the mothballs and stacking them about the country at deactivated facilities. Rifles, machine guns, heavy weapons, armor, munitions of every size and type."

"By God, it sounds like they mean business this time."

"Yes sir, I'm afraid so."

"Don't be afraid, Michael. Hell might descend, yes—but could it be much worse than purgatory? Something good, something *vital*, will come out of this, Mike. You wait and see."

"You, uh, struck a chord there, sir. I've been giving some thought to national vitality myself."

The old man coughed and said, "It's about time someone did. This nation has lost its soul, my boy. It has lost its very soul."

"Yes sir, I agree with that completely. About the Toms, sir. Are you safe here?"

Tromanno laughed quietly. "Yes, I'm as safe as I've ever been. As for Henry and Em, they're like family. Fella I had here a year or so ago, though . . . now he was a hardcase. Temporary help. Used to stand out behind the kitchen and throw the butcher knife into a board, hour after hour. Saw him split a two-by-eight once from a distance of over twenty feet. Had a photo of the Governor, the Governor of Colorado, in his room. Or so Henry told me. Knew the Governor's habits like they came out of the same womb. Went back to town on a weekend off, about a year ago, and never came back. They said he'd died." The old man chuckled. "I don't think he died. I'll bet he's gardening or chauffeuring for the Governor right now. I've been wondering, just wondering, all this time. I'm glad you visited me, Michael. But I don't think I can hold my head up another five minutes. Gravity gets heavier on the old frame every day."

"Well . . . I've enjoyed the visit, sir. And the conversation, as ever, has been entirely stimulating."

"All conversation does is rustle the leaves in the trees, Michael," the ex-president wheezed. "A leaf, you know, falls to the ground and rots or gets burnt. So do a lot of thoughts, produced by stimulating conversation. See to your leaves, Mike. Go on. Go see to your leaves."

CHAPTER 5

The scene at Oakland's Warhole was one of bustling but orderly activity. Ten giant troop copters stood in receiving formation across the artificial turf, great rotary wings whispering softly in a slow idle. Abraham Lincoln Williams sat at the center of the old press box, now a loadmaster's tower, his face close to the glass window in stiff inspection of the activities down on the field. The spectator areas of the massive stadium were filled to capacity with dark young men in U.S. Army combat garb, from which seemingly endless queues extended from all sides to the field.

General Jackson Bogan paced back and forth across the booth behind Williams, speaking occasionally into a hand mike as necessary to give directions to platoon leaders as they moved their troops along the embarkation lines and toward the aircraft.

Suddenly an amplified voice drifted across the stadium, breaking the muted sounds from below. "Aircraft approaching from two o'clock."

Bogan snatched up another headset and spoke briefly into it. He listened for a moment, then instructed, "Let him land if that is his intention. But if he comes within a thousand yards of our traffic pattern and appears to be passing on, then help him land."

The General tossed the headset away and told Abe Williams, "Hover car. Might just be lovers on a moonlight ride." He ran a finger nervously along the base of his nose, then barked into the command net, "Dog Company, take up that slack, move along to Station 10."

"Nuts," he said, glancing at his civilian chief. "Moving this number of troops in such a limited area and keeping this schedule is an exercise I don't care to repeat."

Abe Williams seemed not to have heard. He was gazing into the sky toward San Francisco. "That hover car is coming in," he decided. "And I'll bet I know who's in it. Look at that. He's seen our big birds, and still he comes down. What's the latest from Ritter on that Washington hit?"

"Generally satisfactory," he reported, rather disinterestedly. His main concern was obviously with the operations below. "They lost Winston, though. Just flat lost him. In *church*, of all places. But Ritter believes Winston is neutralized."

"Well I'll bet we're going to find out right quick," Williams declared unemotionally.

"The hovercar wouldn't be one of Ritter's? Don't his people know the recognition signals?"

"No," Williams sighed. "No, I think this must be Mr. Guts himself."

Bogan stared down upon the little hovercar, just beginning to settle onto the turf between two overshadowing copters. "Mr. who?" he muttered.

"Mike Winston. Well that nervy . . . Look at that. That's him, all right. Can you *beat* that nervy . . . ? Give me that headset, Jack—quick!"

The General tossed him the radio gear and Williams jerked the transmitter to his lips. "Leave that whitey breathing and handle him gently! Bring him up here!" His eyes were anxiously on the scene below as a voice crackled back through the earphone. "Yes, this is Top Man. Get him up here!"

He returned the headset to Bogan and told him, "You know, you just have to admire that guy. He's like the old British Empire men—crusty and gutsy and absolutely incorruptible. I wonder how he ever survived the Arlington administration."

"With bruises," the General replied. *"Chopper One, you're loaded. Batten down and get ready."*

Williams was watching the distant approach. He grinned and said, "Our esteemed commissioner has had a very frustrating day. Just look at him. Tired, middle-aged hero, and nobody knows it yet, not even him."

Bogan grunted and resumed his pacing. Presently Mike Winston appeared at the glass door, dwarfed between two enormous black soldiers. One of the escorts opened the door and called in, "You want him in there, sir?"

"Yes, leave him," Williams instructed.

"We took a gun off him, sir. Watch him."

The black leader waved the soldiers away and watched Winston walk into the press box. He glanced at Williams and went directly to the window to gaze soberly upon the scene below.

"Nightmare alley," Winston muttered. "First time I'm sorry to be right."

"If you thought this was happening, why'd you come?" Williams asked, a faint smile playing at his lips.

Winston sighed. "I wasn't *that* sure. I overheard an Air Police signal about troop 'copters over Oakland. I wanted to see for myself."

"Now you see."

"Yeah, now I see. Pretty cute. Wargames cover and all. You feel really ready for this, Abe? You think you can take on the United States of America?"

"What do *you* think, Commissioner?"

"I think you're out of your mind. I can't let you do it, Abe."

Williams laughed. "And just what do you propose to do about it?"

"I didn't come here to plead with you," Winston said. "Reason, maybe. I doubt that you know what you're walking into. Arlington's been onto you for some time. He has some counter-strategy going."

"Like what?"

Winston shook his head. "I don't know like what. But

he's a crafty old fox. I think he's working something on you, Abe."

"He just *thinks* so," Bogan declared, joining the conversation. "*Okay, Chopper One, assume flight station.*"

"Yes, we know Ol' White Devil's master plan," Williams told Winston. "He's been setting us up for a total knockover for the past four years. He'd planned to unveil it a week before election day. You tell me why."

Winston rubbed his forehead and continued staring at the activities on the field. "I don't know why, even assuming your information is correct. But let's hold this operation a moment while we discuss it, eh?"

Abe Williams laughed in his face. "Hear that?" He jerked a thumb toward the playing field and the sound of huge rotary blades whipping the air.

Chopper One rose slowly from the deck, heeled over at sharp angle, and side-slipped beyond the enclosing walls and toward San Francisco.

"Too late for reasoning, or for pleading, or for anything, Commissioner. Oh, and it's even too late to be calling you *Commissioner*. Your commission expired, Winston, three hours ago."

"What?"

"Oh, didn't you hear about that? The President fired you. Publicly."

"*Chopper Two, you're loaded*," Bogan declared, in the background.

"Fired me on what pretense?"

Williams chuckled. "You're an enemy of the state. Carousing around with town niggers, always making trouble for your country, keeping the niggers stirred up all the time and unwilling to accept their heaven-declared fate."

"Well, it figures," Winston said, sighing.

"He said you were even going to marry one once."

A muscle twitched in Winston's jaw. "Did he actually bring her into it?"

Williams nodded. The smile was gone. "He did. On nationwide television."

"Bastard," Winston muttered.

"Chopper Two, assume flight station."

Williams was watching the white man closely. "It's all over for you, Winston. Those men done you wrong, the same way they done me wrong—and I'd guess for precisely the same reason. They don't care if you're black or white. They only know you're weaker than they are, and they're going to do you wrong come hell or fair acres."

"This is all crazy. Arlington is crazy. *You* are crazy."

"Sure I am," Williams replied agreeably. "Crazy enough to play their game, their way. And at dawn, which is just a couple hours away from Washington right now, the balance of power is going to change. The President's cabinet is going to die. Your boss dies. The Inter-Military Coordinator dies—all of the hatchet men, the henchmen, all the crazy devils die at dawn, Mr. Winston. Your friend Fairchild is already dead—his woman too, regrettably. We tried to make *you* die, Winston. You wouldn't stand still long enough. So now here you are, ex-Commissioner, standing still for us."

Winston watched Chopper Two rise from the pad.

"All right, kill me. If I can't stop you, then you'd better kill me. Before I strangle you with my bare hands."

"Talk sensible, man. How could *you* stop it? How could *I* stop it? This thing didn't start today. It didn't start yesterday, or last year. I couldn't stop it right now if I *died* trying, which I wouldn't. You've got twenty million people eating shit, Winston. How long did you expect to get away with it? These are *Americans* you're shitting on, Whitey."

"Yeah, Americans," Winston murmured.

"Chopper Three, you're loaded. Batten down and get ready. Third Platoon! This's no damn drill! Pick it up there. Move on station!"

"You want to know how determined we are? Can you imagine the Chairman of the Joint Chiefs standing out here directing a local combat operation?"

"Whatever logic you want to use, Abe, this is wrong. It's wrong right down to the pit of my stomach and yours. I know you, I know the kind you are. And dammit *you know this is wrong!*"

"Lift off, Chopper Three, lift off!"

"You go to hell, Winston. Don't you stand here in this black town that betrayal built, and argue right and wrong with *me*. We're breaking out. It's that simple. I might let you live awhile. I *might*. But you keep remembering where you are and who you're talking to. You keep *remembering* it!"

"Chopper Four, what the hell! Hold that bird steady. Third Platoon, shake it, shake it!"

Winston sighed and turned away from the terrible sight. "Well," he declared in a hushed voice, "I guess all I can do now is pray for a miracle."

"Won't do any good, Winston," Abe Williams told him. "I tried that twenty years ago, and I tried it ten years ago, and I tried it five years ago—and thousands before me have been trying it for two hundred years. And it never has done any good." He jerked a thumb toward the window as Chopper Four slid past. "There's my prayers now, Winston. Angels with rotary wings, come to carry my people out of hell. You get some prayers like that going, maybe you can do some good." He paused to gaze down at the endless stretch of uniformed men. "Otherwise, Whitey, otherwise . . ." He turned his thumb down, in the classic symbol of death.

And in the background, the steady voice of General Jackson Bogan. *"Batten down, Chopper Five, you're loaded."*

CHAPTER 6

Private Alfred Hannon, California Guard, propped his rifle against the guard shack and dug inside his jacket for cigarettes and lighter. After he'd gotten the cigarette going, he continued to hold the lighter cupped in his hands, warming them by the flickering flame.

What the hell was the need for a guard post way back there anyway? They had a guy on the gate up front, and one at the rear—what'd they want with posts inside the compound?

Being in the military was all right at times. It had its moments. This was not one of them. The good moments were when you got into your dress uniform and went back to the Marin Strip and showed the girls how a white man looks in a jazzy uniform. Yeah. They went into zots over that uniform. But right now Pvt. Hannon was wishing that his six months of Active was over. There was no sense in this stuff . . . standing around out here in the cold, in the middle of the night, with nothing but the coastal fog for company.

As he was thus engrossed in his thoughts, a peculiar sound bore in on his consciousness, a strange flapping as though a million seagulls had appeared overhead at once. What the hell could it be? Hannon peered up into the swirling mist which typifies that portion of coastline at night. A chopper?

Yeah, it could be one of those big troop lifters. Nothing else in his experience would beat the air like that. But the young soldier could see nothing, and now he was not even certain that he had heard anything. Feet crunching gravel, somewhere off in the darkness. Hannon quickly pinched the cigarette out and flicked it away, picked up his rifle, and tried his best to look something like a soldier walking a guard post. Who the hell would be out here, in the . . . ? He could not remember anyone ever inspecting the guard, not once during the two months he'd been Active—but it would be just like that chickenshit sergeant to try to catch him goofing off. Big deal! If the guy wanted to be the big bad military man, then why the hell didn't he darken his skin and get into a *real* outfit? Yeah. Because, dammit, he'd never make the grade in the Regulars, those big mean blacks wouldn't even let him be a private, that's why.

Runnin' around in the middle of the night, trying to catch a guy warming his hands in the cold. Hell, why didn't . . . ? It wasn't the sarge. The shadowy figures of two men, walking rapidly, passed in front of him some fifteen to twenty feet away. "Hey, you guys!" he called out.

The two spun about, hesitated a moment, then slowly approached. Hell, he should have given them the proper military challenge. Maybe they were from Sacramento. Damn, what big bastards! And what th' hell were they doing in *combat* uniform? And walking around out here in the cold mists *this* time of night? Then he thought of the big chopper. New outfit coming in? *Here*? To the *motor pool* for Christ's sake?

The two guys were close enough now to spit on. They halted and eyed him. He lowered his rifle and grinned. "What outfit you guys with?"

"Th' Freedom Brigade," one answered, stepping slightly to one side.

"The what?" He craned forward to get a better look at their insignia. He saw the rifle butt instead, a split-second before it crashed into his mouth.

He fell over onto his back, it seemed like in slow motion,

111

and he was still conscious, but it felt like his face was gone. No pain, just numbness, disbelief. What had they done that for? Just because he wasn't walking his post in a military manner? What did they have to do that for? Didn't they know that he was just Guard, Active?

The roar of the Pacific surf was growing louder and louder. It was taking him over, and he was feeling very poetic. *Cradle me, Mother Sea, hold me in your bosom of eternity.*

He was dimly aware that someone was standing over him, but he neither saw nor felt the long bayonet as it entered his throat.

Private Alfred Hannon, California Guard, Active, age nineteen, died quickly—puzzled and painlessly. And perhaps his soul did join the eternal sea. He was the first military casualty of the Second Civil War.

CHAPTER 7

Patrolman Marvin Taylor, California Traffic Patrol, cruised slowly along the Pacific Park Highway, feeling like the only man alive. He always felt this way when he had the night patrol. This big beautiful six-lane parkway and nobody to use it but the cop on the beat.

It had not forever been this way, of course. He could remember a time when this stretch of the most beautiful scenic highway in the state looked like Bayshore during baseball season, with everybody in the whole damn Bay Area trying to get into Candlestick to watch those slugging Giants. Willy Mays, now *there* had been a power. *Bat* power, not *black* power.

They had lost something when they lost the blacks. *They* meaning the country. They'd lost a lot of grief and turmoil with it, sure, but they'd lost something fine, too.

Yeah, they'd lost a lot. Funny how the human mind never appreciated something until you no longer had it. Like the damn traffic. How he had cussed and sweated the damn freeway traffic back in those days. Now he missed it. Tonight, Marvin Taylor felt like the only man alive. Six beautiful lanes, all for the cop on the beat. It had been this way, especially at night, since the heli-car craze. Then the copters gave way to the hovers. But they didn't use highways, either.

The Patrol had been affected, of course. Most of the younger cops had gone over to the Air Division. That was all right. Let the kids have their damn flying vacuum cleaners. He'd be content as long as there was a berth for an old-fashioned cop in an old-fashioned vehicle. Even if he did feel like the only man alive.

He was coming onto the Sloat Boulevard ramp when an unbelievable sight smote him coming off the loop from Funston. Approaching him was a string of automobile headlamps a mile or more long. He touched his brake and pulled to the shoulder, waiting for the phenomenon to reach him.

And then they were flashing by, and his heart jumped. A *military convoy*? How long had it been since he'd seen a damn . . . ? The patrolman reached for the sheaf of papers clipped to the dashboard and rapidly leafed through them. There was nothing there about a convoy! He reached for his radio mike, then changed his mind and instead cranked the wheel and spun onto the median, up the slight embankment and into the northbound lanes, his rear-end fishtailing wildly for a moment.

Then he was straightened out and tearing along the inside lane, beacon flashing, laying on the coals and passing vehicle after vehicle of the long procession. This was exhilarating! How long had it been since he'd had a chance to be a real cop! Too long, much too long!

The convoy was slowing. In less than a minute the patrol car was running abreast of the command jeep. Yeah, by God, it was Regular Army. Two black mercenaries in that jeep. Taylor touched his siren and gave a friendly wave. The jeep immediately swerved ahead of him, into his lane, and one of the soldiers was standing up in the jeep and waving the convoy on by. Taylor was forced to stand his car on its nose to avoid hitting the slowing jeep, then the little vehicle swung onto the Observation Access and pulled into the Seal Rocks Overlook.

The patrol car followed, Taylor feeling a bit sheepish

about the entire incident. Hell, he hadn't meant to screw them up. The convoy was flashing past, however—maybe the boys had meant to pull off here anyway.

He left the patrol vehicle and walked over to the jeep. A young lieutenant half-stood in the seat beside the driver, watching his convoy by. His eyes flashed to the patrolman and he asked, "Your beacon burning for our benefit, officer?"

"Hadn't meant to stop you," the cop apologized. "Just trying to get up front to clear the way for you. That's all."

"On *this* highway, *this* time of night?"

The cop smiled. "You might've hit some trouble up at the bridge interchange. Where you headed—Presidio?"

"Yes, that's where we're headed."

"Well, hell, I'm sorry you stopped." He turned back toward the patrol car. "I'll call ahead and have a unit take you in."

"Just a minute, officer," the lieutenant said. "Uh . . . the driver thinks his left front wheel is loose. I'm afraid neither of us is very mechanically inclined. I wonder if you'd . . ."

So that was it. "Sure, be glad to," Marvin Taylor assured the military. Hell, he was glad they hadn't stopped on *his* account. "You young people spend all your time floating through the air and in those whiz cars. How could you learn anything about wheels?" He chuckled and walked around the front of the jeep. The driver was already on the ground, his hands gripping the tire. "Well, let's have a look."

The patrolman knelt beside the soldier and examined the lugs of the wheel with his pocket flash. Without warning, he was seized by the neck. Another hand looped into his leather belt, and he felt himself being hoisted into the air.

There was no time to react, nor to assess the situation, nor even to wonder about it. All Marvin Taylor realized was that he was floating free, and that the foam-flecked rocks he'd gazed at so reflectively a few minutes earlier were now rushing up to meet him.

The patrol car followed seconds later, crashing through the guard rail and spinning crazily as it sought to find its place in the law . . . the law of gravity.

But Patrolman Marvin Taylor, California Traffic Patrol—was the first official civilian casualty of the Second Civil War. For this old cop, the day ended before it fully began, when a black cat crossed his path.

CHAPTER 8

Mrs. Floyd Benton Hewgley raised her eyes from the magazine and followed her husband's progression from the door of their bedroom to the window.

"I was wondering if you were ever coming to bed, Governor," she said, pouting a little.

"I've . . . been thinking," he murmured, from the window. His hands were thrust deep into pants pockets, his shoulders slumped, his entire manner one of dejection.

"Thinking? Or drinking?"

"All right, both," he admitted. "Why am I always so depressed, Myra? Isn't this what we always wanted? Look at that out there, those rolling grounds, that beautiful expanse of the best grass in Arkansas, never used by a damn soul but the gardener. No kids to play on it, not even any of our own. Is this the Executive Mansion, Myra, or is it the Executive Jailhouse?"

"You think too deeply for me, Floyd Benton, your excellency," she told him. She returned to her magazine, then looked up again suddenly. "It's going to be daylight soon. Will you get in this bed so we can go to sleep."

"A friend of mine killed himself tonight, Myra."

"Oh? Who this time?"

The Governor swiveled about, leaned a shoulder against

117

the window, and stared at his shoes. "Tom Fairchild. We went to school together. Remember?"

"Of course I remember!" She put down the magazine. "Well imagine that. Isn't he in charge of the federal police?"

"*Was* is the word, my dear. Right now he's in charge of a pine box. Success! Tom was a success! But he blew his brains out. That's success, Myra."

"Well I'm not at all surprised," the Governor's wife declared, knowing-it-all.

"You're not at all surprised," he confirmed with heavy sarcasm.

"Well I'm not. Everybody knows what that wife of his is. Poor man. She's a nympho."

The Governor winced. "Bettina's dead too, Myra."

"Well for God's sake! What'd he do—kill her, then shoot himself?"

"Something like that."

"Well, I'm still not surprised. It's that Washington atmosphere. They allow all those Negruhs to live there, they should run them all out."

"Oh, for God's crying appetite, Myra!"

"Don't you swear at me, Floyd Benton. Next I hear, you'll be wanting to turn Little Rock back over to them."

"I have never expressed any such intention," the Governor replied dully.

"You should run them out of *Nawth* Little Rock. That's too close, Floyd Benton. It's just too close."

"The mighty flowing Arkansas protects you, my dear."

"It doesn't keep away the *stink*!"

"Oh for God's crying. . . . Myra, I believe I will have to get drunk before I come to bed."

"What *ever* is the matter with you, Floyd Benton? Every *time* I try to strike a *serious* conversation with you, you want to go off some place and get *drunk*."

"I don't belong here, Myra. Not in this mansion. I don't know where I belong, but it isn't here."

"You are a *fool*! A *fool*!"

"The Governor is a fool. How true. How true. Arlington's southern fool. I wish I could tell you about his
118

current plot. Maybe I should. Maybe I should tell the whole world."

"Don't talk that way, Floyd Benton. The President has been very kind to us. He needs your support, and you shall continue to give it to him. Do you hear me?"

"I hear you, Mrs. Fool. And the Governor, Mrs. Fool, is for damn sure going to get drunk."

"Don't you *day*-yuh!"

"Oh but that's one thing I *do* dare, my sweet, my executive sweet. Go to hell, Mrs. Governor Fool. The Governor of Arkansas is getting drunk." He stepped to the desk and pushed the intercom signaler and said, "Leroy—bring me a whiskey sour. No—make it a bottle and the mixings." He turned to glare at his wife. "And furthermore, my dear, I am getting out of politics. Just as quickly as I can."

It was the truth she had long dreaded to hear. "You *think* too much, Floyd, that's your trouble, you worry about things that don't concern you. Maybe you *should* have something to drink. I'll even join you, dee-yuh. And listen to me. Nobody ever said it was fun being a governor. But it's a *callin'*. You hear me? A *callin'*. A man, a *man* cannot turn his back to that. You drink some whiskey and come to bed. Mama will make it feel better." She smiled coyly. "You want Mama to make it feel better?"

"Jesus Christ," he muttered.

The house boy rapped gently on the door and came in without awaiting an invitation. He carried a tray, covered with a napkin. The Governor dropped into the chair at his desk. "Put it here, Leroy," he said.

Leroy smiled and set the tray down. He was a small wiry man with delicate features, wavy black hair, and a slightly negroid nose and mouth. He whisked the napkin away, rotated the bottle to show the Governor the label, and set it on the desk. Still in the tray were bottles of mix and some sliced lemons. Alongside the lemon slices lay a long paring knife.

"What'd you bring the knife for, Leroy?" the Governor asked absently. He reached across the tray and snared a bottle of mix.

"To cut you with, Governor," Leroy replied pleasantly. He stepped closer and his hand moved toward the desk.

The Governor chuckled and picked up the bottle of mix. The chuckle turned to a bubbling sound, and the Governor slid forward in his chair, surprised eyes seeking Leroy's face, his throat slit neatly from ear to ear, blood flowing quickly onto the immaculate shirtfront, soaking into the silk lapels of the jacket. Surprise and dejection and depression and disgust and self-loathing and life itself departed from the eyes, then the Governor's head slumped forward onto the desk, spilling the whiskey.

The Governor's wife made a startled sound and raised herself to a half-sit on the bed. "*Le*-roy, did you spill the *whis*-key?" she cried.

"No ma'am," Leroy replied. He stepped quickly to the bed, gave her an instant to see the knife, and then showed her what he'd done.

He left the knife lying beside her on the blood-soaked bed, then he went to the window and looked out. The first fingers of dawn were pushing into the Little Rock sky.

Leroy sighed, smiled, and then quietly went back to his station.

CHAPTER 9

George Reamer had never considered himself a dedicated
civil servant. Actually George had great contempt for civil
servants. "Government workers are the flattest people on
earth," George Reamer always said. And if he happened to
be in a jocular mood, he would usually add, "That's why
the blacks moved in on the field—they were *born* flat."

George actually had no solidified dislike for blacks,
though. He would tell you so, if you should ask him. He
thought they could be made better through technology,
specifically through genetic engineering. "All of us, all life
forms, are just so much electricity solidified," George
would tell you. "In humans there are good circuits and bad
circuits. It isn't the black's fault that he's composed of
mostly bad circuits."

Reamer's greater interests in life lay, however, in
electronic technology, not in human genetics. Another
thing which George always said was, "I'm sure glad the
human race has technology. We sure have nothing else
worthwhile."

George liked machines. Machines he could understand.
Especially electronic machines—and "the more sophis-
ticated, the better," George liked to say. *People* were mere-

ly imperfect machines. George built *perfect* machines. His official title was CATCO, or Chief of Airflow Technical Center Operations. And George was more than a CATCO, George was CATCO at Kansas City, which meant that George Reamer was CATCO of the center of the universe. He was never hesitant to say so. He was proud of it. He had a bachelor's degree in electronic engineering, a master's degree in electronic logic, and a doctorate in electronic philosophy. The thesis he offered for his doctor's degree was titled "Electronic Parallels of Space-Time Continuua." It was to a challenge of Einstein's model of the cosmos, and few minds in the United States would admit to having the faintest idea of what the man was suggesting, though most scientific minds respected George Reamer. George did not like to discuss the thing himself. It seemed to embarrass him—perhaps in the same sense that it would embarrass God to discuss the secrets of creation with mere mortals who could never hope to grasp the heavenly language—and George would always switch the conversation to something more concrete, such as who he picked to win the next World Series or the future of aviation in America.

Once he confided to a friend that "God is unharnessed energy. Whatever portion we harness, dies. Therefore, mankind is daily killing and eating God." But nobody was ever able to tie that idea into his theory of electronic continuua.

At any rate, it seemed somehow fitting, to George's mind, that he be at the center of the universe and, in his mind, that is exactly where he was, electronically speaking and airflow-wise. The Kansas City Airflow Technical Center (KCATO) was actually the "brains" of the entire nation, aviation-wise. It was an electronic wonderland. KCATO occupied a low-slung building comprising more than two-thousand acre-feet. George had engineered the entire feat—or, at any rate, he had been the Project Leader during the entire period of design and development. Fittingly, he was offered the office of CATCO when the project was completed and placed into operation. And, also fittingly, George accepted the position. Even if it was a civil service job. Nobody else really knew just how to keep all the computers properly meshed, or how to keep all the robot stations properly balanced to insure that no two aircraft ever occupied the same precise cube of airspace at the same precise time. In the era of supersonic air transport, which also happened to be the age of heli-cars, hovercars, zot-cars, air busses, air shuttles, and air taxies, this was no small task. George Reamer was the genius of the airflow age, and none would contest this.

One of George's most persistent nightmares always found him standing at the central computer, the *big brain*, feeding a program tape in backwards or upside down. Another one which cropped up now and then involved independent action by the machines he'd created, a dream in which they "took over" and began thinking for themselves. George had his nightmares. It was the price of genius.

There was one man at the Kansas City Central in whom George Reamer had absolute confidence. The man was a mere technician; his name was, incredibly, Archibald Gillingham. George called him "Gilly," and Archibald didn't seem to mind. Gilly, indeed, never seemed to mind anything George did or even suggested doing.

Gilly seemed eager to devote as much of his own life to the KCATO as did Reamer himself, and he had studied diligently under George for three years. He seemed to possess a natural knack for electronic philosophy; indeed, the tutor-student relationship between the two proved so stimulating to George that he had experienced a veritable explosion of consciousness, an expansion of awareness, to use his words, which was far greater and more meaningful than anything the student himself could have gained from the relationship. The explanation, of course, and one which George himself readily recognized, was that he had at last found someone who could understand him when he talked. The student became a sounding-board—George could "talk these things outside"—and, in so doing, he could solidify what may have otherwise amounted to no more than transitory impressions.

On the night of March 9th, 1999, George Reamer experienced a nightmare. It was shortly past midnight. The vision was so realistic, so fraught with the concrete, that he simply could not get back to sleep. He paced about the social of his suburban Kansas City cube for perhaps thirty minutes, drinking warm milk, then warm brandy, then mint-flavored whiskey. But he could not shake the feeling of impending doom. He saw airplanes, throughout the skies of North America, suddenly being diverted electronically into patterns of chaos—large astro-liners flying wingtip formation to shuttle-busses, zot-cars shooting straight upwards into the bellies of chopper-ferries, and thousand-passenger jet commuters diving vertically towards the earth.

And, in his agony, George Reamer began to form another theory of universal mind. He was becoming *psychic*, or *tuned-in*, to the logic circuits—or thought processes—of the airflow computers. He was developing *ESP* with his *machines*! *They were plotting something*!

For another ten minutes the CATCO tried to shake off the nutty idea, and it was a nutty idea, he knew it was. Finally, however, George could stand it no longer. He had to get out to the KCATO and see for himself that the machines had not taken over.

He threw a robe on over his pajamas, tubed up to the roof, stepped into his zot-car and flew a beeline uncontrolled transit to the center. It was shortly after two o'clock, Kansas City time, when he ran into the central computer room, his robe flying out behind him, his hair streaming down across his forehead, for all the world an Einstein on the run.

Then he saw Gilly, standing nonchalantly at the brain console, a faint smile on his face.

"Thank the ohms," George muttered. Had Gilly experienced a similar dream? "Well, well," he called over, trying to sound casual, "the two old philosophers, prowling

124

around the universal center in dead of night. What brings you out here, Gilly?"

The other man flashed him a smile. "I had an idea, just couldn't shake it, thought I'd come out and see about it," he replied.

Sure, okay, so Gilly *did* have the same uneasy feeling. "I think it's continuum-ESP," George told him in a husky voice.

"No, I'm working on another idea," Gilly replied.

"What do you mean?" George asked, a shivery feeling gripping his spine. "What kind of idea?"

"Well . . . come over and take a look," Gilly suggested, the smile widening.

"Hey! Hey hey hey!" George cried, bending low over the console. "What the hell is *this*?"

"I programmed the inductance relay back through the and/or logic to see if I could pick any transients. Look. It's working. See?"

George screamed, *"You crazy bastard do you know what you've done?"* Then the deeper implications crashed into his reeling mind in a blinding expansion of awareness. *"Oh God!"* he gasped. "You've given them an *in*! *You're letting it THINK!"*

George staggered to another console and snatched up a microphone, *"Attention all aircraft, emergency, airflow emergency!"* he gasped. *"Fly dead! Fly dead!* Ohmigod migod, I'm not getting out, I'm not, what's the matter with this goddamn transmitter—*don't tell me they've got it tied up too!"* He rolled frantic eyes toward his student assistant. "Gilly! Goddammit come over here and help me!"

"It's too late, Whitey," Gilly told him, positively beaming as he strolled toward the console.

"What? *What? Whatta you mean?"* Then George saw the small revolver in Gilly's hand, and he immediately began to form a dizzying theory regarding the natural perversity of *animate* objects. But George did not have time to bring in all the parameters and exponentials of the theory and Gilly would not have been inclined to "talk the

125

thing outside" with him anyway.

The revolver reported once, just once, and a tiny hole opened just between George's eyes, and it was the end of another nightmare. It was, perhaps, the price of genius.

Commentary on the National Air Disasters of 1999

Due to the overshadowing events in which they found their context, the air disasters of March 9-10, 1999 were never coherently cemented in the public consciousness. Indeed, a complete assessment of "what happened in the airspace" was not formalized for several years, and then only through a laborious gleaning and inspection of isolated and fragmented news reports originating in various parts of the nation. It is perhaps proper then, that an attempt be made here to determine and document once and for all, the march of events across the continental airspace during those fateful few hours of national history.

The earliest documented disaster involves Oceana Flight 140, enroute from Sydney, Australia to an airdrome outside the old city of Chicago, Illinois. A stratocruiser, this TomFan-80 type aircraft, developed by the Australian government in the middle nineteen-nineties and operated under a charter granted by the Oceanic Alliance in 1997, was a rough equivalent of other atomic-powered craft of that day. Passenger capacity ranged between five hundred and six hundred and fifty, depending upon cargo manifested; it exhibited a cruising range of some 35,000 miles at 2500 knots, with an operating ceiling of 65,000 feet. Flight 140, departing Sydney at one o'clock on the afternoon of March 10 (East Meridian Time), made a hover-stop over the Samoan Republic, enplaning some 40 passengers, then back-tracked for a cargo hover at Guam, in the Mariannas Mandate, and then proceeded along a flight path to make a foodstuffs drop over the offshore islands of Taiwan, where survivors of the China plague-famine belt had been spotted some days earlier.

At 11:55 PM (Pacific Standard Time) on March 9 (West Meridian Date) an APR (Automatic Position Reporter) signal recorded the flight's approach to Vancouver, B.C., in a planned penetration of North America continental airspace. This flight had received prior approval from the U.S. Government to make a port of entry landing at the Chicago airdrome, and there is no reason to believe that this was not the intent. At 12:03 AM, however, tracking tapes show that Flight 140 suddenly veered south from a position near Spokane, Washington, and appeared to be climbing from a programmed altitude of 52,000 feet. An electronic tracker (robot station) near Pocatello, Idaho recorded at 12:09 AM that the flight was at an altitude of 63,000 feet and on a heading of 185° magnetic. No other tracking reports concerning this flight have been found. According to the official record, an eyewitness report filed at Tahoe, California on the morning of March 10, 1999, a TomFan-80 type aircraft, later positively identified as Oceana Flight 140, moving at a speed estimated as supersonic, with navigation and visual display lighting fully operative, appeared suddenly from an alto-cumulus cloudbank and proceeded in a straight vertical dive into the waters of Lake Tahoe, in the Sierra Nevada range, impacting at approximately 12:35 AM. Where the craft had been, and what it had been doing during the intervening twenty-six minutes of supersonic flight since the last APR report, remains a mystery. This flight carried a passenger list of 478 and a crew of 24. There were no survivors.

At the moment when Oceana 140 first exhibited erratic characteristics, it was nearly three o'clock on the U.S. East Coast. At 3:03 a chartered ferry operated by Eastern Consolidated Airways, on the return leg of an excursion from New York to Miami and carrying eight hundred and seventy young women of the Metropolitan Secretarial Society, was executing a routine automated instrument approach to Continental Airdrome on Long Island. This ferry suddenly veered off the base ALS leg, dislocating its course by seventeen degrees southward and climbing nearly three thousand feet in a matter of seconds, colliding in mid-air with a shuttle which was inbound to the Trenton (N.J.) Municipal Airdocks. At best count, 240 lives were lost in this disaster.

Three-seventeen A.M. saw a spectacular four-way

collision in the air over Chillicothe, Ohio, involving a zot-car, two heli-buses, and a small air shuttle. Only eight lives were lost as a direct result of this collision, but a large food processing plant and numerous residences along the Chillicothe Strip were destroyed by flaming debris raining down from the disaster in the air.

A few moments later, or at a recorded time of three-eighteen point seven, a landing strato-cruiser sheared off the local-control tower at Boston National and plowed into three smaller passenger craft then loading for various destinations. Death toll: 982.

At 2:48, Central Time Zone, a collision in the approach lanes to O'Hare Serviceport near the old shell city of Chicago accounted for two strato cruisers of the U.S. Twenty-First Century configuration (full atomic) and a death toll estimated at 1,450.

Meanwhile the disasters continued, in a random, non-pattern sequence. At four-thirty, Washington time, a White House aide declared that the President had been apprised of developments and was "watching the situation."

At four-forty A.M., the White House ordered a cancellation of all penetration clearances by foreign flag air-carriers, and at 4:43 a spectacular mid-air collision occured in the air over Washington, the wreckage falling within sight of the White House.

At best count, the two hours and some odd minutes following the first disaster of record saw the destruction of 17 astro-cruisers, 36 air busses and shuttles, 4 large ferries, an indeterminate number of private craft (though estimated in the several of thousands), and something beyond 14,000 human lives.

A news story filed near Kansas City just before dawn in that area noted that "Dr. George Reamer, genius of the electronic age and CATCO at Kansas City"—had committed suicide in the central computer room at that facility, "perhaps mistakenly blaming himself for the chaos in airspace. A KCATO technician, Archibald Gillingham, demonstrated to this reporter the perfect functioning of the automated equipment which controls all air movements in the continental airspace (above 1,000 feet). Gillingham praised his late Chief, saying, 'Dr. Reamer taught me everything I know about this facility. I don't know what we'll do without him. I'm just a technician myself.' "

The news story concluded, "KCATO is *all systems go.* This reporter saw it for himself. So—what is happening in our airspace?"

What was happening in the airspace, it can now be told, was a result of "random transients" deliberately induced in the master brain computer at the Kansas City ATCO— "establishing an electronic parallel in the airpsace's time-space continuum." Whatever that means.

CHAPTER 10

Howard Silverman, White House correspondent extraordinary and national television commentor, peered glumly at his watch, then shook it at Phil Angelo, the wire services man. "What the hell is wrong with old Arlie this morning," he grumbled. "He's been up, I know, since the sky started falling."

Angelo grinned and commented, "You bitch when he's early, you bitch when he's late, and you bitch when he's on time."

"You'd think a man his age would have enough sense to sleep more," Silverman growled. "Now what the hell can *he* do about falling airplanes? You have any idea how many times I've had to stagger around in the early dawn to cover his breathless announcements?"

Angelo's youthful face drew into a thoughtful frown. "You have to admit, Howie, something damned funny is going on."

"Always has been," Silverman said, sighing. "Ever since Arlie moved into the White House, something damned funny is always going on."

"I don't know why you're complaining," the wire reporter commented. "Since Arlie's been in office you've developed the most distinguished name in television."

"Oh hell, I know that. But as for the most distinguished name on teevee, that's a small honor. I'm afraid there's nothing especially distinguishing about television today. And you can thank the old mountain goat for that, too."

"Well now I wouldn't say that." The telephone rang and Angelo scooped it up. He listened for a moment, grunted something unintelligible into the transmitter, and hung up. "Now, as I was—"

"Who was that?"

"Janie," Angelo replied, rolling his eyes and stroking his leg suggestively. "Arlie's on his way down. He's catching some air on the way, walking around by the terrace. We got a couple minutes. You're all set, aren't you?"

Silverman glanced again at his watch. "Ten 'til eight," he grunted. "She give any clue as to why the twenty minute delay?"

"Yeah. He was waiting for Phillips and Lilienthal. Neither one showed and Arlie has the storm flags flying. So don't cross him."

Silverman's bushy brows came closer together. "The ISC and the African Secretary," he murmured. "He hasn't had those two birds together since, let's see . . . hell I can't remember when. You know what, Angelo? Something big is brewing, and it's not just another dry run either. I feel it in my bones. I saw Fairchild here last night, with Mike Winston. Now Fairchild is dead and Winston is canned. I wonder what . . ." His voice trailed away and he lost himself in thought.

"Aw hell, if you're thinking of foreign intrigue, how the hell could they sabotage all our planes like that?"

Silverman stared at his companion for a moment, then replied, "I'm not saying that anything has been sabotaged. But . . . well, hell. No, I don't believe Africa is involved, I'm not saying that. They're too busy fighting one another. No. No, it's something else. Something's brewing. I feel it in my newsman's bones."

Angelo shivered. "Well, don't look so damned smug about it."

"You're a newsman, aren't you?" Silverman replied, smiling faintly.

131

"Yeah, but I'm a newsman of the Arlington generation," Angelo said, laughing nervously.

"The curiosity of the press is dead, suh," Silverman intoned sarcastically. "Buried beneath the patronage of Ol' Daddy and his Mississippi mud-stompers. Listen, Angelo, there was a time when—"

"Hell don't start that again!" Angelo yelped. He moved restlessly out of his chair and fidgeted about from one foot to the other. "Hang yourself if you want to, but don't ask for a swinging partner. Uh, let's intercept Arlie. We can walk back with him and maybe get some idea of what the address is about. Okay?"

"Okay," Silverman said, sighing. "But he's going to say that little chocolate men are invading us from Alpha Centauri or some place. Wait'n see."

The two men stepped into the hallway and headed towards the door to the terrace, a few hundred feet distant. Before they managed the first ten of those feet, the outside door was flung open and a platoon of Secret Service men came pounding through and down the passageway on a dead run. The leading bodyguard shoved the newsmen back along the hall and into the press room, slamming the heavy glass door on them, then he stood there with arms crossed, his back against the glass. The others ran on past, checking doors along the corridor. Seconds later a thick knot of men walked swiftly past, the President in the center of them.

Arlington was looking a lot older than Silverman remembered ever seeing him; the normally granite jaw had gone slack and was almost trembling. The guard at their door showed the newsmen a grim smile, then fell in behind the entourage.

"What in the political hell?" Silverman exploded.

Angelo carefully opened the door a crack and stuck his head through in a quiet survey of the situation. Jane Bryn, a sleek thirtyish woman and the Presidential Girl Friday, walked slowly up the hall, tears streaming from her eyes. Angelo took her by the arm and yanked her into the press arm, eased her into a chair, and went quickly to the water cooler. He brought the water to her and watched

132

solicitously as she sipped at it.

"What's happened to the President?" Silverman growled.

Jane Byrn slowly shook her head, half-strangling on the water. "I kept trying to get Secretary Lilienthal and Phillips on the telephone after the President left his office. Th-then when I f-found out, I r-ran to catch the President and t-tell him. It's horrible, h-*horrible*."

"Well dammit, *what*?"

"Th-they were both f-found in b-bed, their . . . their . . ."

"Dammit, Janie!"

She cried shrilly, "Their throats had been slashed!"

"Holy Joe!" Angelo exclaimed. He snatched at the desk phone, then changed his mind and scrambled for the turret.

Silverman draped a comforting arm about the woman's shoulders, his own face going ashen. Quietly he commented, "Three men, each close to the President, dead in less than twelve hours. I wonder . . . Janie? . . . do you feel like walking now? Can we go up and try to contact the other cabinet officers?"

She smiled weakly and gripped his hand tightly. They moved out the door and along the hall in an ever-quickening pace. Somehow, though, Silverman knew that he was on a fool's errand. Somehow he knew that the rest of the cabinet was beyond contact. His newsman's bones felt the poultice of ashes clinging to the skeleton of the body politic. Pre-empted air cubes and open jugular veins, on the surface of things, seemed rather remote one from another. But at least one member of the press in whom curiosity survived found a suddenly-twitching nose and an itch for the truth.

Inanely, it seemed, the words to a childish game floated up out of his memory and he recited them under his breath as he hurried toward the Executive Offices with Jane Byrn.

"Ring around the rosies,
Pocket full of posies,
Ashes, ashes,
All fall down!"

133

CHAPTER 11

The police crusier careened wildly between two monster tanks, flashed across Leavenworth, and screeched to a halt in the Federal Center parking area. Two uniformed policemen jumped from the car and marched aggressively toward a cluster of soldiers, crews from the tanks which were lined up at twenty foot intervals facing the building.

"You guys nuts or something?" one of the cops said fiercely. "You got the whole goddam town tied up in knots! What the hell you think you're doing? You get those goddam overgrown tin cans to hell out of here!"

Lieutenant James Woodrow, U.S. Army Regulars, stepped from the cluster. "Haven't you heard, officer?" he replied, big teeth flashing against their dark background. "We're taking over this wonderful city."

The cop thrust his jaw forward, trying to get a better look at the big black in the crash helmet. "Sez who?" he snarled.

"Sez us."

Then the cop noticed the American flag decal on the tank commander's helmet. In place of the field of stars was a clenched black fist. His gaze darted to an ensign waving over the rear of the nearest tank; same thing, a clenched black fist. The cop's jaw dropped and he instinctively went for his gun. The tank commander immediately back-stepped. An automatic weapon chattered briefly from behind him. The two San Francisco cops sprawled to the ground.

"Leave 'em there!" Woodrow commanded gruffly. "Man your vehicles and batten down!" He ran around the line of tanks and climbed aboard a military scout car, an armored vehicle with a fifty-calibre machine-gun mount. Quickly donning a headset, he began hurling last-minute instructions to his crews. "It is now H minus twenty seconds," he announced tersely. "You'll hear the bridge go and that's when *we* go. I want concentrated fire on the Federal Center, then take the auditorium and the opera house. Don't one unit leave the station until the whole thing is rubble. You know where to go then, but one last caution. Do not proceed beyond Taylor Street or you'll be rolling into the fire from Telegraph Hill. You won't want to see that mess down there in the hotel district anyway. I'm going up to scout Van Ness and find out why so many cars are getting through. Big Deal One, you're commanding until I get back. Tally-ho boys, and don't start feeling soft about this old city. It's just her face you're lifting, not her soul."

A distant, echoing rumble of constantly building magnitude approached from the Northwest. Woodrow yelled into his transmitter, *"That's it! Free-fire now, and bring it all down!"*

BOOK III - A CONSIGNMENT TO YESTERDAY

CHAPTER 1

The blast, a rumbling series of explosions, awoke Mike Winston with a start. He dropped his feet from the footstool and sat bolt upright in a chair, confused, trembling, and not immediately certain of his surroundings. Then he recognized the unfamiliar scene deep within the stands of the old Oakland Raider stadium. He'd been brought to Abe Williams' office shortly after midnight, and had paced the floor for hours until fatigue had finally forced him to the chair.

His watch was stopped on a few minutes before twelve, broken during the brief wrestling match with the big troopers when he landed in the Warhole, and he had absolutely no idea of the time of day nor how long he had slept. The small office was windowless. Winston banged on the door and yelled, then paced for several minutes before he heard the snap of the door-lock mechanism. A big trooper stood there, regarding him with a lopsided grin.

"What was that explosion?" Winston asked him.

"Don't worry about that," the soldier replied. "Come on. Mr. Williams says to bring you up."

The guy turned his back on him and walked away. Winston followed him along the network of corridors up the tiered stands of the old press box.

Williams was there with General Bogan and a swarm of uniformed men, all wearing headsets and jotting things on clipboards. Mayor Harvey was there also, bleary-eyed with fatigue but standing stiff and straight and intently watching the fireworks across the bay. The sounds of heavy artillery and rattling gunfire were carrying easily across the miles of waterway, and all eyes in the pressbox were riveted on the towering columns of smoke which were erupting from numerous quarters over there.

Williams showed the new arrival a tired smile and told him, "I thought you deserved a look at this."

"What was the big boom a few minutes ago?" Winston wanted to know.

"That big boom," Williams replied quietly, "was the death knell for the city of San Francisco. Specifically, it was the sound of that once proud engineering masterpiece, the Golden Gate Bridge, withstander of wind and waves and salt-water corrosion, being unceremoniously lowered into the cold waters of the Golden Gate. Splash, splash."

"Congratulations," Winston said drily. "I'm sure you're enjoying the sounds of a civilization collapsing. Pardon me if I don't cheer."

"You hear any cheering up here?" the black leader growled. "Just be quiet and watch, Winston. Some day you can tell your grandkids about it."

"Fat chance," the white man muttered. He left Williams standing there and went on around the curved press box until he reached General Bogan.

The military chief was perched on a stool and almost surrounded by status display boards, grimly watching the action across the bay through a powerful set of binoculars hoisted to his face.

"Now there's a sight for an American ganeral," Winston said by way of greeting.

Bogan lowered the glasses and gave Winston a quick once-over. "For what it's worth, Mike, I'm glad to see you in a single piece."

"What's going on over there, General?"

"Hell is going on over there, Michael. Sheer hell. And don't ever let anyone con you into believing that a general enjoys the sight of bloodshed." He went back to his glasses, and Winston began studying the display boards.

"Kind of Mickey Mouse for a U.S. military operation, isn't it?" he observed quietly. "I mean . . . this command post you've got here."

Without lowering the binoculars, Bogan replied, "You wouldn't think so if you were at the Pentagon right now. We're in full combat order—don't for a moment think otherwise. This is my remote set-up. Mickey Mouse maybe, but good enough."

"So it's nationwide."

"Of course it's nationwide."

Winston raised a hand to his forehead and turned blindly toward Abe Williams. The civil leader caught the look, sighed, and came over to join him.

"Okay, I've seen it," Winston muttered. "Now show me the wall and get it over with."

"Why should I stand you to a wall, Commissioner? You're a talented and versatile man. We can use those talents in the *new* republic."

"That'll be the Goddamned day," Winston replied in a choked voice.

"Maybe, maybe. We'll see. For now you've got free run of the place, Winston. Just don't give us a hard time. The moment for heroics is past. And the moment for soul-searching is fast approaching. Just be ready."

"For what?" Winston growled.

"For saying goodbye to yesterday. We're all going to have to say it sooner or later. May as well be later. Come on, I think the patch is working now to the military command radio. Jackson? You want to listen in?"

General Bogan had been watching the two men in quiet speculation. He responded to the query by sliding off the stool and gently shoving Mike Winston toward the far end of the press box, where a large electronic panel had been emplaced.

"Update me nationally," Williams requested of the General.

"Smooth, very smooth," Bogan replied. "We caught the whole country with its pants down. Not just at half-mast, but flopping about the ankles. No resistance, excepted isolated instances of damn-foolism. Most people don't seem to realize what's happening yet. We moved an armored column from Arlington across to Washington and right down Pennsylvania Avenue. It was past nine o'clock there, streets full of people, buildings filled with workers. People just stood and watched like it was a parade—even waved, some of them. Ritter's man in Washington says everybody's wondering where all the government blacks went—they can't quite grasp the meaning of an all-white Washington—except for troops, of course. We had forty thousand troops in the city as of about ten minutes ago and not a shot has yet been fired."

"Hell, I can't believe that," Winston grumbled.

"Why not?" Williams asked. "You were in that city yourself yesterday. Why can't you believe it?"

"So what's going to happen to them when they wake up?" Winston asked soberly.

"Nothing, absolutely nothing," Bogan told him. "We have no need to get tough. Every military installation in the area is ours—for that matter, in the entire nation. That means every military vehicle, every weapon, every chunk of ammo. They made the mistake of dissolving the standing army and hiring black replacements to mind the store, and they compounded the error by placing all the weapons in storage and placing most of that even in the care of black storekeepers. We simply walked in and took it. Now they can call the militia until they're hoarse. Where will the white militia assemble? What will they use for weapons?"

"All over like that?" Winston asked, choking on the words.

"Sure all over," the General replied. "It was so easy it's almost pitiful. I never saw a country so ripe for a bloodless coup."

"So why are you spilling blood?" Winston wanted to know.

Abe Williams handled that one. "Call it a drum-roll," he said coldly. "We are commanding attention."

"You'll get it," the white man told them. "You guys have bought yourselves more of a war than you realize.

This is a nation of gun lovers. There's hardly a home in the country that doesn't have some sort of gun."

Bogan placed a hand on the white man's shoulder and said, "Listen, Mike. I'll give you the best rifle we have, and all the ammo you can carry on your back. And I'll arm as many of your friends you can round up, in exactly the same manner. Do you think then you'll be ready to go up against military armor and combat-trained troops?"

"I might not be ready, but I'd go," Winston maintained stubbornly.

"You might *think* so. But those who think so have never challenged the authority of a tank, using a 30.06 as his primary weapon. No. Uh-uh. Most men know better. They may throw a clip of ammo into their rabbit guns, but they're not going to go challenging a tank or weapons-company. I'll tell you precisely what they are going to do with those rabbit guns. They will gather their families around them, and they will barricade themselves inside their homes, and they will sit there and dare some black bastard to try to come in and rape their women." The general smiled. "But we don't want their women. We want them to barricade themselves inside their homes and sweat, and maybe even get a little hungry. And a little humble."

"You might be right," Winston said quietly.

"Sure," The General turned his attention to Abe Williams. "Even the civil police are helpless and most of them already know it. We've had a few scraps with them around the country, but as soon as they realize they're up against artillery and massive power, they forget that fierce pride of ownership and decide it's not a police matter."

William nodded curtly, as though hearing nothing surprising. "How about Ritter's operation? Everything neatly dispatched?"

"You don't have to ask me. Just look at Norm. He's getting his reports from Sacramento now. He already told me they got the Governor and the Attorney General, and from the way he's gloating I'd say they got just about everybody on the list. Uh, you know about the Washington side."

Somberly, Williams said, "Yes, I know."

143

"What is this, what's been dispatched?" Winston wanted to know, his eyes sick and already knowing.

"If you want a word," Williams replied in cool tones, "the word is *assassination*. I can't help it if it's in the vocabulary of warfare. Now be quiet and we'll tune in on the command nets." He pushed the white man toward the makeshift console, adding, "I especially want *you* to hear the play by play. I want you to see what we're *capable* of doing, as opposed to what we are *not* doing everywhere. Call it a lesson in black restraint."

Somehow Winston almost expected to awaken any moment and discover that he'd used that packet of Expando at the American Church, after all. He moved woodenly to the console and dropped into a chair offered by General Bogan, then cupped his chin in his hands and glared at the dials and instruments of the console.

"I don't hear anything," he murmured.

"You will," Bogan assured him.

Abruptly, a speaker came alive with a whine and a crackle of background sounds of warfare, and a youthful voice announced, "Big Deal One from Big Deal Leader. What's away down there?"

The reply was muffled and punctuated by the roar of heavy artillery, bringing the war right into the press box. "This's Big Deal One. The Walls of Jericho have tumbled down. Now working on the Tower of Babel."

"Federal Center and Opera House," Bogan quickly explained, for Winston's benefit.

"Roger, Big Deal One. I'm rejoining. Leader out."

"Can I talk to that boy from here?" Abe Williams asked.

The General's eyebrows elevated slightly. "Sure, but . . ." He reached beneath the table and produced a hand mike.

"But what?"

"Well he's busy as a cat covering up shit, you know."

"Yes, I know," Williams murmured. He took the mike and depressed the button. "Big Deal Leader, this is Top Man. Do you read?"

"Top Man from Leader. I read, sir."

"How's the war going?"

144

The only immediate reply was a long burst of rapid fire from a heavy machine gun. Then: "Sorry, Top man, I'm right under the fifty mount. Some nut in a hover, taking potshots with a pistol. Had to bring 'im down. Say again your last, Top Man."

Bogan and Winston exchanged glances, Winston's proclaiming *See, I told you,* and the General's replying, *But who won?*

"I asked how the war is going," Williams was repeating.

"Oh. Going fine, sir. Just like Big Boy said it would."

"Good. How do you feel about the operation?"

"How do *I* feel, sir?" Part of the reply was muffled by the sound of distant artillery. ". . . out of a coccoon, sir. It looks like everything is well in hand."

"Good boy. What's your present position?"

"Just departed Cave Dwellings, sir. Proceeding outbound on Geary, then south on Van Ness to rejoin Big Deal Gang."

Bogan whispered to Wilson, "Cave Dwellings is code for the hotel district around Union Square."

"Standby one, Big Deal Leader," Williams snapped. He released the transmitter button and looked at Jackson Bogan. "What's he doing down around the caves?" he asked.

"Just re-conning," the General replied. "We don't want to start blasting Union Square until the people have had a chance to get out. The public address cars are still in there, urging everyone to evacuate."

"Watch this exercise in restraint, Winston," Williams said. "Jack, get over on the other net and order High Deal to activate Plan Charlie immediately."

Bogan hesitated, his face contorting in some indecision. Williams snapped, "Well is it feasible or not?"

Bogan shrugged his shoulders. "I guess if we watched it closely . . ."

"Then do it!"

The General nodded curtly and grabbed another microphone and stepped around the corner of the console.

"High Deal is the Telegraph Hill Armor," Abe Williams explained to Winston. "Now we'll see about the boys in the

145

heat zone." He punched in the button on the mike and said, "Big Deal Leader, Top Man again. How much resistance are you encountering?"

"Resistance, what's that sir?" came the noisy reply. "A few cops have been trying to write tickets on our foot soldiers. Ha ha. Haven't seen any bluesuits the past ten or twelve blocks, though. Think they've all scurried back to their hutches."

"All right, Big Deal Leader. Call off your dogs as soon as you've rejoined."

"Call 'em off, sir?"

"That's right, call them off. The game has changed. Activate Plan Charlie immediately upon rejoining your element."

A brief pause, then: "Understand, sir, order is to activate Plan Charlie immediately upon rejoining. Switching over to Big Deal net. Big Deal Leader out."

"He sounded a bit disappointed, didn't he?" Abe Williams muttered, smiling wryly at Winston.

"What was that all about," Winston murmured.

Before Williams could explain, the speaker crackled again. "Top Man, Top Man, this is Wet Deal Leader. Do you read, sir?"

"I read, Wet Leader, go ahead," Williams responded.

"Does that order apply to my gang, sir?"

"What's your present situation, Wet Leader?"

"I brought my scouter and two light tanks up from the Embarcadero to look over Bluesuit Hotel. We're in the park opposite at the moment."

"That's the police station on Grant," Williams explained, then spoke into the microphone: "Just what is the situation, Wet Leader?"

General Bogan reappeared around the corner of the console, smiling grimly at Mike Winston.

"Could be bad news, Top Man. Squad cars have been coming in by the droves. Going into the underground garage. My guess is they're loading up with riot guns and tear gas. Biggest piece I have with me is the 37's. I've sent for the self-propelled howitzer and two truckloads of infantry. One of my 37's is zeroed-in on the garage exit. First car trying to come up outta there is getting a hot chunk right on the nose. Figure that'll seal them in. Any further suggestions, Top Man?"

Williams had been studying Jackson Bogan's face during the report. He tossed the mike to the general and said, "Talk to him, Jack."

Bogan depressed the button and frowned into the microphone for a second or two, then announced, "All right, Wet Leader, this is Big Boy. You've done just as I would. But get some more of your light tanks up there, and damn fast. Enough to make the Bluesuits sweat everytime they look out a window. Then use your public address. Let them know they can leave on foot and unarmed. Give them ten minutes to clear the building, jailbirds if any included. Soon as you're satisfied the building is secured, send in a company of infantry to occupy. I want a wilco."

"We don't blow this building to hell, Big Boy?"

"Negative. You do not, not unless your evacuation order is ignored. In any event, activate Plan Charlie as soon as the situation there meets with your satisfaction."

"Wilco, Big Boy. Wet Deal Leader out."

Winston had been listening in utter fascination. "What is Plan Charlie?" he inquired.

"It's a provisional cease-fire," was Abe Williams' tight-lipped reply. "We sit and watch, and fire only when fired upon. Each element has preassigned stations where they'll do their sitting and watching. Call it psychological warfare."

Winston smiled wanly. His hands shook as he lit a cigarette. Williams took the cigarette from Winston's lips and put it between his own. Winston automatically lit another. Jackson Bogan nervously cleared his throat.

"Well, Jack?" Williams asked, slowly exhaling a lung full of smoke.

"I approve, of course," the General replied.

"All right. Have the word passed on the All-Cal Net. Emphasize that each element must use discretion in activating the plan. They are not to jeopardize their situation. Then you'd better pass the word on the All-States Net. See if you can get a positive wilco from at least each town command."

"We'll probably have some back-yak from the southern tong."

Williams sighed heavily. "This isn't a war, Jackson. It's a slaughter. I had no idea it would go off this smoothly. Try to sell them that idea. We've showed Whitey our capability. Now let's show him our restraint. Push that line."

"Right."

"And Jack. This wll help the political war. Make sure they understand that. It will help. We don't want to inherit chaos. Push that idea."

Bogan smiled, squeezed Williams' shoulder, and disappeared once again behind the console.

Norman Ritter sailed up, his face set in angry lines, glaring at the black leader with baleful eyes. "What's this shit?" he asked loudly.

Williams took a drag on his cigarette, then said calmly, "What shit?"

"This Plan Charlie shit! We're not ready for that yet!"

"No?" His glance flashed to Winston, then back to Ritter. "Who says we're not?"

Ritter was glaring at the white man. "What's this fuckin' guy doing here, lolling around the command post!"

"He's lolling here at my invitation, Norm," Williams said smoothly. "Now if you've got something to say, get it off your chest."

Ritter's fury was building by the moment. "Historians will call this the ten-minute war!" he snarled. "They think those Jews and Arabs had it quick, wait'll they get ahold of *this*!"

"I'm not worried about war historians, Norm. Are you?"

"We can't do this, Abe. Now we just can't do it." The redhead was still in high dudgeon, but he was now working at controlling it. "These boys have a right to a bit of mayhem. You just can't take that away from them. God look how easy it's going. We're like steam-rolling them. Let's keep hitting them while they're off balance. Dammit, Abe. Dammit!"

He turned his rage on Mike Winston. "I can see I should have seen this bastard dead last night! He's got you all fucked up!"

"Maybe," Williams said, his eyes on the floor. "I won't claim that Winston hasn't influenced me. I saw it all there in his face, the misery that we were buying ourselves. I started off showing something to this whitey, an exercise in restraint is what I fancied it. I wound up showing something to myself, Norm. I watched Winston squirm, I watched him tremble and suffer, and I saw a man dying inside. Just like this country would die inside, Norm, if I turned people like you loose on it. Now you calm yourself—goddammit." The eyes were up now, and blazing at the intelligence man. "As an exercise in vengeance, I had Winston by the ass. I knew it, and he knew it. But as an exercise in *tomorrow*, Winston has *me* by the ass, and I know that also, so does he. *Tomorrow* is going to be made by men like Mike Winston and me. Isn't that right, Winston?"

"I suppose so," Winston replied woodenly. His voice sounded hollow in his ears. "Unless you want to spend the rest of your life 'sitting and watching.' You can't kill us all, Abe. And those you don't kill, you're going to have to watch for a long long time. Unless . . . unless some accomodation can be made—as much as I detest that word."

The conversation was getting away from Ritter. His eyes snapped rapidly back and forth between the two men. Presently he opened his mouth and said one word. "Bullshit!" he growled.

"I'll accept that, Norman," Abe Williams said, chuckling. "I'll accept that as your farewell address to yesterday . . . a damn long and a damn black and a damn miserable yesterday. Now let's hear your welcome word to *tomorrow*."

CHAPTER 2

Howard Silverman's eyes danced excitedly above the mouthpiece of the control headset. "Look, Andy, I'm telling you. The Press Secretary is dead. Cold, dead and already gray. No, I cannot get to Arlie. Now we're just going to have to go without the clearance. Well don't be chickenshit about it, I'll take full responsibility. Okay, then, okay. I'll say it again, and you record it. I, Howard Silverman, accept full responsibility for the White House telecast of March 10th, 1999.

"Now shut up and listen to me. The units are set up. Camera One is positioned atop the steps. Two and Three are here in the press room.

"Dammit, can't you understand anything I've been telling you? The President is *not* going to appear! I don't know how I know . . . but I am *here*, aren't I? And *you* are *there*. Okay so I'm telling you that Arlie is not going to appear this morning.

"Now listen to me, Andy. With the biggest story in ten years maybe breaking right under our noses, we're not going to let the network setup go to waste. Are we, Andy?

"Dammit stop thinking and just do what I say. Yes, I'll give you your cues, but you keep your eyes on the monitors and select anything that looks interesting.

"Whattaya mean, technical direction? You fuzzy-ass gosling, can't you do anything without a script? Listen, we just have twenty seconds . . . just smile now and say goodbye. Leave the worrying to me. Are you with me? Well *are* you? Fine. Good boy. Here goes."

Silverman quickly adjusted the headset and stepped to a mark on the floor, a few feet to the side of the Presidential box. He checked the remote relay, a small box studded with pearl buttons designed to fit the palm of the hand, then gazed into the lens of a television camera a few yards away. A red light atop the camera illuminated. Silverman released half the air from his lungs and began speaking in the round tones of the seasoned broadcaster.

The men at Oakland's Warhole had moved to the more comfortable quarters at Operations Control, in the converted locker rooms of the stadium. A full OpCon crew was on duty there in the miniature duplicate of the Pentagon's war room. Huge floor-to-ceiling sliding wall charts were providing intelligence display, and these were being continually posted by a swarm of control specialists.

Michael Winston sat in the company of Abraham Lincoln Williams, General Jackson Bogan, Intelligence Chief Norman Ritter, and Oakland Mayor John Harvey. The mayor was half-asleep, his chin drooping onto his chest and eyes fluttering in an effort to remain open. The other three blacks were quietly sober, their faces reflecting the strain of the past twenty-four hours. The white man appeared somber, morose and emotionally wearied. He was quietly smoking a cigarette and watching the postings on the status boards when a radio engineer strode over to announce, "The Presidential Address is coming up. I'm throwing it on the big screen."

"Wouldn't want to miss Arlie's big moment of truth," Williams declared, sighing. He swiveled his chair about and pointed to the telescreen set into the far wall. The others turned expectant eyes toward the screen, Winston scooting his chair around to stare morosely across the room as an image of the Presidential pressbox appeared,

151

the Seal of the United States emblazoned across the front of it.

The box, empty and silent, occupied the screen for perhaps five seconds, the battery of microphones almost poignantly telling their story of desertion and neglect. Then the camera panned slowly to the figure of a suave man of about sixty.

"Good morning, America, this is Howard Silverman at the White House." How often, thought Winston, he had heard those familiar words. "There is hardly anything *good* about *this* morning in the nation's capital. The scheduled address by the President has been temporarily cancelled. In just a moment, you will understand why this has been necessary."

Silverman paused to gaze soberly at the millions of viewers across the country, then went on in a gravely urgent tone. "At this sad moment in national history, ladies and gentlemen, the President of the United States stands alone at the helm of government. At this time yesterday, the President enjoyed the support of ten cabinet members and twenty-two able men and women of the White House staff. This morning, there remains only the President and his personal administrative aide, Miss Jane Byrn. All the others are dead. I repeat. The President's entire cabinet and staff are dead. These thirty-two members of the Federal Executive were murdered in their beds sometime during this past night. The word, of course, is not murder. The word, America, is *assassination*."

The newsman again paused to allow the disclosure to register on the viewing audience. Then he resumed in a voice of choked restraint. "These grim discoveries are but a few minutes old. There has not yet been time to fully assess the implications of this stunning situation. But mark this day on your calendars, America. Draw a circle around March 10th, 1999, and draw that circle in blood. Today the President stands alone. The Congress is not in session. The Supreme Court of the United States stands adjourned. And the Federal Executive, but for the Chief, is no more.

"Information gleaned from reliable sources inside the Executive Office indicate that the President is attempting

152

to contact the Speaker of the House of Representatives and the President *pro tem* of the Senate. These men are, of course, in the line of presidential succession, an important item to remember in view of the death last year of Vice President Burridge.

"The Chief of the White House Secret Service Detail has emphasized, however, that the President has not been threatened, nor is he considered to be in immediate danger. The presidential apartment is fully protected, and it should be noted that the military garrison at Arlington has already commenced movements to safeguard the city of Washington."

Norman Ritter chuckled.

"It is hinted," Silverman continued, "that last night's dirty work was either inspired by, or carried out by, certain elements of the political lunatic fringe which was forced underground some years back. Arrests may be announced at any moment."

"Don't bet on that, Howie," Ritter commented, with a grin at Bogan.

"Perhaps connected somehow to the savage blood-letting in the nation's capital are the inexplicable events in our airspace a few hours ago. The Federal Broadcasting System is at this moment attempting to piece together a coherent analysis of these events. It is noted, by the way, that the father of electronic airways control, George Reamer, is dead—also as of several hours ago. Perhaps there is a connection here with the chaos in our skies last night. Perhaps not. But let us not be programmed by wild rumor. Let us, Americans, await the facts and then act with reason and common sense."

"You'll need more than common sense, buddy," Ritter told the televised image.

"FBS is pre-empting all local programming to maintain this vital communications link with the nation. We shall endeavor to keep the public fully abreast of developments in this stunning situation. In the meantime, our editorial staff at the network studios in New York have prepared special video clips of the murdered officials. Stay tuned. This is Howard Silverman at the White House, just a zot

153

away. And now to Andy Anderson in New York."

A likeness of the late Attorney-General appeared on the screen, and a nervous voice began a recounting of the dead man's career.

"They still don't know," Norman Ritter declared in a somewhat disappointed tone.

Abe Williams smiled faintly, winked at Ritter, then returned his attention to the viewer. Ritter was on the verge of saying something else; Williams cleared his throat, impaled the intelligence man with a harsh stare, and shot a meaningful glance toward Mike Winston.

Winston himself was totally preoccupied with the television program. His chin rested in a cupped palm and he was staring somberly at the likeness of his late alcoholic boss of the Urban Bureau, Chuck Waring.

Ritter studied the wan face of Mike Winston for a moment, then he lit a cigarette, blew the smoke toward the ceiling, watched it dissipate, and stared thoughtfully at the glowing tip of the cigarette.

"I was just going to say that I always thought of Howard Silverman as pretty sharp," he quietly declared. "Now I don't know. Hell. He doesn't even know yet that Washington is occupied!"

"Wait!" Abe Williams said loudly, sliding forward in his chair. "Something's coming off."

The usual procedure of network television was going amiss. A photo of the Secretary of State occupied the screen. Some unseen person was cursing with hushed eloquence. The Secretary of State disappeared, to be replaced by the likeness of the White House commentator in a rear-angle shot as he stared gravely into a television monitor. There followed an instant of startled reaction as Silverman saw his own backside in the monitor, then the scene shifted abruptly to outside the White House, the camera picking up a procession of U.S. Army tanks as they rumbled along Pennsylvania Avenue. After another second or two of silence, the voice of Howard Silverman was once again in command of the situation.

"We wished to bring you this shot of military activity," he announced smoothly. "It looks like . . . yes you'll notice that two of the larger tanks, updated M-60's I believe have dropped out of the formation and have stationed themselves in front of the White House. You can see how seriously the military view the current situation in Washington. They are taking no chances with the life of the President. We have been attempting to contact the office of the joint chiefs without success. All incoming calls to the Pentagon are being automatically rejected.

"John Tetrazini, of our technical staff, is outside the White House at this moment with the mobile equipment. Can you pick up a long shot, John, with the telescopic lens? We'd like to see . . . it appears that there are some covered military trucks a half-block or so down the street . . . can you bring those in closer?"

The lens of a long-distance camera was moving slowly into focus on a military column which was moving along Pennsylvania Avenue toward the White House. The commentator's voice was telling the viewers, "Yes, that's what they are. Troop transports. I would not be surprised to learn that they are a special White House guard. Can you give us a better angle, John? Oh . . . there . . . what's that? An armored car. A *scout* car, I believe they are called in the military. Just look at those fellows. Our stalwart Blacks, often the butt of jokes and ridicule, but when the cards are on the table, America . . . Well, they certainly look businesslike now, don't they? Our nation should take pride in these young men, dedicating their lives to the defense of their nation . . . a nation which has not always been particularly kind or understanding. . . . Uh, John . . . that ensign flying from the scout car, can you get a. . . ?"

A muscle had been working in General Bogan's jaw. His eyes clashed with Mike Winston's eyes and locked there momentarily, then fell away.

"The Stars and Stripes, ladies and gentlemen. Take comfort in that. . . . But. . . . Sharpen that focus, John! *Stars* and stripes? That's not Old Glory! What *is* that design in the. . . ?"

Norman Ritter was wheezing in an attempt to remain silent. Williams and Bogan were staring intently at the television screen and Mike Winston was impassive. Mayor

Harvey reached over and slapped Ritter lightly on the shoulder and the two men erupted in spasms of repressed laughter.

"But how could it . . . ? That's a *fist,* a *black fist! That's not the stars and stripes!*"

A confusion of sound followed, accompanied by microphone-feedback squeals and the clatter of a chair being upset. Someone whispered loudly, "Get that other camera outside! *Outside!*"

And back at Oakland Town, Norman Ritter was hunched over in his chair, shuddering and gasping in the emotional release of the moment and struggling for control. Mayor Harvey had a hand to his face, dabbing at tears and chuckling merrily. General Bogan had risen to his feet and was watching the confusion on the telescreen with dignified amusement.

Abraham Williams was watching Mike Winston. The white man's eyes were watery; he felt Williams' attention and turned to him with a gaze of abject pathos. Williams was smiling faintly. His eyes sent a message which Winston received, understood and returned. Then the two men turned their attention to the viewer.

Howard Silverman's excited face appeared on the screen. His headset was askew, one earphone dangling and the mouthpiece perching jauntily midway between nose and ear. Then the screen went black and a new voice, crisp and unemotional, uttered two words, very calmly: "Please stand by."

Now they knew.

CHAPTER 3

Oakland, California
March 10, 1999

Dear Michael,
  Just a short few hours ago, before my world disappeared, a very wise and noble man instructed me in the matter of leaf-tending. He likened mental stimulation to the wind that sets leaves free, and noble thoughts to the leaves themselves.
  "See to your leaves, Michael," was his admonishment to me.
  In this first letter to myself, I must confess a lack of experience in this matter of leaf-tending. And perhaps this is why I gropingly set out to press my first leaf with a borrowed pencil and some crumpled paper salvaged from a wastebasket in the War Room of the Oakland headquarters.
  After such an introduction, how do I begin this letter to myself? What am I trying to accomplish by this? I must confess, Michael, that I do not know what or why. I believe I am groping for myself. Yet all there seems to be to work on, as I sit here amidst the litter of coffee cups and overflowing ashtrays, are rambling emotions and stirring

impulses. I am frightened. I am sad. I am unhappy. I am brave. I am courageous. I am bold. I am frustrated. I am challenged. I am defeated. I have not yet begun the fight.

I feel that I am standing on the Universal Date Line, an artificial device which marks the gateway between yesterday and tomorrow. I stand here a ghost, in no-time, with one eye fixed upon yesterday, the other upon tomorrow, and wondering what has become of today. I know that I cannot stand here for long, because the world continues to turn, and no-time is also no-place. I am momentarily suspended, and I must very quickly come down in some-time and some-place.

I have been wrong, Michael. How difficult a thing to say! But, yes, I have been very long wrong. I have known it for some time. I could just not say it, not even to myself. So why, Michael? Why have I drifted along in wrongness, clasping weakness to me in a forge of ignorance, and in dedication to a basic immorality? If anything of life be of value to the human mind, can it be found in any such framework?

No, it cannot. And I know now that I am about to step outside that framework. I knew it a little while ago, as I sat watching television in the War Room. What these men have done, as terrible as it may seem, is no more than a natural expression of the human spirit. They are right, and we have been wrong. So, now Michael. Will I find the courage to take the proper side in this dispute? In the face of those who call me Quisling, or traitor, or coward—or in the mere prospect of such—will I be human enough and man enough to suffer through the courage of my convictions? We shall see, Michael, my lifelong companion. We shall see.

So I have disposed of one vein of the leaf. There is no issue here between right and wrong. That issue is settled. I know now where my sympathies lie. So now I am pursuing a new growth tickling at the fibres of my leaf. Here goes, Michael, just for thee and me. I do not know every Negro in the United States. I am acquainted with a few. I strongly admire one or two. I once loved very much, a fraction of one, and I still cherish that memory. It is not necessary that

158

I know every Negro to understand that a terrible wrong has been visited upon a few, or upon one or two, or upon a fraction of one. I can find no rationalizers to justify the wrongs committed. Within the realm of my personal observation and experience, the Negro race—personified by that small number whom I have known—has, with great dedication and vigor, been thoroughly and unequivocally crapped on. Excuse my earthiness of expression, Michael. This is an earthy matter, and no other expression quite fits the crime.

So here goes. I, Michael Winston, with my own bare hands, in whatever pit is opened to me, and without worrying about what creeps beneath my fingernails, must begin the task of shovelling that crap from my brothers' heads. I do not flatter myself that much will be accomplished by my hands alone. My black brothers have a rather formidable steam shovel of their own at the moment. But I must get my hands down in there just the same. They belong there.

And now, what is this? Another vein for the leaf? Let us pursue it, Michael. I cannot condone the spilling of American blood this day. Yet, at the same time, I cannot condemn it. It is as though the nation has been marching inexorably toward this moment since the day the nation began. We came to these shores, in the beginning, as mistreated men with lofty ideals concerning justice and freedom and human dignity. But we also carted over with us some rather confused ideas about this business of justice and dignity. And we bound men, and took slaves, and lorded our supposed superiority over the poor and the weak and the black ... and especially the black. And God what a landscape of misery and injustice and human cruelty lies about the edifice of this democratic nation, Michael. There is no more pervading form of tyranny than that exercised over a minority by an unconscionable majority.

So, yes, the nation has been marching toward today, and to the blood that has been shed, and to all the other horrors. And all of us here are so many actors in the drama that is America. We change our costumes, apply our make-

up, make our entrance upon the proper cue, speak our lines, add our part to the action, bring whatever life we may to the role being played, then exit. Some of us will be around for the curtain call, some will not; but this has no bearing upon the success of the play itself. I cannot rationalize my cue, I cannot write my own lines. I can only bring vigor and clarity to the role as allowed by the depth of scene and action.

Thank you, Michael. I guess that's one leaf abstracted and blown free. Since I cannot read my own scribbling, I will hand it to Abigail Foster, John Harvey's secretary, in the hopes that she can . . . and that she will type it up for me.

Don't return this to me, Abby. Drop it into a drawer, or press it in a book, or mail it—To Whom It May Concern, in care of the Universal Date Line. Someday I hope someone will send it on to me, but not too soon a someday, so that I may determine whether this, my first freed leaf, fell into the mud to rot with yesterday, or was borne aloft upon the cleansing winds of tomorrow.

Michael Winston
Oakland, March 10, 1999

CHAPTER 4

Claudia Sanderson was feeling vaguely disoriented on that Wednesday morning of March 10th. She had a Tuesday feeling, and the children of her fifth-grade class were exhibiting a Friday exuberance. She rechecked the calendar on her desk, then looked at the date on the stack of papers she'd graded the evening before.

An airplane had crashed a few blocks over from her house the night before. She had not been able to sleep the rest of the night. Leaping flames of the burning building it had fallen onto—the container factory—had filled her bedroom with a yellow glow and flickering shadows until the sun came up. Perhaps this was why she was still in Tuesday; she had not been allowed to consummate Tuesday in the usual routine. Claudia wondered vaguely how she would catch up to Wednesday.

She was drawn out of her thoughts by the solemn face of blonde Melanie, who had approached the teacher's desk and was now standing in quiet non-assertiveness at the edge of authority. "Yes, Melanie?" Claudia said, acknowledging the fair presence.

The ten-year-old mumbled, "It's nearly recess, Miss Sanderson."

Claudia's eyes darted to the wall clock. "Thank you for

161

reminding me, Melanie," she said quietly. "You go ahead."

The child nodded her head and went softly to the door, opened it and stepped into the hallway. Claudia watched her disappear from view, and thought of the progress the shy little thing had made in such a short time. When Melanie had first come to Lake Charles, at the beginning of the second semester, the soberfaced little newcomer had hung back from the smallest participation in group activities. She had been shyly withdrawn to the point of a practiced anti-sociality, even in the important area of student-teacher relationships.

Claudia had made a project of the fair Melanie and she had broken through. Appointment to the important post of "door monitor" had marked the break-through. The burdens of social responsibility often had a way of subjugating personal self-consciousness. Claudia had witnessed the simple psychology work time and again, in a time-worn formula.

Her inward smile turned grimly at the corners. *Physician, heal thyself!* But where was a good time-worn formula for the distress of a twenty-eight-year-old unmarried schoolteacher? And especially in an age when the population balance of the world had gone haywire?

She had been reading some fascinating statistics concerning the population question. In the year of her birth, 1971, the combined population of the world had been around 3600 millions, and forward-looking scientists were then trying to figure out some way to outwit the population explosion which expected to see some 40% more people crowding the globe by the turn of the century. Well, the turn was here—and the explosion had been outwitted, all right—in *this* country. North America had "stabilized" scientifically—and *ughh*, what price stability? Nature was working her own balance in China, India and Africa—thousands and tens of thousands were dying daily of starvation and disease. Certainly that was tragic, and no sensitive person could think of such a thing without feeling terribly sad. But what about the method of balance in *this* country? Was it really any better? What in the world had the scientists *done* to the American men? In the matter of

162

balance—balance of the sexes, a subject near and dear to Claudia's heart, the American statistics were more alarming than the death rates of Asia and Africa.

In the year of Claudia's birth, the balance of young adults was at about 98 males to every 100 females. This could be disconcerting enough thinking in terms of equal opportunity for a woman seeking a mate. One woman in fifty, in that era, would either go without or would be required to play musical-husbands with some of her sisters. But look at 1999! Yipes! One woman in *ten* was faced with this terrible truth! What sort of sadistic balance was *that*! Birth control, *si*—but, for God's sake—*male* control, *no*! It certainly was no world for the *shy* female. Natural selection, survival of the fittest, adapt or perish—these were primeval jungle conditions! Claudia—unsure, shy, retiring Claudia was certainly no candidate for survival.

She had ceased to care. Or, at any rate, she had ceased to be concerned. Except sometimes in the night. And sometimes in the early evening. And sometimes in the light of dawn. And then there were those embittered moments when she evinced a quiet anger with the male sex. What had they let happen to them? There had been a steady drop in the live-birth rate of American males for as far back into history as the records went. Why? Wasn't the male the primary determinant of sex in the conception of new life? What nefarious plot was this against the female, who wanted naught but a man of her own? Had the scientists done this? Or was it some twisted mechanism of the male psyche which was responsible? Did men resent this concept of female ownership? Had the female possessively screwed herself out of the possessive position? She smiled at the Freudian vulgarism suggested by that last structure, then blushed flame-red and looked up to see what her class was doing.

The class was gone! She realized with a wrenching start that the recess bell had sounded somewhere back there in her borderline consciousness; she had dismissed the class in one of those automatic rituals without even realizing what she was doing. How unforgivable! The State of Louisiana deserved at the very least a conscious teacher, even at this meager salary. The children deserved more. Yes, the children—most of all—deserved more than this!

Claudia got out of her chair, smoothed her dress against the backs of her legs, and walked slowly to the window. The children. In God's name, would it forever be someone else's children? Would there never be a fair little Melanie, or a mischievious-eyed little Tommy for Claudia to tuck into bed at night? Would she never read a story to a child of her own?

She watched the pair through the window, Melanie and Tommy, noting their seeming obliviousness to one another and yet the obvious deep awareness each had of the other. Tommy was showing off, as usual, climbing the steel support of the zot-swings, haughtily and busily aloof to the mere girl below, the fair Melanie, the once-confirmed anti-sosh, now doggedly maintaining her position beneath the daring astrogator. Did children ever change, Claudia wondered, from one generation to another? The times changed, the toys changed, the styles of dress and speech changed . . . but did the children themselves actually change? Claudia believed that they did not. The children represented the hopes of mankind. If somebody—some brilliant genius of a thinker or a scientist could figure out what happened, what went wrong, what slipped the track or jumped the cog, in that startling transition from childhood to grownup, and could figure some way to correct the deformation . . . maybe the jungles could be left behind mankind once and for all. But, to Claudia, it seemed that each new generation of adults found some new corner of that vast and beloved jungleland to resurrect and re-explore. Wouldn't it be romantic if Tommy and Melanie were to grow up together all the way into adulthood, and marry, and produce more little Tommies and Melanies? Wouldn't that be so precious? And so utterly impossible!

She thought of Melanie, Melanie the golden, walking into a CAC with a warmth in her thighs and an ache in her heart, and Claudia nearly cried.

Well, she told herself, perhaps that would be preferable to the solo accomodation Claudia had made for herself. Who could say which was the lesser of two evils? An evil is an evil, and none is lesser nor greater, an evil is an equal thing.

Perhaps, some day, Claudia herself would go into New Orleans with some of the girls and see for herself what this man-woman thing was really all about. After all, she'd given up the dreams, hadn't she? Why not accomodate the reality? But she knew that she was kidding herself. She knew that she would never visit a CAC, not in New Orleans or anywhere else. There was one right there in Lake Charles. Why go clear into New Orleans? The evil is in the doing, not in someone finding out.

Claudia knew, however, with the logic that is a woman's heart, that the only accomodation truly required by every woman was the abiding presence of a man of her own. Sex yes, but sex with love, with affection, with *caring*. All else was imitation. It was defamatory, the expansion and perpetuation of bitterness. And Claudia Sanderson desired an application of sweetness to a life already edged with the bitter.

She brushed away a tear and swung away from the window just as Dorothy Brannon, the Principal, entered the room. The usually bright and grandmotherly Mrs. Brannan had a peculiar look about her on this visit. Her face was drawn in tight lines of suppressed emotion as she told the teacher, "Claudia, come here."

Claudia went to the door like a sleepwalker. She had expected something unpleasant today. She hadn't shaken Tuesday yet and she was utterly unprepared for Wednesday. When a person eked out a lifetime on a day-by-hopeful-day basis, these things became important. Somehow Claudia knew that Dorothy Brannan was the bearer of a terrible unpleasantness.

The older woman moved her lips close to Claudia's ear and spoke in a half-whisper. "We are dismissing classes for the day. Go and help bring the children back inside so we can get them on their way quietly and orderly."

Claudia's heart flopped painfully and she gasped, "Wh-what has happened?"

"The Governor and most of the government at Baton Rouge were murdered in their sleep last night. Something is going on in Washington, also. Andrew has the tel-ed switched over to FBS if you want to come into the office after the children have left. But hurry, Claudia. Let us get these children into their own homes where they belong." Mrs. Brannan's composure was rapidly leaving her. She fought trembling lips and told the teacher, "For God's sake, Claudia, don't go to pieces now. Remember the children."

The elderly woman hurried out, leaving Claudia wringing her hands in stunned confusion. Then Claudia pulled her hands across her face, using a trick her father had taught her many years earlier, and as the hands slid away, a bright and smiling face was revealed, like the sun breaking through a dark cloud. She opened the outside door, marched calmly into the play yard, and began calmly and methodically rounding up the little mavericks and sending them into the old corral.

The playground was about emptied, some minutes later, when young Cecile Greene, the first-grade teacher, came running up. "I can't find Jimmy Hartman!" she cried, dancing about in a near panic.

Claudia placed a steadying hand on the younger teacher's shoulder and told her, "Go on back to your class. I'll find Jimmy. Look in on my gang, will you? Make them behave."

Claudia watched Cecile spring back towards the building, then she rounded the corner by the zap-ball court in search of strays. A little girl of about seven collided with her. "Say, you're supposed to be inside," Claudia told her. "Didn't you hear the bell?"

The dimpled doll gave Claudia a con-girl smile and declared, "I didn't have time."

"Well you go on in. Do you know Jimmy Hartman?"

"Nope I don't."

"Well have you seen a little boy out here any place where he should not be?"

"Yes'm I did." She leaned far to the right, as though compensating for the perverse obscurities of geometric objects, and tried to point around the building, the corner

166

of which was several yards beyond her outstretched hand. "Talkin' to a chok-lut man."

Claudia pantomined a gross reaction to a stretched truth, patted the little girl on her bottom, and sent her on her way. Then Claudia went looking for the boy who talked to chocolate men.

And she found him, talking to a chocolate man. Claudia did not realize at once that this was indeed the truth of the matter. She could see that there was a soldier involved in Jimmy's AWOL status. He was a large man, kneeling in front of the boy, an automatic weapon slung onto his back, muzzle down, his helmet riding loosely at the back of his neck, and he was talking earnestly to the six-year-old.

Somehow the sight of military virility and the armed jeep which stood at the curb just beyond was not nearly so disconcerting, nor did it seem so unusual to Claudia's mind on this particular morning as it would have been on, say—Tuesday morning. Somehow, what with her failure to properly discharge Tuesday, and with the incomprehensible disclosure by Dorothy Brannan such a short while earlier, the military seemed quite fitting and entirely proper. Even if they were, indeed, "chok-lut." Claudia could almost, in fact, have passed her hands back across her face and wept in the sudden joy of released responsibility.

Claudia was one of those rare whites who actually *missed* the black presence in Louisiana. One rarely saw a soldier and there were but two black towns in the entire state—no one went there. She found herself gazing at the soldier with a welling sentimentality. He looked *good*, by golly, no matter what anyone said—black *was* beautiful.

Jimmy Hartman's chubby little hand was placed trustingly upon the cheek of the soldier, and Jimmy was staring into the soldier's eyes with that unpaintable gaze of childoood fascination.

"Sure," Claudia heard the soldier saying in that soft organ voice of the black man, "I like to be a soldier and shoot guns. Haven't you ever shot a gun before?"

Then Claudia moved in and took charge. Little boys

167

could not be expected to distinguish between black and white . . . not when a uniform entered the equation especially. Chocolate and vanilla were simply flavors of ice cream, and what child did not like chocolate best of all? Claudia placed a hand atop the fair head and quietly announced, "You're needed inside, mister. You skedaddle."

Jimmy reached out and touched the sergeant's chevrons on the OD sleeve, shot a reproachful glance at his shepherd. and ran a looping trail toward the building.

The soldier rose slowly to his full height, gazed down upon the white woman with the shining hair, smiled faintly and flicked a glance toward the school. "Sentimental sidetrip," he said softly. "I went to this school once, long time ago."

"I—I did too," Claudia stammered, suddenly aware that she was actually conversing with a *black*. She managed a bright smile and went on in a rush. "I mean, I was a student here, also. Now I teach here." She felt the need to keep talking, as though if she stopped for a moment it would suddenly be Tuesday again. "I was here from '77 to '83—as a student, I mean. And I've been here since '94 as a teacher. Fifth grade, now. I started all over again, you see, in '94, with the first grade. Now I have made it up to the fifth. Maybe some day I will—"

The soldier seemed to understand that she was running without a brake. "I was here then," he told her, giving her a chance to breathe. "I mean, '77 to '80, or part of '80. Say, I'll bet we were in the same room together some of that time."

Claudia stared at the big man, her eyes searching his face for a clue to yesterday, all the while wondering why she was not fleeing back across that schoolyard toward the safety of today.

"My name is Paul Fulton," the soldier volunteered, looking at her strangely. "They used to call me Buck Rogers, cause I always had a toy space gun stashed on the playground, and I ran around zapping everybody during recess."

Bucky? Claudia's inner voice screamed. *Black Bucky*
168

Fulton? "I remember a l-little boy like that . . . vaguely," she said aloud, feeling faint.

Sergeant Fulton was watching her now with ill-concealed friendliness. "I remember a little red headed girl," he said. "Don't remember the name but I used to zap hell out of her with that gun of mine. She was, uh, a whitey, you know, a little white girl, and she wouldn't pay me no attention, but uh . . ."

Children do not change from one generation to another. Of course she paid you no attention, Bucky, but not for the reason you think! Claudia was certain that she was going to faint.

The sergeant pulled his eyes away from her and gazed again at the school building. "Well . . . I'm not supposed to be over here. But I was just a few blocks away. Thought I'd come over and take a look, for old times sake." He laughed softly. "Believe it or not, I liked this place."

"Yes, I know," Claudia whispered through bloodless lips.

"Got to thinking about my old zap gun. I still remember where I kept it stashed. Things don't really change that much, do they. You think the world must've flopped finally all the way over for good, then you come back to a little bit of yesterday, and there it all still is, just the way you left it. I, uh, you'll think I'm silly. I thought I'd look for that old toy gun. After all these years. Silly, huh. Things do change, just like people."

"Your gun isn't here, Bucky," Claudia heard herself saying. "I knew where you kept it. And I took it home with me. But I . . . I forgot what ever became of it."

"Well I'll be," the soldier said, his voice awed. "You're her, the little redheaded white girl. I knew there was something. . . . Well I'll be. So you're a teacher here now. I don't even remember your name."

"Claudia," she replied quietly. "Claudia Sanderson."

"Well sure! Claudia Sanderson! You're as pretty as ever, Claudia. I, uh, I guess I shouldn't say that, huh. Well listen, I have to get back to my unit. You, uh, take a tip from an old buddy, eh? You go back in that school house and you stay there. Don't come out all day or all night. You stay there and you'll be safe. Do you know what I mean?"

Vaguely, Claudia knew what Bucky Fulton meant. It had something to do with a crossover from yesterday, it had something to do with Dorothy Brannan's overwrought face and the loss of a government and the sudden appearance of black troops in Lake Charles. Yes, she knew—somehow—just about what Bucky meant.

She told him, "Thank you. And I'm sorry I lost your zap gun."

He smiled, a big happy showplace of his soul, and he told her, "Nothing is ever lost forever, is it? There's always tomorrow."

"Yes, there's always a tomorrow," she agreed breathlessly. With sudden fervor, she cried, "You come back, Bucky. You hear me? You come back!" Then she spun about and ran blindly across the play yard. Not once did she look back, and when she reached the door of her classroom she passed her hands in a slow slide across her face and went inside. Dorothy Brannan stood inpatiently just inside the other door.

"For goodness sake, Miss Sanderson," the Principal greeted her in standard classroom formality, "we thought you'd become lost. Didn't we, children?"

"Lost or found or something," Claudia replied quietly, not giving a damn for classroom formality. "I'll take over now. Thank you, Miss Brannan."

The Principal edged out the door, leaving it standing ajar. Claudia went over and firmly closed it. Yes—lost or found or something. She had finally become rid of Tuesday.

Claudia faced her class and told them, "All right, you luckies, no more school today, but you must go straight home, *straight* hone, and no fooling around on the way. I want you to dismiss orderly, file out by rows just like in a fire drill. Go out through the playyard door, go *straight* home, and do not stop to talk to any chocolate soldiers."

A titter of giggling rippled through the class. "Oh, oh, I almost forgot, didn't I?" Claudia quickly caught herself. "Just because you go home early doesn't mean you get off without the daily message. Live all of today there is to live before you get in bed tonight. Then, when you get into bed, let go of today. When you wake up tomorrow, be sure you find tomorrow, and not a left-over yesterday."

The teacher clapped her hands smartly together. "That's it, you lucky stiffs. Melanie, get the door, dear. Tommy . . . Tommy Grayson, you help her. Get up there and help that poor little thing with that heavy old door, what's a man for in this world anyway? You stand right there with Melanie and help her hold that door. That's my man. Row One, rise now and file out, orderly I said, orderly. Goodnight, you lucky stiffs. God bless tomorrow. God bless all our tomorrows."

CHAPTER 5

"Niggers! Sure they're niggers! What'd you think? Overdone beach boys? Hey, monkey face! Who let you out of the cage?"

"It's some kinda stunt. I bet they're making a movie."

"Hey, Nig! Where's your cotton sack?"

"Where's your banjo?"

"Lookout for that gun, jungle boy! It's a nigger-eater!"

"Got any ivory for sale, boy?"

"I don't think they're niggers. I think they're made up for something."

"You guys got AMS cards for this town? Ain't you about fifty miles lost?"

Sergeant Basie Davidson fingered the safety of his automatic weapon and watched the faces of his squad. The boys sure weren't liking this. Well, they hadn't expected to find roses strewn in their path. They should have been prepared for this kind of stuff.

"Don't one man get down off this tank," the squad leader growled, then he crawled over to the hatch and grinned at the tank commander. "Getting hot in there?" he asked.

"It's great in here," Sgt. Ringer replied. "I'd say it's hotter out where you are." He gazed solemnly at the rapidly building congregation of white youths in the parking lot of the shopping center, just opposite their position. "I don't like the looks of this at all, not at all," he added grimly.

"Too quick on Plan Charlie," the infantry squadleader muttered.

"I'm gonna disperse them," Ringer said. The words had not left his mouth when a small rock banged off the turret. "Yeah, I think I am."

Davidson grunted, "They're not hurting anything yet. Just kids. Leave 'em be for awhile, let's see what happens."

"*Hey! You jungle boys want a snack? I think I got some dried monkey's nuts you can have!*"

Sergeant Ringer's face wrinkled in a troubled frown. "What do they want to talk like that for? Now what's that gonna get them?"

"They're just showing off," Davidson calmly suggested. "Let 'em scream. Long as they're screaming they're not doing anything else."

"I think I'll throw a round of HE into that tower there on the corner."

"The shopping center marquee?"

"Yeah. That thing must weigh a couple of tons. That'd scatter them."

"Those are just kids, Al."

"Yeah, and this is Florence, Alabama too. My Daddy was tore apart by a gang of kids like that."

"Yeah?"

"*Damn* yeah. Not thirty miles from here. I'm not going to give 'em too much steam, Basie. They start making threatening motions, I'm going to clean 'em out."

"Well let's just wait awhile and see," Basie Davidson urged, squinting anxiously across the way.

"That's what I'm telling you, Sheriff," Warren Mallory said excitedly. "There's a tank sitting out there and there's a bunch of nigger soldiers sitting on top of it. It's not white militia, it's black regulars and they're sitting in our city and armed to the teeth!"

Sheriff Butch Cunningham smiled indulgently, took

another sip of his coffee, and stepped casually over to his fax-vue message box. "I told Don Spain to take it easy on those promotion stunts," he declared good-naturedly. "Last time he decided to double his sales he had little fuzzy purple people from Venus on top of the marquee."

"This's no stunt, I'm telling you!" Mallory cried, smashing his fist onto the sheriff's desk.

"Well, it's right on the city line. Why don't you go tell Chief Welch about it." The sheriff turned the vue knob on the message box, slowly rolling the messages out of sight as he quickly scanned the routine notices which daily seeped out of Montgomery. Suddenly he stiffened and bent hawkishly over the small box. His coffee cup slid around on his fingers, up-ending. Coffee poured onto the floor, onto his shoes, splattering onto the cuffs of his immaculate trousers. He turned to Warren Mallory, his face ashen. "The Governor's dead, Warren."

"*What*?"

"Assassinated, it says. Him and the whole bunch. All of 'em."

Mallory lunged toward the fax-vue, gaped at the message, then exclaimed, "Well Jesus Christ!"

"You weren't kidding about those niggers, were you, Warren," the sheriff said, his voice suddenly coldly composed. "That's regular army out there. Now why are they. . . ?"

"God, do you think we're at *war*?" Mallory cried.

At that moment, the radio dispatcher appeared in the doorway, his face white and confused. He steadied himself against the doorjamb and gasped, "Howard Silverman says all of Arlington's people were murdered last night. *Assassinated*!"

"Same thing in Montgomery," Warren Mallory yelled back. "We're being attacked! I bet it's China!"

"Hold it, hold it," came the cold tones of Sheriff Cunningham. "Let's take this one phenomenon at a time. Sparky, you contact all the units, tell them to meet me at the south side of Spain's Center." The sheriff was moving quickly toward the gun rack. He paused to twist around toward Warren Mallory and snap, "Run down and tell

174

Chief Welch! I want every man he's got!"

"At *Spain's*?"

"That's right."

"But the black army makes sense now, Butch! They're here to protect the——"

"How the hell do you know that?" Cunningham yelled. "How do you know we're not in a *civil* war?"

"Oh my God!" Mallory exclaimed. He jerked his head toward the radio dispatcher, lurched around the sheriff's desk and ran out of the office.

The crowd at the shopping center had more than doubled in less than five minutes. It was not just kids now, either. Adult men and women could be seen here and there throughout the throng, casting glances at the tank, talking quietly among themselves. And Basie Davidson had about reached his moment of truth. Something would have to be done. He sure wished they'd been able to Phase II a bit of this town before Plan Charlie had gone into effect You don't just rumble into a town this size, one lone tank and one weapons squad, to occupy the whole damn town. You had to smash them up a little first, soften them up, shock them out of old habit patterns, put some fear into them, make them wonder if they're going to live or die, let them know that it could be either way. Maybe then a tank and a handful of foot soldiers could have some influence. A hurting man doesn't go looking for more hurt. He likes to lie back and lick awhile.

The sergeant crawled back to the hatch and stuck a hand inside. Ringer's head popped into view immediately.

"I guess we better do something about now," Davidson muttered. "The natives are getting restless."

"Well, I'm ready. You wanta give me the targets? Or you want me to pick my own?"

"I think your first idea was good. Probably wouldn't hurt too many people, and it'd show them what a big rifle can do." He stared out over the crowd Man, it was point blank range. "Yeah, I guess that's best. Go ahead and bring that tower down. That's easy. Line up on it slow, though. Let them see what you're doing. Let them watch

175

this big baby track up onto the target. And let's give them a double feature. See that truck over to the left, the delivery truck?"

"You mean that cold drink truck?"

"Yeah. Work your coordinates for a quick second round. Give them a good show. Set it up for automatic second round onto the truck. They won't know any better, they'll think you're shooting from the hip, like the fastest gun in the west."

Ringer grinned. "Okay. Better get your boys down. This turret will be swinging."

Davidson slid off the side of the big tank, with an arm-signal to his squad. They quickly regrouped on the ground beside the vehicle. The sergeant moved them into a line formation, on the sidewalk and to the safe flank of the mammoth, then he quickly moved along the line, repeating the brisk command, "Fire only on command, then fire for effect." He swung his own weapon out of the shoulder-sling, slipped off the safety, and held it poised in the crook of the arm, the muzzle up. Then he walked back to the tank and raised his palm to slap it smartly in the all-clear signal. He hesitated, however, to watch a police car whiz across the intersection, light flashing, and pull in at the edge of the crowd.

Ringer's head popped out of the hatch and he glared down at Davidson. "What the hell are you waiting for?" he snapped.

"The law just arrived." The sergeant flicked his eyes in the direction of the police car. "Let's see what they're going to do. Maybe they'll save us some trouble."

Ringer grunted. "I'm calling it from here on out. I'll be watching." He disappeared from view and the hatch clanged shut.

The door to the police car had opened and a tall stringbean of a man in a khaki uniform was standing beside it, both arms draped atop the open door. Two more police cars came up and swung into a cartwheel effect around the first car. Blue-suited policemen were erupting from the open doors of both cars and milling about in some confusion—throwing dark looks across the street at the

176

disturbing picture of black military might.

Davidson made a quick count of the enemy and decided there were no more than a dozen cops on hand. He could take the whole bunch with one sweep of his weapon before they could get their holsters open. He tensed, watching to see their intent, to anticipate it if possible. He did not want to die right here, at the edge of tomorrow.

The cops were going into a huddle. Davidson raised his right arm and made a sign with his fingers. A tall boy wearing corporal's stripes quickly stepped out of line and moved beside the sergeant. The corporal wore a square box on his back. A small sunflower-like gadget, attached by a cord to the box, was in his hand.

"I better talk," the sergeant muttered.

The corporal handed him the sunflower. Davidson accepted it, raised it to his lips and began speaking. His voice floated out across the heads of the assembled crowd in cooly modulated tones.

"I am Sergeant Davidson, United States Army Special Corps, Occupation Forces. This city is under military occupation. No citizens will be harmed if instructions are followed to the letter. Disperse and go immediately to your homes. Close all businesses except those essential to the public health and welfare. Go to your homes, watch your tele-viewers, and await instructions. I repeat—no citizens will be harmed if instructions are followed."

A loud murmur arose from the crowd. Two of the blue-suited cops stepped forward into the street, chins thrust forward belligerently. A bottle whizzed through the air and broke at Davidson's feet. The sergeant tossed the sunflower to the corporal. "Keep those boys cool," he cautioned.

The corporal jerked his hand in understanding and fell quickly back to the line of troops. The two policemen who had moved into the street exchanged quick glances and went for ther guns.

Davidson swung his auto down. It burped briefly, the sound nearly lost in the swelling murmur of the crowd. The two policemen went down, clutching at their chests, falling onto their faces in the street. Another, just behind the two, grabbed his arm and spun about into the midst of his fellow officers.

At the same instant the air vibrated under the roar of a big gun. The shopping center marquee angled forward crazily at the top and exploded downwards onto the crowd. Davidson caught a flicker of motion behind him as the long barrel swung down and left, roared again and a soft-drink truck in the parking lot became a fireball.

Police were scampering behind squad cars and the crowd was hysterical. Davidson could hear the piercing shrieks of a woman, somewhere in the direction of the marquee wreckage, and a loud male basso was yelling for help.

The tank lurched forward then clanked out to the center of the street—the big turret angling back and forth like the head of an angry bull elephant—seeking another target. It squared off less than twenty feet opposite the collection of police cars and the long barrel projecting out from the turret yawned onto the official vehicles with a portent of doomsday.

Davidson waved his men into a fan stack behind the behemoth. He again snatched the sunflower and announced, as calmly as he could manage, "Disperse, disperse. Go to your homes. Clear this area. Disperse."

The announcement was unnecessary. The crowd was already moving and flowing toward the back of the parking lot. There was no hint of activity from behind the police cars.

Presently the man in the khaki uniform appeared slowly above the hood of his vehicle. He stood there with a perplexed face, empty hands pressing grimly against the gleaming painted surface of the automobile. He glanced at the yawning chasm of spiraled steel which was staring down on him from the tank, then quickly averted his eyes, opened his mouth, then closed it and stared helplessly at the big sergeant with the machine pistol.

Then he called over, "There's some people hurt here."

"You can send for medics if you want to," the Negro called back.

The Sheriff hesitated ever so slightly, then he climbed into his car and began speaking into a radio. When he left the car again, the parking lot was practically empty except for a few stragglers at the far edge, a dozen or so people who lay moaning in the wreckage of the marquee, and police officers who still crouched behind the cruisers.

The Sheriff and the Sergeant stared at each other across the silence. "We didn't want to do that," the Negro announced.

"Yeah, yeah," the Sheriff replied quietly.

"You can keep it from happening again."

"I'll try."

"Fine. We don't want to hurt anyone. But we will, if they make us."

"Yeah, yeah."

The chopping noise of a small helicopter stole into the silence, then grew in volume, and presently the whirly-bird swung into view over some treetops, swept once over the parking lot, then settled alongside the police cars. Two white-jacketed men ran out, crouching beneath the still-twirling blades, and began moving swiftly among the wounded. Another helicopter appeared moments later, then another. In a matter of minutes, they had borne up their fallen and were rising into the sky with them.

There was no one left but the soldiers and the cops. The cops got into their vehicles, turned off the flashing beacons, and quietly departed.

The hatch to the tank opened and a smiling black face popped out. "Now that's what I call authority," Ringer said, chuckling solemnly.

"That's what *I* call not wanting to die," Sgt. Davidson declared softly.

No sir. If somebody wanted to die on the edge of tomorrow, it wasn't going to be the heirs to tomorrow. It'd been too damn long a yesterday, indeed.

MANIFESTO

The Negro Race of the United States, through their agents, the United Negro Army Corps of the United States, hereby declare a state of military occupation through the fifty United States.

All citizens are hereby ordered to desist from violence and to go about their daily routines in an attitude of peacefulness and acceptance of this occupation program.

No arrests will be made by military occupation forces; however, resistance of any nature and from any source shall be met with immediate and forceful suppression.

No laws nor civil programs shall be instituted by the occupation forces. All citizens are urged to go about their business in the usual manner. Law enforcement agencies are enjoined to protect the public good.

A provisional federal government has been appointed by the occupation forces to administrate the re-formation of the nation. State governments have been incapacitated and shall remain so throughout the occupation period. County and municipal authorities are enjoined to continue their functions in the public interest.

Foreign nationals presently residing or visiting within the national boundaries of the United States are ordered to report to their nearest embassy for immediate trans-portation to their country of origin.

Representatives of foreign powers presently exercising diplomatic relations on United States soil are invited to remain, but will be subject to any restrictive provisions of this manifesto.

Early formation of active and free political parties by the American citizenry is encouraged. Charters and platforms of prospective political parties must be presented to the provisional government in Washington within fifteen days of the date of this manifesto. No more than three and no less that two such parties shall be commissioned by the provisional government. Party conventions shall be held no later than ninety days and no earlier than forty-five days from the date of this manifesto. National elections, for the purpose of instituting a new federal structure and government of the United States, shall be held as ordered by the provisional government; in no event shall they occur later than one hundred and eighty days following the date of this manifesto.

Members of the Negro Race shall participate in neither the provisional government nor in the aforementioned political activities. The American citizenry is reminded that the Negro Race of the United States has been systematically stripped of all such responsibilities by The People of the United States. The Military Occupation shall remain in effect, however, until full and equal rights of citizenship have been restored to the American Negro by The People of the United States; and, furthermore, until such time as all rights of equality are guaranteed by unalterable constitutional provisions.

The United Negro Army Corps hereby undertakes full responsibility for military defense of the United States of America, and hereby so serves such notice to all foreign powers. The Autotomic Defense System of this nation remains in full operation, and shall so remain throughout the period of military occupation.

All Americans, white and black alike, are urged to turn the final page of the painful Book of Yesterday, and to go immediately to the clean and unspoiled first page of our nation's promising Book of Tomorrow.

/s/ Abraham Lincoln Williams
   for the Negro Race of the United States
   this Tenth day of March, Nineteen Hundred and Ninety
    Nine

BOOK IV - TOMORROW, PAGE ONE

CHAPTER 1

"Ladies and Gentlemen, this is Howard Silverman speaking to you from the nation's capital. It is noon in Washington, an unbelievable, nightmarish noon. The questions now on all lips are: Why? How could it happen? Precisely what *has* happened? What do they want? What will they do next?

"FBS has attempted to answer some of these questions, and to piece together the incredible events of these, the darkest hours of this republic's history. But the information is meager; no one seems to know anything other than 'I woke up and there they were.' Even the gentlemen in the White House remain silent, except for vague charges of treason in high places. Obviously, there has been treason. Just as obviously, it has been committed in high places.

"The President has named few names: Thomas Fairchild, the late chief of the Federal Police Bureau; Michael Winston, an administrator in the Urban Bureau; General Jackson T. Bogan, the nation's highest ranking combat officer. Treason . . . perhaps. But this is no explanation of what happened. This is certainly not the sort of information we desire from our President at such a time.

"As I look out my window, I see United States Army tanks and troops. The airplanes that whistle low through our skies bear the markings of the United States Air Force. Warships steam along our east coast, just a few miles away, flying commission pennants of the United States Navy. We are a nation occupied . . . by our own armed forces.

"I have, on my desk, wire reports from around the nation. This is another curiosity. Our communications networks have remained virtually intact. Only in isolated instances have we lost contact with the parts of our nation. I shall not attempt to read to you all of the wire reports that continue to flood this newsdesk. That job would require a team of broadcasters, speaking continuously around the clock for days. Just know that wherever you are in this country, the events taking place there are being repeated everywhere.

"Our nation is occupied by military might. In each of our states at least one city has sustained massive destruction of property—though, oddly enough, with very small loss of life. Assassins have been at work, however, in each of the state capitals and of course, here in Washington. And everywhere, if these reports are any indication, black troops with massive firepower and certainly with the capability for rampaging terrorism merely sit and watch. What are they watching for? Eyes upon the nation, America. *Eyes* more than *hands*.

"The facts seem to be these. A sort of limited and unusual form of military coup has taken place. Limited and unusual, I say, because there have been no direct moves upon the chief seat of government. Our Congress remains intact, though adjourned. Our President remains in the White House. No proclamations have as yet been issued to establish military rule. No attempt has been made to seize communications networks.

"We *are*, however, very definitely a nation occupied. And something more than a coup is suggested by our present situation. Using simple mathematical extrapolation, FBS has established an estimate of the number of troops in the occupying forces. This reliable estimate amounts to a staggering sum, nearly one hundred times more than the known strength of our army regular combat forces.

"This nation is blanketed, ocean to ocean, Canada to Mexico, with grimfaced soldiers of an occupation force. If all the black, uniformed men who now calmly gaze upon America are indeed themselves Americans, then it would seem that the entire black nation is participating in this action. And this, it appears, is indeed the case. The only alternative is much worse. If these black troops are not Americans . . . then they are Africans. And if they are Africans, then the charges of treason in high places are indeed ominous. Let us pray that these are American blacks wearing our uniforms . . . and let us so assume.

"Perhaps it is now appropriate that the people of the United States re-direct their questions. Perhaps now we should ask the White House: what do *you* intend to do? Black soldiers are camped on the White House grounds, directly outside your windows. Their tanks prowl our streets, unopposed and unchallenged. Their bayonets point at our unprotected bellies. Dozens of our great cities lie in rubble. Every executive branch of government throughout these states has ceased to exist, including your very own.

"How does the AMS Society get itself out of this predicament, Mr. President? Which slot do we feed for personal protection? Which one for national survival? You have been telling us for most of two decades that AMS is the purest form of democracy and the most certain solution to our racial problems. Look out your window, Mr. President, and tell us: do we still have that solution?

"And please, sir, do not speak to us in vague terms of foreign plots, of unlikely traitors or of the great American dream. Do not flower your answer with mentions of patriots, of fine old institutions, of inferior and superior races, of noble instruments of government. Simply look out your window, Mr. President, and tell us where we go from here.

"This is Howard Silverman saying good day from Washington. May we—God willing—meet again."

Silverman peered somberly into the camera until the red light winked out, then he sighed and pushed his chair away

187

from the desk. Lou Washburn, the technical director, moved nervously to the desk and declared, "Jesus, Howie, you're going to get hanged from the highest point in Washington."

Silverman sighed and tried to fish a cigarette from a crumpled pack. "It's the end of an era, Louie," he said, with a tired smile. "For us, anyway. All I've done for twenty years is bitch about things. But never where it could be heard."

The cigarette package was empty. Washburn handed the newsman a smoke and lit it, then peered at him with troubles eyes. "The word is run. *Run*, Howie, not walk."

"What's that you have there?" Silverman asked, glancing at the paper.

"Came in just as you were winding up, so I held it. It's their manifesto."

The newsman took the creased message paper and opened it, grunted something unintelligible, then began reading intently. He finished the reading, then raised clouded eyes to his companion. "Well, that answers all the questions," he quietly declared. "But it's not the end to anything."

CHAPTER 2

Abraham Williams was bringing Mike Winston up to date regarding the history of Negro thought during fifteen years of institutionalized servitude. "AMS was the final straw," he pointed out. "That's what really broke our backs. Just as Arlington knew it would. The guy that controls your pocketbook controls *you*, and I guess it's the oldest idea in history. All the kings and emperors used it, the commies used it, and I guess every power bloc has used it, consciously or not. Economic power is the ultimate power. When Arlington AMS'd this country he knew exactly what he was doing."

"The first American *coup d'etat*," Winston commented.

"That's right. I don't think he could have pulled it off except for the condition the country was in. Everyone in panic, people going hungry, the economy in disarray. The population flowing back to the land. AMS seemed like the logical blueprint to a lot of people to get the country back in shape. Not many people realized they were selling their souls to a devil machine. The *black* people least of all. We couldn't get anyone to believe that those little cards weren't the goldmines Arlington promised. The majority of blacks had gone to the cities anyway, and nobody would take them back on the land. The minority of us who still owned

189

land were pushovers for the power bloc. They AMS'd us right out of there and into the Towns, and it wasn't done all that gently either."

Winston murmured, "Yes I remember the land sweeps."

"So do a lot of us," Williams said, sighing. "I had twenty acres of the prettiest, rolling. . . . Ah don't let me start talking about that."

"They threw you off," Winston said quietly.

"Yeah. The law of eminent domain. Sounds nice and legal, doesn't it." The black man smiled ruefully. "Well, I'm digressing. What was I. . . ? Oh yeah. It was in the autumn of '88 when most of us finally started singing the same tune. By then most of the hotheads had cooled somewhat and the upbeat ideas were beginning to sound more inspirational than the 'burn, baby, burn' dialogue. Don't—uh—don't think that Norm Ritter's attitudes are the prevailing ones. And don't sell Ritter himself short. He runs around making bad noises, I know, but I believe most of it is show. He's a deep one, really. You never know what the man is really thinking. Personally, I admire Ritter.

"To give you a bit of insight into this guy, Mike . . . he lost his wife and baby in the Oregon land purge of '87. Not to violence, nothing like that. But conditions were appalling in some of those temporary relocation centers. You'd have to live through it to know. Gertrude Ritter and the baby just weren't physically up to it. They died of pneumonia. And they weren't the only ones to go that way. I had it better than some. I was at the Camp Roberts Center, for three months only .The weather was pretty good, and there happened to be a health service medic there who believed that nigger babies needed vitamins and things the same as white babies. My kids came through okay. But this is all old history. I want to give you the late history.

"After the agreement of '88 we began quietly bringing the scattered black community together—in the soul, I mean. And we began to understand just what it was they'd done to us. And we decided that we were not going to accept it this time. No more slavery, not by any name. We got a dialogue going with the government niggers, and Ritter became our go-between with the military. He arranged the first meeting between General Bogan and me. We've had direct rapport now since the summer of '92 with all elements of the government community—the blacks, I mean. What few holdouts there were came over quickly when Arlington entered the White House."

"You were going to tell me about the philosophy," Winston quietly reminded his host.

"Yes. Well we thought, see, maybe this entire terrible thing could be worked for the eventual good of the black man in America. What have we ever had, Michael? I mean, actually *had*? Nothing. Except a few dreams, a lot of promises, much talk about equality and freedom and opportunity. But it was all emptiness. They niggered us to death. The white people really did not want us to have those things, you see. They didn't applaud our few advances. They niggered us about them. And they squealed with delight every time we fell on our faces. And we began to realize that we'd come full circle in this country. We started in slavery, as nothing more than the white man's tool, we'd gone around the horn and landed on the shores all over again, and nothing had changed.

"These towns are nothing more than government reservations, Michael. So, like I said, we got to thinking. Maybe the thing could be turned to our better good. And that was the way we went at it. We began to look at all the suffering of the seventies and the frustrations of the eighties as the nicest thing anybody had ever done for us. They'd given us *back* to *ourselves*, you see.

"And we began to build hope again. We'd been running around half crazy from the forties to the seventies, three decades of insanity, trying to hack a trail through that white jungle out there. And, in the process, we'd lost sight of ourselves and of our true place in the American society. The white man had lost sight of us, also. The Negro image was terribly distorted, entirely out of focus.

"Most Negroes, Michael—and I say this in all sincerity, most Negroes want the same things that most white people want. We want food on the table when we're hungry. We want nice clothes. We want things and opportunities for our kids. We want to feel a bit of pride now and then, and—well, just like all people everywhere, Michael, we

191

want the respect of our fellow man. And what really rankled, you see, was the terrible feeling that the white man was determined that we weren't going to have those things. If it hadn't been for that, the Rap Browns and Stokely Carmichaels and the black bigots could have yelled until they were blue in the face and nobody would have paid them any mind. But, see, that's what made Rap and Stokely scream too. Those same things."

"I guess so," Winston murmured.

"Yeah. Well, this was the framework we hung everything together on. We knew we had to have the power, first of all. And the way Arlington immediately began demilitarizing, we knew we'd have no real trouble in that area. The only reason, now the *only* reason that the old man cut back so severely on the armed forces is because he was scared silly at the thought of all those armed blacks. And he wasn't willing to pay the price to hire good white men to bear arms. So he demilitarized. We had Automated Defense anyway, he reasoned, so who the hell needed a standing army—especially a standing army of *blacks*.

"Well, General Bogan could tell you something about that decision. He says that there was no way, not with ADS or anything else, that we could've turned back a determined massive invasion by the Chinese—not the way Arlington went. And the old man knew it, too. Yet he played dice with national security in his determination to keep us pent up in those towns.

"We got the power and we knew we could come out of those towns any damn time we wanted to. But there was a rub. Power could get us out, yeah. But it couldn't *keep* us out, not unless we wanted to become prisoners to our own freedom. See? We don't want to *occupy* this country, 'til doomsday, Mike. We want to *live* here as equal American citizens, in dignity and with respect. We knew that we needed a political base. We needed someone to stand up and arouse the conscience of the nation all over again—and this time, by God, we'd make it work right. We'd make them give us good government and rockbound guarantees that this sort of crap would never happen again.

"And that was the hardest part, getting a political base. Most people in the white community who we knew would be receptive to our cause had just run flat out of time. They were old. They wanted no part in any hairbrained scheme to overthrow the nation by force. They could see themselves, I'm sure, hanging from their wheelchairs. And I couldn't blame them.

"The point is, we had a tough time. We very strongly considered asking President Tromanno to represent us—he was the greatest white friend we'd ever had, and I guess we damn near got him hung the first time around. But . . . we were thinking about asking him to lay it out for us again. Our contacts told us the old man was just barely clinging to life, so we left him alone. He's got a place up in—"

"Yes I know," Winston cut in. "I saw him just last night. He's alive and well, and he's probably still your greatest friend. But your information was correct. He is very frail."

Williams shrugged. "So you see our problem. There were some we could have recruited whom I wouldn't have had on a bet. The wild-eyes ones, you know. Those guys are suffering their own special brand of insanity. *We* sure didn't need it. Anyway, Arlington knows about that bunch, and they're kept under pretty close watch.

"So we started in '96 trying to line up some intelligent white sympathy to our plan. As of yesterday, when you walked in on us unannounced, I had enlisted five white men to help. Good men. I have them now, and they constitute the provisional government." The big black man sighed and, added, "They're far from the best I would like to have . . . but they're good men."

"Who?" Winston wanted to know.

"The top man is Simpson Barnes Bancroft."

Winston's eyes showed his surprise. "*Senator* Bancroft?"

Williams nodded. "He's not the smartest man in the country, but he's honest. I trust him implicitly. Anyway, he knows politics, and he knows politicians, and I guess he's the world's greatest living authority on the U.S. Constitution. I'm depending on him to help set up the new permanent government—*under* the constitution. Or, rather, under the constitution as it existed in 1980. He can do that. And then I expect the people—*the people,* Michael—to make the real decision. The people will make the only decisions the Negro will accept."

"Are these men in Washington now?" Winston wondered.

Williams glanced at the clock. "They'll be arriving there most any minute. We are going to leave Arlington in the White House until the people run him out. The provisional government will work around him. But the niggers are not going to drag that old man out of the White House. Hell no. Wait'll you hear about *his* plot. He was planning on niggering *us* into another stand for himself in the White House. He thought *he* was setting *us* up, and we let him keep on thinking it. He was going to strike at election time, declare a national emergency, and declare himself in for an illegal third term."

"Is that honest-to-God fact, Abe?" Winston asked solemnly.

"That, Michael, is honest-to-God fact."

"Well . . . isn't that a hell of a footnote!"

"Call it what you want, but we're not dragging him out of there. The white man will have to handle his own garbage."

"What a hell of a footnote," Winston repeated.

CHAPTER 3

Norman Ritter charged into the office with his nostrils
flaring and eyes blazing. "That damned Arlington!" he
raged. "*He* hasn't given up yet!"

Abe Williams glared at the intelligence man for a
moment, waiting for him to continue, then demanded, "All
right, spit it out. What's up?"

"What's up is just maybe the whole damned show, that's
what's up! He got them! Simpson Barnes Bancroft and all
the others, he got 'em all!"

"What do you mean, he *got* them?" Williams asked, his
voice suddenly very quiet.

"I mean that he splattered their guts all over
Pennsylvania Avenue, that's what I mean! Hell, it's my
fault, *all* my fault. I thought the damn war was over. But
it's not, Abe. It's a hell of a long way from over!"

Williams placed both hands on Ritter's arm, led him to a
chair, sat him down, and said, "Now, Norman. Exactly
what happened?"

"I had my Washington man, John Douglas, meet them
at the airport," Ritter mournfully reported. "Thought it
might look better that way. I mean, instead of having them
marched in by a squad of black troops. And I screwed up.
My counter-intel slipped, that's all, it must have. Nobody
should have known about those guys."

"Tell me what happened, Norm," Abe Williams said patiently.

"Just like a twenty's movie of Chicago. This car comes up alongside our car, a machine pistol pokes out the window, and down goes the provisional government . . . every damn one of them, Abe. *Every one.* So what do we do now? Draft old Arlington for a third term?"

Abe Williams was scrutinizing his friend's troubled face. He mused, "Maybe . . . maybe, Norm. . . ."

"Yeah, maybe Norm Ritter is slipping," the other growled. "It's a miracle I didn't lose John Douglas, too. The limousine smacked into a light standard and rolled twice. I don't know how he managed to walk away from that."

"There's a psychological overtone to this thing, Norm," Williams commented faintly. "This marks the first decisive and successful retort for the white establishment. We have to play this very carefully. It could snowball. It could snowball fast."

"Well I won't mention it if you won't," Ritter said.

"Neither of us will have to. Arlington will be screaming it over the rooftops."

"Then let's cut their communications."

Williams shook his head. "Wouldn't help. Might even hurt. No, we can't cover it up."

"Then let's disclaim Senator Bancroft. Let's say that—"

"Uh uh, no good," Williams said quickly. "We need a better hand than that. Tell me something, Norman. In view of all that's been said publicly by the White House today . . . if you were Whitey, who would you expect the niggers to move into the White House?"

"Well . . . let's see . . . I don't know if I follow your line of . . . hey! Of course! The traitorous jackal! The nigger-tender! Old Uncle Mose himself!"

"Right," Williams replied softly. "So right."

"I know what you're thinking!" Ritter said. "I *know* what you're thinking!"

"Go get him for me, Norm. He's all pegged-out, exhausted, over-used, soul-sick, but he's the only one can turn this for us now. Go get him, Norm."

Mike Winston peered glumly at his fingertips and told Abe Williams, "You don't know what you're asking me to do. You're asking me to confirm to every white person in the country that I sold them out. You're asking me to stand up there and say, 'Well, I screwed you, Charlie. Now I'm going to lead you.' I don't think I can do it, Abe. Besides, I'm simply not qualified. I've never run a nation before."

"You've run the entire black nation for the past three years," Williams pointed out "Almost single-handedly. That requires considerable ability. Now that I think of it, you're a whole hell of a lot better equipped for the job than Bancroft. He was a good man, and I am sincerely shaken by his death—I hate to lose him in that manner. But face it, Michael. I was looking to Bancroft primarily for his organizing talents and his political footwork. We can find someone else for that part of it, after we get a provisional establishment in operation. I'm sure that many good men will come over, and gladly. But right now we need a *head* of *government*. Right now! And before Arlington can make any political capital from this brief little victory of his."

Winston sighed. "I just don't know, Abe," he muttered. He ran a hand across his forehead. "I'm liable to botch things for good, you realize that. Hell, I'm just not in that league. Not anywhere near it. I wouldn't know where to start."

"You start by seizing the reins of government. That's where every man starts. Then you take each problem as it presents itself. I know you can do it. But that isn't what is really worrying you, is it? It's the traitor tag that is chewing you to pieces, isn't it?"

Winston went to the desk and helped himself to one of the black leader's cigarettes, lit it with steady hands, and exhaled vigorously. "I guess I could live through that part of it," he declared.

"Then don't worry about the rest. Men grow, Michael. I've seen men grow from midgets to giants in the space of a heartbeat. All it takes to lead is the wisdom to *know* what is right and the *strength* to do it. I believe that you have both those qualities. Growth is a natural consequence of

197

that exercise. How many men enter the White House with presidential experience?"

Winston took another slow drag on the cigarette, then angled an oblique gaze to the status boards depicting the progress of the occupation forces. "You think you really need me, Abe?" he asked quietly.

"There is no one else, Michael."

"Well . . . I believe I feel a wind at my back."

"What does that mean?"

Winston grimaced. "I guess it means that the show must go on."

Williams' face split into a restrained grin. "I never thought for a minute you'd say anything else."

"Yeah," Winston growled. "Me too, I guess. But . . . back when I made that decision, Abe, I didn't realize that such a big role was being written."

"I don't get you," the black man replied, smiling quizzically.

"Private joke. I'll explain it to you some day. If I don't fall flat on my face. But . . . brrrr, what a hell of a bitter wind."

CHAPTER 4

Howard Silverman had the full staff of film librarians working feverishly. Two editors, flanking him at the long table, were peering at rolls of video film and jotting notes on large program sheets.

Silverman snagged a passing librarian and told her, "Bring me this S-87-121."

The girl stopped to consult the catalog in Silverman's hand. "That one's in the security file, also," she informed him. "It's never been cleared for release."

"Hell, I know that," he snapped. "Bring it."

The librarian walked away, resignedly shaking her head. Silverman stabbed his pencil toward the film editor to his left. "I remember that S-121 very well," he ruminated. "Now here's what I want out of it. There are some good shots of old nigger patients being carried out of a Virginia hospital on stretchers. That's when they were moving them into the relocation centers. Later on, there are some shots of the field hospitals they set up at Parris Island. I want you to splice that up to show the continuity between the county hospital and Parris Island. Got it?"

The editor nodded and nervously cleared his throat.

"Okay. And there's one shot in there that shows daylight right through the ceiling where they're setting up the cots.

No wonder we never got this stuff cleared, eh? All right. You run those frames along with that statement in his speech." He leaned forward and stabbed the program sheet with an index finger.

The editor scribbled a note on the program sheet and murmured, "Christ."

"You getting the general slant now?" Silverman asked. "See this right here? Where Arlie is saying, 'with all due regard to the needs and welfare of these people. . . ? All right, there's your continuity slice. You bang it in there."

He turned to the man at his other side. "Now look, Eddie. This film you're working was shot while the Appalachin Plateau was being built. Early construction phase. See these cats in the plows and dozers? It's hard to tell here, but it shows clear as hell in projection. Those guys are niggers. Yeah, all of them, the whole mess. Now run on down . . . a little more . . . okay, here. See these cops beating hell out of these guys? Know what that is? Got any idea? That, Eddie, is the end of organized labor in America. This was the last picket line. Arlie used all nigger labor on those land recycles. How do you think he got the job done so cheap? Like making a man dig his own grave, isn't it. Think on that angle and try to work it in. And remember that no black man has ever lived in Appalachin Strip, or raised so much as a single apple on that plateau. You know how to play it? All right, you guys get busy."

"This scares the hell out of me, Howie," the editor said quietly. "Leavenworth, here I come."

"You got more to worry about than Leavenworth, Eddie. A whole hell of a lot more. You just do the job. I'll take the responsibility."

An excited older man hurried into the room. "Hey, Howie! You're wanted over in the communications section."

"What's up?" Silverman asked, struggling to his feet.

"Damnedest thing I ever saw. This MCW transmission blasts into our monitor right on top of our press carrier. They must have fifty gillion watts of output. We cut our transmitter and listened. This guy says it's Oakland Warhole, calling for Howard Silverman."

"Well Christ let's *go*!" Silverman cried, pushing the other man along with him. "You got MCW capability on that transmitter, Walt?"

"Sure. Harry's peaking it up for voice now. The guy says that a Michael Winston wants to talk to you, Howie. Do you know a Michael Winston?"

Silverman's face was beaming like the northern lights. "Not personally, Walt, no—not personally. But I guess I'm going to. I'll bet you an old fashioned American dollar that I'm going to."

The time had arrived for the long-awaited presidential address to the nation. Howard Silverman entered the large control booth and stood slightly to one side of the technical director. The countdown clock had moved to the ninety-two-second mark. "You all set?" Silverman asked.

"All is ready," the director replied tensely. "I just hope you know what you're doing."

"Let me worry. You just concentrate on mixing this stuff according to the script."

"You're blocking my Central Station monitor."

"Sorry." Silverman moved slightly aside. "Hope everything goes smooth."

"It will, unless the cops descend on us. I filtered the background noise out of the Winston recording. The guy speaks well." The director jabbed a finger toward the wall clock. "Better get on your mark."

Silverman hurried out the door and down the short flight of stairs. When the red light flashed on, he was starely somberly into the camera, his lungs ready. "Good evening, this is Howard Silverman in Washington, speaking to you from the studios of the Federal Broadcasting System. It is eight o'clock here in the nation's capital. In just a moment, FBS will present an address to the nation by the President.

"This message was video-taped earlier this morning for more effective presentation at this time. Please stay tuned for another surprise presentation immediately following the President's address.

"Ladies and gentlemen of America, I give you the President of the United States."

The red light winked off. Silverman strode rapidly to a chair which had been placed in front of the studio monitor. The nation had been waiting all day for this, this word of advice from their *Big Daddy* Arlington. Silverman felt a little sorry for them; perhaps a bit guilty for the trick he'd played on them. He sighed and sat back in the chair. They'd get Big Daddy, all right. But just his voice. Presently occupying the screen was a still photo of the President. The familiar Arlington oratory was flowing smoothly, the velvety tones which had charmed a nation were still rich and elegant despite the passage of years.

And while the words flowed on unchecked from their recorded sound track, the presidential image vanished from the screen, to be immediately replaced by the latest thing in television re-runs—from an era dead and nearly forgotten.

There were films of Maryland and Mississippi, of Arkansas and Detroit, of San Francisco and New York—the bloody integration riots of the fifties, sixties, and early seventies. The Presidential syrup flowed on, oblivious of the scenes of horror which filled the screen. Police dogs bared snarling fangs and nightsticks crunched onto black skulls as the President was saying, "Those we have succored and fed, those we have housed and employed, those for whom we have assumed normal and financial responsibility have closed their hearts to their benefactors and have opened their ears to the evil whispers of those beyond the seas who would pillage our blessed land of plenty.

"Those in whom we have entrusted the defense and protection of our nation have raised their own black fists against us. This is indeed a dark day, not only for the white citizens of this republic, but for the misguided and misused blacks as well. Let us . . ."

Silverman blinked back unbidden tears as the Grand Central Heli cameras came on. Thousands of Americans were gathered there to watch the giant screen—and in the background could occasionally be seen a movement of black troops carrying formidable weapons. The white faces showed bewilderment—then, here and there, a smile or a frown as understanding dawned.

Arlington was just warming up; as he moved into the next familiar argument, montages of Booker T. Washington, Paul Dunbar, Phyllis Wheatley, Marian Anderson, Paul Robeson, Satchmo Armstrong, Nat Cole, Peter Salem, George Washington Carver, Ralph Bunche, Jackie Robinson, Joe Louis, Willie Mays, Whitney Young —on and on and on, each appropriately subtitled —marched across the television screens of the nation.

". . . and the Negruh has built no civilizations, has made no really significant contributions to the arts and sciences, has had little impact upon the American culture and way of life."

(The technical script: DUB IN BACKGROUND MUSIC, NEW ORLEANS JAZZ).

"No, Americans, the white man has no debt to the Negruh. Quite the reverse is true. The Negruhs of this continent have done nothing but take from the white man, and the more he has received the more he has demanded. For more than one hundred years he has despoiled our citics, filled our charity lists, profaned our womanhood, and bloated our labor markets with useless manpower."

(The technical script: MIX IN APPALACHIN PLATEAU CONSTRUCTION SHOTS. SPLIT, CUT TO. . . .)

"In the nineteen hundred and sixties, a juvenile and febrile government administration, which I cannot bear to mention by name, (KENNEDY FUNERAL CORTEGE. SWELL IN BACKGROUND SOUND.) nourished and encouraged the Negruh influence in our affairs of state to the absolute zenith of intolerability. This was followed closely by another coddling administration which set this nation afire, my friends, *afire*—and then another and another. *This* party found its strength in the ashes of America's 20th century fools, and we followed the dictates of the *majority* of our people, as we sought to place the Negruh in a true perspective to the American Dream. We sought to free the average American citizens of the burden and pain of daily confrontation with an irresponsible rabble . . ."

The nation's viewers were treated to long-suppressed

views of the Negro roundup of the '80s—of crying, frightened children—of the aged and sick, of pregnant women and weeping men, of the truckloads jammed to overflowing with suffocating cargo, bound beyond the barbed wire of various "relocation centers"—and the President was saying, "Even so, this program was not undertaken with malice but with humane and sincere consideration and with all due regard to the needs and welfare of these people. In a tremendous public works program designed to both fulfill Negruh needs and to . . ."

Howard Silverman unashamedly dabbed at his eyes with a handkerchief. He was thinking of another probable viewer of the program, a handsome old man who sat alone but for the cordon of Secret Service bodyguards; he was thinking of the many years of close association, of the campaigns, of the days of glory gone forever.

". . . they want to live in *your* neighborhood, they want to meddle in *your* affairs of government, they want to dilute *your* fine educational systems with their backward children. They want what *you* have and this has been the story of the American Negruh for over two hundred years."

The television audience was being shown a forty-year-old film of Mississippi's one-room unpainted clapboard shacks, of incredible big-city ghettoes, and the President was saying: "What *they* have is never *good* enough. They will never be content to take what is theirs and leave the white man alone. They want the fruits of *your* labors, my people. Are you going to give it to them?"

Video tape recordings of the destruction of Los Angeles and San Francisco appeared on the viewer, followed by still shots from around the nation, hospital scenes, morgue scenes, horror scenes from March 10th, 1999. One shot showed an armored column as it moved ponderously along Pennsylvania Avenue in Washington, this quickly replaced by motion picture footage of another armored column speeding along the Hollywood Freeway, spitting death and destruction to each side of the raised structure. And the President was telling the nation, ". . . no, we will not open the doors of the nation to this rabble. We are going to let them sit in their metal prisons and fry, we are going to let them gnaw on the wooden stocks of their rifles in hunger. And we are going to sit with butcher knives and paring knives, and with squirrel rifles and target pistols, and we are going to wait them out. Let them *dare* try opening the doors to America.

"In this entire country there are less than twenty million of them. *We* number a full two hundred strong, my friends. So *courage*, America. Already your President is pleased to announce that the traitors among us have been destroyed. The provisional government named in the Negro Manifesto is no longer in existence. *We have wiped them out*! And now we say to the military, *throw down your arms* and go back to where you belong. Do so immediately or suffer the consequences of your ill-considered and infantile actions.

"And I say to my people, *my people, stand up*. Stand up with your President, stand up in freedom and in dignity, *stand up* and stare the savages back into their holes! Give them not a foothold, *not one*, or they will take all that you have.

"Goodnight, America. God be with us all. God *is* with us all."

Howard Silverman was back on his mark, right on cue, staring somberly into the camera. "Ladies and gentlemen, please be assured that no one at FBS is gloating over the technical triumphs implied in this evening's programming. None of us have found any pleasure in making a fool and a liar of the President of the United States. But truth must out, and this day in our destiny is certainly no time for any American to attempt to find comfort in half-truths, in deliberate distortions, or in meaningless rationalizations. The harsh truth, quite simply stated, is this: We are a nation occupied. Those of us who have missed death thus far have missed it very narrowly indeed. All of us, if we simply admit the truth to ourselves, know that the American Negro has suffered a long history of injustice and mistreatment at the hands of the white majority. And now the Negro holds *our* fate in his hands. These are not stupid hands, as the President implied. They are not children's hands, nor obviously are they frightened hands.

But they are very angry and very powerful hands.

"Before responding to the President's call to combat, every American has a right to know the true circumstances of our present situation. The black forces have complete and uncontested control of every military installation in the nation, including even the Automated systems. The Negro holds all the weapons, and therefore all the cards. The President has pointed out the fact that we outnumber the Negro. What comfort can we find in this sort of number's game? How long would numerical superiority prevail in a duel between target pistols and heavy artillery? And how much comfort would the citizens of Los Angeles and other of our cities have found in butcher knives on this fateful morning?

"No, I found no joy in my task this evening. But I would find even less joy tomorrow in the total and complete destruction of this nation. And, of course, this is the course being demanded by the President. The annihilation of a people. After a quarter-century of close association with the President, I feel that his address tonight had nothing whatever to do with the responsibilities of his office. I feel most strongly, in fact, that President Arlington is suffering from some form of mental derangement, and that his plea to the nation tonight represents nothing more than a madman's folly, a desperate and emotional bid for support of his personal and lifelong and perhaps psychotic grievances with the black race. In short, I feel the President was not thinking in the best interests of the nation. I believe that he would rather see the nation perish than to admit his and our mistreatment of the Negro citizens of this country. This is the way Howard Silverman sees it. With so much at stake, this is the way Howard Silverman must *say* it.

"I promised you a surprise presentation to follow the presidential message I have been in short-wave radio contact with one of the men who stands accused of treason. Contrary to the President's claim, the provisional government of the occupation has not ceased to exist, not by any means. It was this man's wish to deliver a personal statement to the nation. FBS engineers recorded that statement directly from the short wave. It is my good pleasure to present that radio transcription at this time. There is no video accompanying this presentation. Your screens will go black. No adjustments to your sets are necessary. May I suggest that you extinguish or dim all lights wherever you may be, and that you listen with great attention to the following message. It is time for each American to deliberate the fate of his nation. Please do so now.

"Ladies and gentlemen, I give you the new Director of National Affairs, representing the provisional government of the United States, Mr. Michael Winston."

TEXT OF MICHAEL WINSTON'S STATEMENT

My name is Michael Winston. I am a native-born citizen of the United States. I have been a government employee for the past fourteen years. My position for the past three years was that of National Commissioner of Urban Affairs. I exerted government controls over approximately eighteen million human beings. *Black* human beings. My AMS passcard carries an FVIP override. I am not married. I have no family living. A few hours ago, I was officially charged with high treason against my country.

The preceding statements are factual, and are given only to indicate that I have been a quite comfortable member of the American society—which, in itself, is certainly the most comfortable society in the history of the world . . . for many of us. I am not a revolutionary. I am not a wild-eyed fanatic, reformer, or zealot. What I am, or what I was until a few hours ago, was a comfortable American.

As this moment, I am anything but comfortable. I have found myself suddenly thrust forward into the consciousness of my fellow Americans in a setting which could hardly be considered comfortable. I stand before you an accused traitor. I am speaking at this moment from within the military stronghold of the Black forces in Oakland, California. And I come to you as an appointee to the provisional government established by the occupation forces. No . . . at this moment, I am not a comfortable American.

The rest of my own personal story is of little importance to the present moment. The present state and ultimate fate of the American Republic far outweigh any personal considerations or discomfort of Michael Winston and of any other individual citizen of this land. Only the most careful handling and sensitive understanding of the present situation can prevent further violence, bloodshed, and destruction of the nation.

The American Negro has searched his conscience. He desires no pound of flesh. He does desire reinstatement into the American community. He has come out of these towns where the people had, in effect, imprisoned him, and he has come out fighting, as would any of us indeed. And now the Negro is out of the towns and back onto the main streets of the nation. He belongs there, he has a right to be there, and—believe me—he intends to remain there. I applaud him.

I applaud the Negro because . . . at a moment when he has the power and the ability, for the first time, to fully avenge the unspeakable crimes committed against his race for centuries, he has exercised a humane restraint and a love of country that is difficult for me, a comfortable American, to understand. He came out of those towns and he lashed out in a brief—believe me, a very brief—destructive trumpet-blast of freedom found. But he has not run amuck. Blood does not flow in rivers through the streets of America. The Negro has withdrawn that big fist. He came out, he bade us look at him, and now he stands back, waiting to see what we intend to do about it.

Make no mistake, however, that black fist is still cocked. It could lash out again, either in blind reflexive action or in cool calculation. Whatever the mode, the results for the white American and for the nation as a whole can be nothing but destruction, disaster and genocide.

This is my primary message to the people of the United States. Think. Act rationally. Consider the state of the nation, and conduct yourselves accordingly. Make no mistake . . . this is no mere uprising or momentary flare-up. What has happened in this country today is a military operation of the highest calibre, the fruits of painstaking

208

years of planning and preparation. The Negro controls the military might of this nation today. He controls us.

I stated earlier that my own personal involvements were of no consequence to our present situation. But I want to be entirely honest, and I want every citizen of this nation to know precisely where my sympathies lie. I am not sure, you see, that I would erase the events of the past twenty-four hours even if I had the power to do so. I feel that what has happened has served as an awakening from some hallucinogenic dream or illusion. I have no desire to return to that dream. The air is clean and crisp out here in reality. There is a noticeable tugging at the soul and a vigorous recognition of the values of life . . . out here in reality.

I am not a child, I am thirty-six years of age. I am not an idiot, my present station in life attests to that. I am not politically naive . . . my survival through fourteen years of government service should verify that. Yet . . . in the most important issues of life itself I have habitually surrendered my thinking mind to the emotional braying of the jackasses among us. I have accepted—no, I have *welcomed* the fanatic and his hatreds, the opportunist and his greed, the professional hater and his ruthlessness. I have wrapped these in a mantle about me and walked among you as a responsible citizen, as an average American, as a patriot. And of these guises, only one is true. The one of average American. I have, you see, been like you. At this moment, I am only like myself. I intend to think for myself. I will not surrender that unique consciousness of mine to a dream of national narcosis.

The President has said that the present *quote* unrest *unquote* is foreign inspired. My reply to the President is that unrest is an American institution, or it was at one time. I would remind the President that these people who have risen up in our midst were not born into a slave consciousness. They were born with American minds, and they were educated in American ideals and philosophies.

Since when, Mr. President, does the home of the free and the land of the brave require an injection of foreign inspiration to produce a feeling of anger, frustration, and rebellion against tyranny and injustice? But this is the saddest part of all, for it seems that this reaction can be felt only by those Americans who are themselves suffering the fruits of tyranny and injustice. Is the American Negro the only one who can lift his head and cry out against the things this nation has come to stand for? Is this true, America? Can we look at our brothers, and seeing that they are black, *forget* that they are *Americans*? Can we look at tyranny and degradation of the American ideal and, secure in the knowledge that it is not being directed against ourselves, *forget American principles*?

A wise old man in Denver told me, not many hours ago, that character is an exercise of principle, and that an exercise of principle usually amounts to doing something we don't particularly want to do, or something that we will not personally profit from. Is the principle of freedom and equality still alive in the home of the free?

As the black man searches his conscience for the right course of action in this, his moment of triumph, cannot the white man do likewise in this, *his* moment of *truth*? Let us each, white and black alike, paraphrase an early American patriot, and say: I may not like the color of your skin, American, but I shall defend to the death your right to wear it, in freedom and with pride.

CHAPTER 5 - THE CHANGING OF THE GUARD

President Arlington stared searchingly at the Chief of the White House Secret Service detail. "Are you telling me, Bill, that the people are doing nothing, absolutely nothing? They are simply sitting and waiting for the end to come?"

"It appears that way, Mr. President," the head bodyguard admitted. "But after the way they treated you on television last night, I guess it isn't too surprising. The nation has become accustomed to listening to Mr. Silverman. I guess most people are rather confused about the whole thing."

"Nonsense," the President said calmly. "They aren't confused. They are frightened. Frightened rabbits. They have deserted their President, they have deserted their country, and they are sitting around waiting for someone to deliver them from their difficulties once again.

"Well, it won't be me this time, Bill. I am too old for that task this time, I simply cannot handle it. How soon can you get me out of here?"

"Any time you'd like to leave, sir. Where are we going?"

"I want to go to Streamhaven, Bill. Let the Negruhs have the damn country. Apparently nobody cares but me, and now *I* don't care either. I simply do not care about a thing. But the Negruhs did *not* beat me, Bill. *Old age.* Old

211

age beat me. I have given this nation my very life. I will not give it my death as well."

"I'll contact the FPB and set up a convoy right away, sir."

"No, Bill, no convoy. Tell the boys over at the bureau to close up shop and get out of town. It's every man for himself, and I suppose the Negruhs have a list a mile long."

"I suppose so, sir."

"Do you realize, Bill? I am the first American President to be run out of his office."

"Yes sir," the bodyguard replied. "I guess that's true."

Arlington laughed. "Don't take it so hard, old friend. It's a distinction, of sorts. Hump Arlington, the last father of the country. Last in war, last in peace, and last in the hearts of his countrymen."

Abe Williams examined his protege critically and quietly told him, "You're looking frisky as a colt this morning, Michael."

Winston grinned and replied, "Shows what one good night's sleep can do for a guy."

"You mean you were actually able to sleep?"

"I mean I lay down, died, and was resurrected twelve hours later. Or that's the way it feels." He accepted a glass of juice from his host and added, "By the way, to whomever brought me the clothing, thanks."

"You can thank her yourself when you get to Washington."

"What?"

"A very anxious young lady came dragging in here in the middle of the night." Williams was smiling hugely. "From Connecticut, she said. And she left the clothing with love."

"Well I'll be damned," Winston commented.

"Yeah. Said you'd know where to find her, in Washington, when you got the time. I invited her to stay and travel with you this morning, but she seemed to think she'd be in the way. I wish I had someone like that dragging clothes around for *me*."

"Yes, she's quite a woman," Winston said, smiling modestly. "You'll be seeing more of her."

212

"I want you to know how very pleased I am, Michael," Williams told him. "About the way things have shaped up, I mean. I am very happy that you are in our corner."

"I guess I am, too," Winston admitted. "And I guess I'm ready to travel. Is the General ready?"

"He is."

"Then I guess there's just one last item."

"What's that?" Williams asked.

"I want a letter of authority."

"From whom and over whom?"

"I'm going to be running this country for awhile. Right?"

"So right."

"In case I ever get into a stare-down with one of your people, I want to know who's boss."

"And you want a letter of authority?"

Winston nodded. "Or an equivalent instrument."

The black man sighed. "I can't give you anything like that, Michael. I've named you head of the provisional government. How much can I add to that?"

"You can add that my authority extends to all the occupational and/or insurgent forces. I'm going to need that, Abe. And you know it."

"I don't have that to give, Michael," Williams told him. "I've been running this black show by virtue of self-evident authority, and no more. It's nothing that has been given me, or accorded me, therefore it is not a power nor even an influence that I can pass along to someone else."

Winston gave an unhappy grunt and said, "Then my task may be all that more impossible. If I have no influence over the black—"

"You'll just have to exert influence, the same as I have done. Anyway, don't worry about the black support. You'll have that. Your big worries are with the white populace, don't you think?"

Winston frowned. "I guess you could be right. Well, okay. I'll play it by ear. How about my task force? Is it all set?"

The black leader soberly nodded his head. "All but the economist from UCLA. Unfortunately, he was killed during the strike on Los Angeles yesterday. But I contacted the alternate, Dr. Mackay. He agreed to join you in Washington."

Winston's face had fallen over the news of the death. A muscle bunched in his jaw and he said, "Okay, that's fine." He glanced at his watch. "I guess it's time to be shoving off."

"Uh, there's one more thing, Michael. Concerning Ritter."

"What about Ritter?"

Williams seemed mildly embarrassed. "He, uh, felt terrible about that goof-up in Washington yesterday. When we lost Senator Bancroft and company. He, uh . . . I believe that he wishes to hover about your person. He wants to accompany you to Washington."

"It's fine with me," Winston declared soberly. "So long as he knows who's boss."

"You'll have no trouble from Norm Ritter," Williams assured him. He chuckled suddenly and lowered his voice to a conspiratorial tone. "Know what that big faker told me this morning?"

Winston grinned and shook his head.

"He told me he could almost pass as white, with that red hair, if I was worried about having a bunch of niggers around the White House."

The two men laughed together. Then Mike Winston took a last look around, as though perhaps he would never see the place again. History had been made at this unlikely place. Living history. *Vital* history. Williams noted the "last look" expression on Winston's face. Their glances crossed, and each other saw the other, for a fleeting instant, through the other's eyes. Then they went out, side by side—one white, one black—to step upon the stage of another chapter of America.

The helicopter settled gently to the White House lawn, in the center of a circle of black infantrymen. Norman Ritter was the first man out, leaping energetically to the ground before the ladder was emplaced, and he was engaged in an animated conversation with the troop commander when Mike Winston and General Bogan de-planed. A special security guard, provided by Ritter, swept in to enclose them in a protective circle, then the thick knot of men set off rapidly for the main building. The infantry ranks split to let them pass, performing a ceremonial salute with their rifles, then regrouped into a wedge-shaped escort formation.

Ritter maneuvered alongside Winston and told him, "The troop commander says that Arlington bailed out a few hours ago, bag and baggage. They have your offices set up in the east wing, per your request. Silverman accepted the job as press secretary, and he's already selected a White House press corps. I understand he's pretty happy about that. Hasn't been an official press corps here since Arlington took office. He's got them assembled and waiting, requests that you step in and at least say hello to them right away. Thinks it's important."

Winston nodded his head mechanically. "I'd sooner not. But I agree with Silverman. It's probably very important to get off on the right foot with the press."

The military escort was left behind at the south portico. As the party moved up the steps, a tall dignified-appearing man ran down to greet them. He swung in beside Ritter, who performed perfunctory introductions. "Mike Winston, General Bogan, this is John Douglas, heads up the Washington intelligence unit. How's it going, John?"

"Very well," Douglas replied, panting a little. He was a graceful man with silvery hair who carried his Negro heritage proudly. "The entire White House staff volunteered to remain on—for awhile, anyway. I mean, the cooks and bottle washers, you know, the . . ." He chuckled. ". . . the important ones. The President checked out about eight o'clock. I hear he's gone to his farm in Virginia. There's about a hundred newspapermen and magazine writers waiting in there. Silverman has been outlining the ground rules to them." He leaned forward to smile at Winston. "I believe you have a good man there, Mr. Director. He's been berating them for thirty minutes now. I don't think they'll be giving you a hard time."

Winston smiled and stared stonily forward. John Douglas was the first to address him as *Mr. Director*. The title had a hollow ring to it. For a guy who had been gloating about the thrill of reality just last night, Winston was wondering why everything seemed so unreal to him at the moment. It had been less than forty-eight hours since he'd last come into these hallowed halls and then he'd had to scream, stomp, yell, and finally pull a gun to get in. Now here he was, the very same guy, casually strolling in to take over the joint. And as *Mr. Director*.

And then the gravity of the moment descended fully upon him. The entourage was sweeping along the broad passageway toward the press room. Winston called a sudden halt and took Jackson Bogan by the arm. "General," he said quietly, "the first thing I want you to do is get those troops off the White House grounds. I want things to look as nearly normal as possible around here. Okay? The White House is *not* under military occupation."

"You're right," Bogan agreed. "It does look bad."

"Fine. And then you'd better doublecheck your communications with your field commanders around the country. I have a feeling way down inside my bones and . . . well, just be sure you know how to talk to the army any time you need to, wherever you need to."

Winston then turned to John Douglas. "John, I guess I can't avoid this press conference—I may as well get it over with and get it all up on the line. While I'm in there, try to get a line on the status of my executive task force. I want to huddle with those people as soon as possible. As they get aboard, get them collected some place where I can find them all together. Now, let's break up right here. I'll rejoin as soon as I can shake the fourth estate."

Bogan and Douglas dropped out of the group and the remainder of the party went on to the press room. Winston was shaken by the very size of the place. A confused rumble of sound, the concert of a hundred or more busy voices, further intensified the tension within the new chief of state.

Howard Silverman came forward, smiling, and introduced himself. The two men shook hands and exchanged pleasantries. Then they moved together to the rostrum. Silverman held up a hand for attention, though the gesture was totally unnecessary. The beehive of sound had dropped off completely moments after Winston entered the room, and all eyes were glued silently to the largely unknown individual who had suddenly taken over the executive mansion of the United States.

"Just one quick reminder, gentlemen," Silverman intoned. "No questions of a personal nature. You'll get all that in a bio handout later today. Please confine all queries to the present and planned state of the nation. Gentlemen . . . the Provisional Director of U.S. National Affairs, Mr. Michael Winston."

Silverman left Winston standing there alone, and *Mr. Director* looked out upon the sea of faces with a growing feeling of panic. *What the hell am I doing here?* screamed an inner voice. His hands were clammy and unsteady as he lay them on the rostrum—his mouth was dry and he felt somewhat dizzy. Then he pointed blindly to a man in the front row of seats, wondering as he did if he was supposed to do so. At least the gesture was understood. The man stood up, cleared his throat, and said, "Uh, do we call you. . . ? Uh, how do we address you, sir?"

"The name is Winston," he replied tightly. He grinned and added, "Why don't you just use that?"

The newsman grinned back, and Winston mentally scored one for his side. "All right . . . Mr. Winston . . . I think most of us are surprised that a military *junta* didn't move into the White House. Would you care to discuss that?"

Winston looked into the man's eyes, and saw something there he'd discovered in himself a few hours earlier. He allowed himself a few seconds to gaze at some of the other expectant faces raised to him and he felt himself thawing inside, felt the rapport of human beings caught up in the same nightmare, and when his voice came it was pleasant and warm. "There is no military *junta*. Not in Washington,

217

not anywhere in this country. This is not a military coup, gentlemen. It was a citizen's uprising. Abe Lincoln Williams, the man who planned and led that uprising, told me a short while ago that he could not give me a letter of authority over the black military establishment. His own authority, he said, was self-evident. I accepted that. I hope that you will accept it. Self-evident authority is a rare thing. It bespeaks a rare state of leadership. Abe Williams is not a soldier. He is as anxious to preserve the American system of civil government as is anyone in this room. I'm sure you've all read the *manifesto*. If so, you'll know that I am here simply to coordinate the formation of the new civil government. There is not, and will not be, I hope, a military *junta*. Does that answer your question?"

"Yes sir, I guess it does. Thank you." The man sat down and said something beneath his breath to the man beside him.

Winston fingered another. The man only half rose and asked, "This manifesto the Negroes issued . . . is it really on the level? Are they really going to allow a continuation of political freedom?"

"A continuation?" Winston replied, smiling. "I would use the word *resumption*. Politics in this nation, for the past twelve years, have been a mockery of the constitution. Yes sir, the manifesto is on the level. As for the resumption of free politics, this all depends upon how *we* react to this situation. If the next few weeks are marked by active white resistance to black demands . . . if we do not make a sincere effort to re-orient our thinking and to organize a constructive and conscionable government . . . then I'd say we'll never see another ballot box.

"Even if we remain peaceful yet fail to repudiate the present political climate of this nation—that is to say, if we bring in a new regime with the same ills and goals as the old one, then we surely cannot expect the blacks to merely fold up their tents and return to their towns. If that were to happen, then the blacks will have no recourse except to continue in occupation, throw out the government again, and make us try again. Or as an alternative, they could

218

decide to put their own people in power, double the guard, and tear up the U.S. constitution. They could do that. They could do it right now.

"I'd like to say this, though. I am convinced that if we behave ourselves and do the right things, no matter how much they may hurt, then the entire nation will profit and grow from this experience. If we do not, then this nation, as constituted, will cease to exist."

Another man arose, out of order, and sneered. "Why did the niggers appoint *you* as their mouthpiece?"

Silverman's feet scraped the floor, as though he were about to leap into the act. Winston headed him off. "I'm glad you asked that," he replied, smiling. "It gives me the chance to assure you that I am *not* their mouthpiece. The Negro, right now, is all eyes and ears. No mouth. He has said all he's going to say. It's all in the manifesto. Now he is listening for some dialogue from the white side."

Another man leapt from his chair and cried, "Are you telling us that you're not just a nigger puppet?" Disorder descended.

This time Silverman did hit the deck, both feet planted solidly beside the rostrum and raising his hands for order. Winston's eyes were slightly glazed but his grin was hanging on. He touched Silverman lightly on the arm and winked. The veteran newsman gave him an odd look, dropped his hands, and returned to his chair. Winston stood straight, both hands clasped lightly atop the rostrum. Presently the noise began to subside Not until silence completely gripped the room did *Mr. Director* open his mouth.

Then he said, "Okay, I'm glad to see that the American Press is finding its guts again. Just keep it up. Ride me all the way, watch me as though I were about to steal your most precious possession. . . . This is what you should have been doing, and did not do, for the past twenty years. You allowed the government to scare you into silence. Don't ever let that happen again. Your nation needs you, gentlemen. *I* need you. But let's keep the dialogue intelligent. Does anyone out there have an intelligent question to ask, or shall we call this whole thing off?"

An older man sitting halfway up the center aisle began quietly applauding. Several others picked it up and soon most of the assembled newsmen were on their feet, quietly beating their hands together. The sound swelled, and held for most of a minute. Howard Silverman's face was a study in baffled wonderment, but he was on his feet applauding also.

Norman Ritter leaned toward one of his agents. "I'm starting to see why Abe Williams is so sold on this guy," he muttered. "Gutsy. More than that. Something else. But guts too."

Winston tossed a meaningful glance to Howard Silverman. The new press secretary began calling for order, and quiet quickly returned.

Winston then told the assemblage, "I'm going to answer that last charge just the same and as honestly as I can. because I believe it to be an important point. The question—or the charge—had to do with puppets. I want you all to know that I am not a puppet. Nor are any of you out there. Not at this moment. The day before yesterday, I believe I was a puppet. And you. All of us, the entire nation. Someone pulled a string, or programmed a machine, and we all danced to the tune. Isn't that right?"

Winston was gazing out across the sea of faces, and he was liking what he saw. "Ask Mr. Silverman here," he added. "Ask him how it felt, yesterday, to exercise a prerogative of the free press. Ask him how long it had been since he'd felt that way."

Dead silence gripped the large room. Winston had touched an open nerve. A mild-appearing man at mid-center rose to his feet, gazing steadily at the rostrum. Winston recognized the man with a nod of his head.

"My name is Butterfield, Mr. Winston. Federated Wire Press. In your mention of free press, is this an indication that the provisional government is abolishing the censorship regulations which have been in effect since 1993?"

"Precisely," Winston immediately replied. "How can a

press be both free and censored?"

Pandemonium erupted in the press room. Winston looked at Howard Silverman and grinned. Silverman returned the grin, sat back, lit a cigarette, and let pandemonium reign.

CHAPTER 6

In the corner of his vision, Mike Winston saw the black colonel in the U.S. Army uniform quietly enter the press room and huddle with Normal Ritter, and the look on the colonel's face left little doubt that his business was gravely urgent. So Winston was prepared for bad news when Ritter swung beside him at the rostrum to whisper, "Bogan says you should come to the War Room right away. Something's up."

Winston turned the press proceedings over to Howard Silverman and made a quick exit. He had only the vaguest idea as to the location of the White House War Room, but the colonel was in the vanguard of the little procession of bodyguards and all the new chief of state had to do was follow the parade. They packed themselves into an elevator and descended to the subterranean level.

General Bogan awaited him. The place was a duplicate in miniature of the big combat central at the Pentagon. Uniformed men sat quietly at consoles and peered into viewscreens. Each of them, Winston noted, were commissioned officers and—of course—black.

Bogan was telling him, in that quietly authoritative voice, "Our Automated Pacific Line is picking up some unusual activity in the air over Eastern China. Automated Defense Command says it's a positive airlift. They can even tell you the type of aircraft if you're interested."

"So what does it mean to you?" Winston asked the military mind.

"It means an airborne invasion, Mr. Winston," the General replied.

"What would be your normal reaction to intelligence of this sort?"

"Our normal course would be to notify the President. With his concurrence, we would then hot-line a formal warning to the offending government and immediately activate the appropriate thermo-magnetic screens."

Winston frowned. "Now unscramble that for me as it applies to this specific instance."

"Our WestPac TM screen follows roughly the 180th longitude, the International Date Line. We need to notify Peking and get those air barriers activated."

"Then do it."

Bogan smiled faintly. "I was hoping you'd be that decisive." He passed brief orders to the colonel who had come for Winston, and the man went quickly to a command console. Then the General told Winston, "The screens aren't that perfect, of course. We can't cover the entire line continuously. We work an alternating pattern, and the Chinese have instruments which can locate those magnetic fields several hundred miles in advance of their flight paths. But this at least serves notice that we are in defense posture. And we'll know pretty soon if they are simply probing us or if they are committed to an all-out attack."

"And suppose they are committed?" Winston wanted to know.

"Then there will be a lot of Chinese buried at sea. Some will get through, perhaps forty percent of their airlift. We could get another twenty percent with our missiles. Even so, they could land a formidable force for us to contend with. It depends on just how badly they need our foodstuffs."

Winston was fervently wishing that he knew a bit more about the national defense apparatus. He asked Bogan,

"What are the chances of this becoming a nuclear conflict?"

"You mean bombers and missiles?" The General screwed his face into a grimace. "Very remote, I'd say. They wouldn't be gaining much by destroying or contaminating our agriculture. That's their only interest, you know. Food."

"Okay," Winston said. "But let's keep a close eye on that possibility, just the same. Are we equipped to handle a nuclear attack?"

The General showed him an expression of pathos and replied, "Is anyone ever prepared to handle nuclear war, Mr. Winston? I believe we could survive, if that's what you mean."

"I'm leaving it in your hands," the Director told the General. "I'm not qualified to even make decisions of this nature. You are. I've got to be up there with my task force and get busy on the domestic problems. But you keep me—"

Winston was interrupted by the sudden appearance in the War Room of John Douglas, the Washington Intelligence Chief. Douglas seemed less immaculate than before, disheveled almost, and he seemed out of breath as he hastily crossed the room toward the Winston group.

"What the hell is it now?" Winston muttered.

"Must be bad," Ritter commented. "John doesn't heat up easily."

The intelligence man paused to catch his breath, with both arms draped across the top of a console desk, then panted, "Just got word! Came quick as I could. They're running wild! Ripping through everything like crazy men."

"They *who*?" Winston barked.

"The *tong*, the southern tong. They've gone crazy. They've disavowed Abe Williams and the manifesto. And they're running wild in Dixie!"

Mike Winston restlessly paced the floors of the War Room, the lines of his face drawn in deep concern. General Bogan was manning a communications console. Howard Silverman sat in a telephone turret, near the door, scribbling notes on a large pad.

Ritter hurtled in from an adjoining conference room. "I talked to Abe!" he announced. "It's no good. They told him to get screwed. He says he's lost them!"

"How many towns are involved in the revolt?" Shelton snapped.

"So far just Hattiesburg."

"Then by God we've got to pull some regulars in there and sit on those people! General Bogan! How many troops can we airlift to—"

"No good, Michael," the General told him. "I've thought of that, and it won't work. It's something of a miracle that only Hattiesburg has pulled out. We start showing muscle down there, the others will line up damn quick behind the rebels. They're all more sympathetic to Hattiesburg than they are to us."

"Hell yes," Ritter chimed in. "Abe's been using every persuader in the book to keep that tong in line. He says they could go the other way any time. Just *any* time. He's afraid we could have a full southern revolt on our hands before the day's over."

"I want to know how it happened," Winston muttered. "Just how the hell *did it happen*?"

"God, I don't know, Winston," Ritter said meekly.

Howard Silverman stepped out of the turret, frowningly consulting his note pad. "Don't know *how* it happened," he told Winston, "but here's a pretty accurate recap of *what* has happened. Jackson is in flames. The dead and the dying litter the streets—men, women, kids—it's a slaughter. They're using Patton's tactics in the business district, throwing heavy armor-piercing shells down through a line of buildings to breach the front walls. Most of the town is a rubble already.

"Same story at Meridian, only maybe twice as bad on the death toll. They're driving those big Sherman tanks right through the houses, block after block of them. And at the port of Mobile . . . they're even sinking shipping. And they're racing through the countryside in armored columns, demolishing strip cities and farming villages one after another; isolated farmhouses are being assaulted. It's

225

a terrible picture . . . terrible."

Bogan looked up from his console and reported, "Well, the story is beginning to emerge. Sounds like it started with a vendetta list which someone with a long memory and a festering hate has been keeping alive all these years. Names of Klansmen and other hate merchants very well preserved. Ritter, I believe your man down there—what's the name, Hatfield? Uh-huh, that's the guy. He hates long and hard, I guess. They've been keeping very quiet tabs on their old enemies down there. They began rounding up the ones who were still living early this morning."

"I know nothing of any vendetta lists," Ritter protested.

"Didn't say you did. Just reporting what's going on."

"Nothing new there," Silverman put in. "Israel was still hunting Nazis in the seventies."

"Well it's about the same thing we got here now," Bogan declared. "The Klans are still active down there. I guess they've just been hating one another all these years but they're still organized. Here's the story as it came through my liaison man with Hattiesburg. These people have a klavern or something near Yazoo City. That's in Mississippi. Now when Hatfield began rounding up his old enemies, these guys cut loose. Ambushed a couple truckloads of infantry that were headed for a bivouac outside of Jackson. Killed 'em all, about sixty men. But it wasn't just the killing that sent Hattiesburg blood crazy. It was the atrocities. Those bodies were mutilated, hanging from trees all along the highway. Their genitals hung around their necks or stuffed into their own mouths."

Winston smacked a console with his open palm, drew the hand up, stared at it, cussed at it, massaged, then cussed some more while he lit a cigarette. He growled, "Insanity. It never ends."

Ritter commented, "Nobody ever said the world was perfect."

A light on Bogan's console was flashing. The General responded quickly, speaking into a headset. Presently he said, "Yes, I have that. Thank you, Jacksonville." He turned to the others with a forlorn face and mumbled, "It's spreading. Little town in northern Florida just got taken off the map."

Winston squeezed the General's shoulder, then gently relieved him of the headset and dropped it onto the console. "All right," he said heavily, "we're not going to get anywhere merely tracking the insanity. We have to stop it. How are we going to do that? Does anyone have any bright ideas?"

All eyes were staring at Winston, but no one ventured a suggestion. His gaze fastened firmly upon Jackson Bogan. "I'll want a talk with your missiles man," he said quietly.

The General replied, "You mean Automated Defense?"

"Whatever you call it. Get your expert over here, and get him here damn quick."

"What's the idea?" Ritter inquired. "We can't use ADS. Can we?"

"That," said Mike Winston, "is precisely what I intend to explore."

CHAPTER 7

Colonel Melvin Stanley was a moderately young career officer, and he was Jackson Bogan's handpicked CADC, Chief of the Automated Defense Command. He awkwardly shook hands with the new white leader and diffidently told him, "We are watching this Chinese thing very closely, sir."

"Good," Winston replied. "ADC is a joint forces thing, isn't it? Army, Navy, Air Force?"

"Yes sir."

"And you run the whole show?"

"Yes sir."

Winston studied the man for a moment, than abruptly asked him, "Are you a soldier or a scientist?"

"I'm both, sir. Well . . . I'm a systems officer."

"I see. And you thoroughly understand the automated system? The mechanics of the thing? The missiles themselves, even?"

"Yes sir."

"How good are our missiles?"

"Very good, sir. But they constitute a small part of the overall automated systems."

"Yes, I understand that," Winston replied. "But right now I'm particularly interested in the missiles. Do you have some sort of manual control over things? I mean, can you put a missile into the outer atmosphere and detonate the warhead anytime you wish? Or do you have to wait for the monster to think?"

"It thinks what we tell it to think, sir," Stanley said, his voice showing wonder at what the hell was going on. "We can program our birds into any hole in space, or any quarter of the globe, and at any time we wish."

Winston smiled grimly at the colonel and told him, "All right, that's exactly what I wanted to know. Now tell me about these 'clean' warheads. Suppose we did detonate a missile over the Atlantic or over the Gulf of Mexico at an altitude of . . . oh, say twenty miles or so. What would be the ground effect and the atmosphere effect over our land areas?"

The Colonel looked perplexed. "I'm not sure I understand the question. Did you have a specific application in mind, sir?"

Winston measured the man again, then sighed and told him, "I want to scare the pants off of some people. I don't want to knock any chunks of land off into the sea, or start any volcanoes in Mexico, or contaminate any crops, and I don't want to kill any one. I just want to scare the hell out of them."

Stanley did not have to even think about it. "We could use light tactical weapons for that purpose, sir. We have a type with a small nuclear warhead. It has never been operationally tested with the warhead aboard—they took away our funds for that purpose—but this bird was designed for use over continental areas and for close range, last-ditch missile defense. It is regarded as a feasible defense at altitudes as low as 30,000 feet."

"Fine," Winston said. "Keep talking."

"We could get some contamination of our atmospheres, but only in certain unfavorable weather conditions. Also we might get some barely tolerable heat generated by this weapon, but it is really of very low yield—very clean—and with most of the shock waves traveling horizontally through the atmosphere. That's the *theory*. As I said, we've never op-tested this warhead."

"But such a shot would be seen and perhaps experienced physically for quite a few miles?"

The officer nodded. "Oh absolutely. It would be a spectacular display at about ten miles up. In a night shot, the entire eastern half of the United States would be brightly illuminated from a coastal window. It would be like sudden sunlight—a new sun, you might say, and for a period of several minutes. Also, at that altitude, the horizontal shock waves would ripple along for hundreds of miles, creating a tremendous rumble like thunder you've never heard. Yes, it would be a spectacular shot. It would certainly command plenty of attention, if that's what you're looking for."

"Thank you, Colonel," Winston said. "That is exactly what I am looking for." He turned to regard the General. "Jack? What do you think?"

"It sounds feasible," Bogan admitted. "But you know what you're playing with, don't you? Atomic weaponry. That's the dirtiest word this planet has ever come up with." He fixed Colonel Stanley with a sharp gaze. "Tell me, Mel, are your emplacements so located that you could target these tactical birds over the Gulf at such a point that it could be experienced into the interiors of Mississippi and Alabama?"

"We can put that bird any damn place you want it, General."

"That doesn't answer my question, Mel. Can we keep the detonations over ocean areas and still get the effect as far inland as northern Mississippi?"

"No, sir, we cannot. But I can put a ring of fire any damn place you want it. In any event, damage to land areas would be limited to minor shock wave effect. And perhaps a bit of heat."

"No radioactive fallout?"

"I can't guarantee that, General," Stanley replied. "But . . . for what my professional opinion is worth, I'd say it's a negligible risk. Will some one tell me what this is all about? Is this a hypothetical drill, or are we seriously contemplating such an action?"

"It's no drill, Mel," the General said. His gaze was on

Mike Winston. "Remember, Mr. Winston," he warned, "it's the dirtiest word there is. And it's your decision."

"The hell it is," Winston said quietly. "I want a joint decision, and you'll remember that it's covered in your manifesto. Actually, it's more your decision than mine."

The two men locked gazes for an instant, then Bogan's eyes deflected. He sighed and said, "All right, Michael. You're right. If you want to try it, go ahead. I concur."

"There's actually no decision to it," Winston told him. "We have a human-type nuclear reaction racing through the south right now. And it seems as though ADS is our only deterrent force. Colonel Stanley?"

"Yes, sir?"

Howard Silverman yelled from the turret at that instant. "Okay! There she goes! It's a crown fire! Little town just across the border into Arkansas just got hit, a place called Eudora. Also a couple in Alabama. It's a crown fire!"

"Or a nuclear reaction," Winston muttered. He took Colonel Stanley by the arm and marched him to a wall display of the United States. With a grease pencil he drew a circle in the southeast portion of the country. "Bracket them," he commanded simply. He jerked the map off the wall and gave it to the Colonel.

"Yes sir, I understand."

"You know what I want. Put some birds up there. The total number I leave entirely to your superior knowledge. But I want every person in that area to know without any doubt whatever that nuclear devices are exploding above their heads."

"Yes sir."

"All right. How long, Colonel?"

"How long, sir?"

"Before your birds are aloft."

The Colonel frowned. "These will be manual mode launchings. I'll have to program the coordinates and select the appropriate sites. Say ten minutes."

"All right, let's say *twenty*, and the timing is all-important. I want those warheads felt in *exactly* twenty minutes."

"Can you give me a written order to cover this, sir?"

"Who the hell gave me any written orders?" Winston snapped. "Twenty minutes, Stanley, or I'll have it written all over your ass!"

"Yes sir. Exactly twenty minutes, sir." The Colonel back-stepped, threw *Mr. Director* a smart salute, and went to talk to his birds.

Winston, Bogan, Silverman, and Ritter had retired to the conference alcove adjoining the War Room. Now a dead calm prevailed there. Winston had gone to a wall map and was silently staring at it, hands on his hips, lips pursed thoughtfully.

The rattle of diaphragms in telephone receivers scattered along the conference table could be plainly heard. Silverman was slumped in a chair, staring at the telephone, a perplexity working at his craggy features, hands crossed on one knee.

Norman Ritter was staring at the back of Michael Winston, and he was quieter than perhaps at any other time during his adult life.

General Bogan watched the play of emotion across the redhead's face, then he moved alongside him and asked, "Something bothering you, Norm?"

Ritter's eyes swiveled about to rest lightly on the old soldier, then they returned abruptly to the object of his intent interest. "That man there bothers me," he said softly. "I just realized what he's doing. He's atom bombing us. He's attacking my country with nuclear weapons."

"Would you care to depose him and take his place for awhile?" Bogan asked calmly.

"He scares the shit out of me," Ritter said, ignoring the sarcastic query. "I've been watching him all day." He tossed a quick look at the General and added, "But I'm not scared of the damn *bombs.* I'm scared of *him!*"

"I don't believe it," Bogan said, with faint amusement. "The tiger of the towns, afraid of a mere white man?"

"That's just it," Ritter muttered. "There's nothing *mere* about this white man. Nothing even nearly *mere.* And he scares the shit out of me, Jackson."

Bogan heaved a long sigh and said, "It's a phenomenon

232

I've seen many times. Norm. In Korea. In Southeast Asia. Many places. It's called *growing into your hat*. I'd say that Mr. Winston has *mushroomed* into his."

Winston turned from the wall and caught the two men staring at him. "What am I now?" he growled. "The new ogre of Pennsylvania Avenue?"

General Bogan smiled and told him, "I guess so, Mr. Director. Yes, I guess that must be it. Welcome to the club."

CHAPTER 8

Henry Chambers was thankful that he had dug that drainage ditch, after all. When Dixie Agro began the condemnation proceedings that Spring, wanting to swallow up Chambers and the other handful of independent farmers in the area—he'd thought, what the heck, why dig ditches or anything else now? No one could fight Dixie Agro, certainly not a poor independent like Henry Chambers.

But now Chambers was glad he'd gone ahead and dug the ditch. It seemed highly unlikely now that Dixie's claims would ever come before a court—unless it was a *black* court. And that ditch now provided a near-perfect front line defense entrenchment for himself and his two boys, Wayne and Pete, and they'd by God fight the blacks for their land . . . in a way they could have never hoped to fight the agricultural conglomerate.

They had filled some old fifty-gallon steel drums with dirt and lined them along the road side of the ditch, just for extra added protection, and Chambers figured they were pretty well dug in . . . if only them coons didn't start pitching heavy stuff at them. He carefully positioned his old 30.06 between two of the drums, then smiled grimly at his boys and double-checked their positions.

"Think they'll be coming soon, Dad?" asked thirteen-year-old Pete, his voice quivering with the excitement of the moment.

"Soon enough," his father grunted. "And don't sound so anxious. We got about one chance in a million if they come up here with tanks or with heavy artillery."

"You're not scared of them, are you Dad?" Wayne asked, the seventeen-year-old's eyes probing into his father for the truth of the matter.

Chambers glared at his eldest son for a moment. Then he smiled reassuringly and told him, "Course I'm scared, Wayne. Think I'm an idiot? Man has to be an idiot not to be scared at a time like this." He pulled a coarse blue handkerchief from his hip pocket and mopped his face with it, then sat on the side of the trench with a loud sigh.

"Now look here, you boys," he said softly. "Let's not play games with ourselves. We got a hell of a chore coming up here. But it *is* a chore, just like milking a cow or slopping the hogs. We got a chore. And that chore is to keep those coons away from your mother and your sisters. Now that's the whole thing, pure and simple. You know what those coons will do to our women. So we can't let them past us. Understand? That's all there is to it. We don't let 'em past us."

"We won't," Wayne replied staunchly.

"We'll probably die, boys. Face that. We'll die. But if we hurt the coons enough first . . . well . . . maybe they won't be in no mood for anything else. I know this is a bitter pill for boys your age to swallow. But the worst can happen to *us* is that we'll die. Your mother and sisters . . . well, you know what I mean. Some things are *worse* than death."

"I ain't afraid t'die!" young Pete declared fiercely.

"Just don't be in no hurry to do it. We gotta hurt 'em all we can first. Remember that. We got to keep our heads."

Wayne cried out a warning and pointed down the dirt road. A faint cloud of dust was lifting above the treetops, far down the hillside.

Henry Chambers huskily cleared his throat and told his troops, "All right, that might be them coming now. Petey, you run back and make sure the women are in the storm cellar. And you make 'em lock it from the inside, now. And

235

then you get right back here. Wayne, you come with me. We'll set the gas trap now."

Young Pete dashed off toward the house, some thirty yards up the hill. Chambers and the older boy ran down the rutted farm road to a point about fifty yards below the entrenchment. Four large gasoline cans occupied the center of the narrow road. The two men feverishly dumped three of the cans, saturating a fifteen-foot stretch of freshly plowed roadbed, then used the fourth can to spew a careful trail back to the entrenchment. Pete had returned from his task when they reached the trench, and he was grunting with exertion and restrained anxiety.

"Now listen to me," Chambers panted. "Don't do any shooting until I light off that gas. And then make every damn shot count. I mean every one. Don't lose your heads. Putting a bullet through a coon's head is no different than putting one through a squirrel's head. Remember that. And maybe we'll even come through this. They're going to be coming upgrade and that fresh earth will slow them even more. If we're lucky, and I mean damn lucky, we'll blow them to kingdom come, or at least roast their tails good. Okay now. Get your heads down. Here they come."

Henry Chambers took a last long look at his two sons, his throat constricting with a swelling pride as he noted the unflinching determination upon their too-young faces. His eyes roved slowly and wetly across the fields he'd spent his sweat on for so many years, finally coming to rest upon the big house he'd built with his own two hands.

He tried to visualize his Judith and the two girls, huddled together in the storm cellar, awaiting God only knew what—but he simply could not call up a vision of such an impossible thing. *What a funny thing*, he thought. What a funny thing to be happening to him and his on their own land and in their own country. It simply could not be happening. But it was.

The cloud of dust was no more than a city block away now. They would be coming over the rise any second now. *God help me!* he cried out in the anguish of his mind. *God help me do what I got to do!*

236

Several minutes before Wayne Chambers had spotted the dust cloud, a small armored column moved swiftly northwest along the highway out of Yazoo City, Mississippi. Then suddenly the column came to a quick and unexpected halt. The point jeep, which had a good hundred-yard lead on the heavier vehicles of the column, burned rubber on the deserted asphalt pavement for thirty feet or more before halting its forward motion.

Sergeant Paul Bartel, seated alongside the driver, rose to gaze back at the column. He conversed briefly with the C.O. through a two-way radio, then commanded the driver, "Okay, let's go back."

The little vehicle weaved wildly in reverse motion, coming to rest beside the scout car at the head of the column. Bartel stood up in the floor of the jeep and gazed back along the column, taking a mental inventory of the six light tanks and three troop-carriers, then he shifted puzzled eyes to the lieutenant who sat in the observation turret of the scout. "What's up, sir?" he asked.

The C.O. pointed to a rural mail box which was supported by an unpainted post just off the shoulder of the highway. A deeply rutted dirt road led off just beyond the mail box, disappearing over a small hill several hundred yards distant. "Must be a farmhouse up in there, maybe a bunch," the lieutenant said. "Go on up and spot for us. If there's a decent target, call back the coordinates. Otherwise just chop up what's there with your fifties and get on back here."

Sergeant Bartel grimaced distastefully. "One lousy farmhouse, Lieutenant?"

"One lousy pigpen, Sergeant, if that's all there is up there. You know our orders and you've got yours. Now get to it."

Bartel touched his helmet in a limp salute, slid into the seat, and motioned resignedly to the driver. The jeep leaped forward, swerved onto the dusty roadway, then jounced along in second gear up the incline.

To Sergeant Bartel, this was not a war. Nothing in all his years of training had prepared him for the horrors he'd witnessed this day. The lieutenant was sure a cold one.

Hell, Bartel had seen that road when they passed. But, God, what was going to be gained by slaughtering everything they passed? What a great new start for the bright new future of the American Negro! Be happy, children. Laugh, sing, and be merry. You're dancing in a graveyard—but we can't help that. The whole damn country is a graveyard. A couple hundred million dead people are under your feet, and that squishy feeling between your toes is nothing but millions of gallons of whitey blood trying to soak into the earth. It never will, of course. It'll never soak in. You'll be walking around ankle deep in blood for the rest of your lives. But we couldn't help that. That's what war is like.

He swiveled about to glare back into the motionless line of armor on the highway and he sighed. This courageous and powerful armored light attack force was gonna slaughter the enemy—boy wasn't that something! Probably one lousy farmhouse, probably an old weatherbeaten man and woman and a bunch of raggedy kids. And this was the enemy. Hell, what an enemy. These people out here probably didn't even know the war was on. Bartel smiled grimly, smarting at the taste of dust in his mouth. The cause of liberty and equality must not falter. The sergeant grunted and tried to find a comfortable hand grip. They topped the rise and plunged down the other side, the little jeep shuddering and jouncing along the washboard roadbed, then started up another gentler incline.

Bartel stood up, gripping the top of the windshield with both hands, trying to get above the dust and get a better look at the terrain ahead. The private who was manning the rear-fifty swore loudly. He was all but obscured in the backwash of finely powdered dust being kicked up by the jeep's wheels.

"Slow the sunabitch down!" the gunner cried. "You're bouncing my balls off!"

The driver grinned and shifted into first gear, slowing to a crawl. Bartel leaned forward suddenly and waved violently at the driver. The jeep jerked to a halt, swinging almost broadside across the road as the brakes grabbed and held.

The Sergeant stepped onto the road and took several paces up the incline. They had halted just a few feet short of what appeared to be a mudhole. He was thankful he'd seen it in time. Nothing he'd like worse than getting stuck in the mud in this forsaken spot. He dropped to one knee and dug his fingers into the soft earth, plumbing for depth, then withdrew his hand quickly in surprise and raised it to his nose. Gasoline? A gasoline-soaked country road?

He slowly stood up and cautiously surveyed the surroundings. He noted the steel barrels alongside the road a short distance ahead, stared at them thoughtfully for a long moment, then he walked around to the driver's side and stood silently rolling the wet earth between thumb and forefinger.

"What's the matter?" the driver inquired, dabbing at dusted eyes.

"Ambush, I bet," Bartel said softly. "Don't let on we know. Act casual. Behind those barrels up there, I'd say." He took a backward step and placed a hand on the gunner's knee. "See those barrels up there on the right, Smitty? Well just look for now, but get that baby-doll of yours limber and ready and do it casual-like."

The Sergeant went to the rear of the jeep and pretended to inspect the undercarriage, then he moved back alongside the gunner. "When Ace and me hit the dirt, you tear hell out of those barrels and everything within five yards to either side. Ace and me will be sweeping in from the flanks, so keep us in sight. Now. Wait until I get around to the front. I want them to think I'm going around to climb back in. Get ready. The instant we hit the dirt, you cut loose—and man don't stop to wonder what you're shooting at, just do it."

He stepped back to stand beside the driver. "Lucky we're not fireballs already," he said. "Swing your feet out, Acey, but keep the upper part of your body straight ahead until you jump. Roll under the jeep if you—"

The world suddenly seemed to come aglow, as though a new sun had been added to the heavens, halting Bartel's instructions in mid-speech. The face of Ace Jenkens, behind the wheel of the jeep, glowed bright despite his heavy pigmentation. Jenkins' jaw dropped and he was staring mutely into the sky behind the Sergeant's head. Bartel whirled around and immediately clapped a hand across his face.

"Cover your eyes!" he cried. "Don't look at it!"

But the Sergeant did not heed his own warning. Spreading his fingers carefully, he peered through at the awesome mushroom-shaped cloud of fire boiling up into the higher heavens, growing and spreading in silent majesty, many miles to the northeast.

The gunner had come to his feet with both hands clenched in front of him, his lips moving soundlessly in unspoken tribute which mere mortals reserve for absolute power. In a small corner of his awareness, Bartel heard the shrilly terrified piping of a young boy's voice crying, "What is it? Dad, what is that?"

Then *the sound* arrived, like ten thousand freight trains thundering overhead at once.

"Hit the deck!" Bartel screamed. He flung himself forward into the new-plowed earth and burrowed frantically with his body, burying his face nose-down in the smelly mixture.

Something seemed to be tearing at his backside. He pulled his face out of the mud, gulped air wildly, then fought the unseen centrifugal-like force to get his head back down again. His right leg was suddenly ripped from the mud mooring and he found himself tumbling madly across an open field.

Then, as suddenly as it had come, it was gone. Bartel raised to an elbow and gazed into the sky. The ball of fire was still there and still expanding, but it seemed higher than before. The sound continued, but distant now and like constant thunder.

Bartel shivered, shook his head viciously, ran fingers into both ears and manipulated his numbed organs, his jaws straining in an effort to unblock the ears. His eyes smarted and he felt like he'd been trampled by a herd of steers. He pulled himself erect, examined his person gingerly, then set off at a slow and uneven trot across the field and towards the jeep. His two companions were nowhere to be seen.

Three white people stood in the roadway, gazing with hand-shaded eyes into the heavens.

One of these, a middle-aged man wearing Levi's and a flannel shirt, turned to stare dumbly at the sergeant.

"What do you make of it?" Henry Chambers asked the black soldier.

"Damnedest thing I ever saw," Bartel exclaimed.

"But what do you think it means?"

"Damned if I know. Carried me into the middle of that field over there. I don't see my buddies anywhere. You see them?"

The man was shaking his head and continuing to stare into the sky. He told the soldier, "*We* were lucky. We had good cover in that ditch. Thought for a minute it was going to pull us all out, though. Would've sucked Petey out for sure if *I* hadn't had hold of him. Man . . . would you *look* at that thing. What the hell could it mean?"

"It's the Asians, Dad," Wayne Chambers solemnly declared. "They're attacking us."

"God I bet . . ." Bartel said.

"Look look!" yelled young Pete. He was pointing toward the northwest, in the general direction of Arkansas, where another mushroom was boiling into view.

"Guess I'd better get back to my outfit," the soldier muttered.

"Good God, what could it mean?" Henry Chambers asked in a horrified voice.

"I guess it means we got a *real* war on our hands now," the Sergeant told him. "Listen. Are you folks going to be all right here? I mean . . . maybe we could give you shelter."

"No . . . no . . . we'll be okay. We have the storm cellar. Thanks, we'll be all right." Chambers was like a man in trance. "Good Lord, *look* at those things!"

"Well, I better find my buddies and rejoin." Bartel fidgeted slightly, realizing for the first time the bizarre nature of this conversation on a rutted farm road. "Uh, listen. If you folks need it, we got a field hospital outside Yazoo City. You come there if you have to. Hear?"

"Yes, I hear," said Henry Chambers.

The black sergeant turned his back on the white people and walked dazedly to his jeep. It wasn't until he'd crawled behind the wheel that he realized that his face was caked with evil-smelling mud. He clawed at it with his fingertips as he backed the little vehicle down the torturous road. He leaned on the horn, hoping his driver and gunner were somewhere within earshot and able to hear.

And far to the south, another sun appeared in the sky.

CHAPTER 9

Some ten minutes before Sergeant Bartel collected his dazed and battered comrades, Abraham Williams pushed a microphone back across his desk and sagged wearily forward onto his elbows. "It's all lost, Ned," he told the radio engineer. "Just when we had it all wrapped up, just when a bright new tomorrow was in sight for the black man, the damned hooligans messed it up again."

"Sort of like history repeating itself, Mr. Williams," the engineer replied quietly.

"I backed the wrong men down there. Damn me. I let the wrong element get in control down there."

"Well . . . you're not God, Mr. Williams."

"That's for sure," Williams snorted. "I guess I thought I was, though. I ordained myself one and look what it's turned into."

The engineer was trying to be comforting. He obviously did not believe his own words as he said, "Maybe something will happen yet. Maybe it can still turn out okay."

Williams raised his head with a grim smile. "And maybe not. You heard them, Ned. You heard the way they talked to me."

"Well . . ."

"All of them. Jacksonville, New Orleans, Atlanta, Birmingham, all of them. They've lined up solidly behind Hatty. The *tong*, Bogan calls them. Small men of narrow vision who cannot handle power. How much longer can the world survive such men, Ned? Dammit. *Dammit*! I don't know what to do now. I've forgotten how to pray."

"Aw, you never forget how to do that, Mr. Williams. Tell you what . . . I'll get us some coffee." The engineer departed, disappearing around a Rube Goldberg arrangement of radio sending and receiving equipment.

Williams stared around him, as though seeing for the first time the immensity of what had been accomplished by a defeated people in such an incredibly short time. All the years, all the work, all the ingenuity, all the prayers, all being tossed away for one glorious day of vengeance and insanity.

He pushed a pencil idly about the desk, wondering how Winston was taking the situation. How many hours ago had it been that he'd told the gutsy whitey that he needn't worry about Negro cooperation? Williams grunted with the memory of that scene. A letter of authority. Mr. Guts had wanted a letter of authority. Well, Winston was on the spot now. Maybe he'd come up with something. Only God knew what . . . but just maybe the man would come up with something.

Ned Clemmons came scooting around the corner, coffee slopping from two cups. "Mike Winston is coming up on television," he announced excitedly. "Radio too. They're clearing everything off all the broadcast channels, telling everyone to stand by for an important announcement from the White House."

Williams lunged out of his chair and followed Clemmons into the lounge. He had just re-settled on a leather couch, a cup of coffee at his knee, when Michael Winston was introduced and the familiar face of his friend, the ex-nigger-tender, filled the big TV screen.

Winston had grown already, Williams decided, or else TV made people look different. A new expression seemed to frame his eyes, the lines about his mouth were firmer, there was even something different in the slope of the shoulders.

"Approximately twenty minutes ago," Winston began, without preamble, "or at about 4:10 P.M., Eastern Standard Time, I ordered the Chief of the Automated Defense Command to launch a nuclear attack upon the United States of America." Then he paused, gazing steadily into the camera, apparently to give the nation's viewers a chance to assimilate the startling announcement."

He looks ready to eat nails, Williams mused. *Did he say nuclear attack?*"

"Before I conclude this announcement, the citizens of some of our southern states shall see evidence to confirm what I have just said. Now pay attention to my words and hear me all the way through. I have had no time to prepare this statement, so the words will not be fancy—only factual. These nuclear devices are to be triggered at extremely high altitudes. They will cause little or no damage to the land areas. There is no intent to harm any citizen, nor to damage any property. That is, in this first salvo. I repeat, in this *first* salvo. Call it a shot across the bow, if you wish. A warning salvo.

"The government of the United States, of which I am at this moment the sole authority, serves notice that it will not stand idly by and see the slaughter of Americans—whatever the race, whatever the reasons, whatever the provocation. It must stop, and it must stop immediately.

"I have just been given the sign that the first missiles have been launched. To any of you who cannot place love of country above personal grievances and animosities, I am telling you to look to the southern skies. *There* is more destruction than your mind can grasp. *There* is more power than you could experience in a lifetime. *There* is more authority than all the hatreds in the nation can assemble collectively. And *there* is the power and the authority of the United States government.

"And now I speak directly to the citizens of Florida,

245

Mississippi, Georgia, Alabama, Arkansas and South Carolina. Stop the killing! Black man, go back to your military base. White man, go to your home. Do so immediately. I am a surgeon, and at this moment you are a cancerous growth upon the tail of this country. I will not hesitate to cut off the offending growth—tail and all—if that is what is required to save the rest of the body.

"The next salvo of nuclear-tipped missiles fired by direction of this government will not be across the bow. They will not explode harmlessly in the heavens. They will come in at their level of maximum effect.

"This ultimatum has already been communicated to Negro Army Commands. This is the only means I have of communicating with the white community. You've got until five o'clock, Eastern time. Five o'clock. That's all the time you've got."

Winston glared balefully into the camera for a brief moment of silence, then he whirled and walked away. Howard Silverman took his place in front of the camera and began amplifying Winston's remarks.

Ned Clemmons turned an owlish stare to Abraham Williams. "God damn," he said in an awed voice. "An atomic shot across the bow. What do you think of that?"

"That gutsy bastard," Williams said, grinning. "He's found his letter of authority."

CHAPTER 10

Michael Winston was at his office window, one hand clenching the heavy folds of drapery, staring silently out upon the southern skies. His shoulders were slumped wearily, his shirt open at the neck and tie dangling, his eyes red-rimmed with anxiety and fatigue.

He turned away from the window and let his eyes travel slowly about the provisional office of the United States. Jackson Bogan, in rumpled khakis, reclined stiffly on a leather couch. Howard Silverman sat slumped across the telephone turret, his head resting on crossed arms. Colonel Stanley sat stiffly in a straight wooden chair, a red telephone on his lap.

That red phone had been in use a few hours earlier. Peking had called to announce the discontinuance of their "war games exercise" and to inform the new U.S. government that China stood solidly beside them in their bid for freedom. The head of the provisional government had thanked Peking for their good wishes and had assured them that the U.S. would do its best in the future to relieve the Asian peoples in their food crisis.

But now the red phone and all phones sat silent in disuse. Other than Winston, Normal Ritter appeared to be the one man aboard with his eyes open. The tough little

247

redhead was reared-back in a swivel chair, his feet crossed atop a draw-leaf of the executive desk, his eyes on the man at the window. "You look like hell," he told Winston quietly. "You want some coffee?"

The head country-tender shook his head negative. "What time is it?" he croaked.

"It's three o'clock in the morning," Ritter replied. "Ten hours and ten minutes since the truce."

"I had them on the run," Winston said wearily. "I shouldn't have let them hold this parley before a complete withdrawal. They've got two more hours. They damn sure better get with it. I'm not giving them another damn inch."

"Sure you don't want some coffee?"

"No, but I'd like a cigarette."

A loud buzzer sounded. The room leapt to immediate attention. Bogan was bolt upright on the couch. Ritter's feet pounded to the floor. Stanley half rose, then sat back down. Howard Silverman lurched toward a toggle switch on the turret. He flipped the switch and gave a high-sign to Winston.

Winston picked up a telephone at his side, held it to his head, and his lips moved in quiet, barely audible sounds. "All right," he said. "All right, yes, I accept that. You have those assurances. Of course. Yes, I'll be down early next week."

He hung up the instrument, smiled, let his eyes rest lightly on each of his companions, and announced, "The council of war is over. They accept our assurances of full redress of grievances. They will commence withdrawal to military bases immediately. Abe Williams is down there. That's him I was talking to. He says it's A-OK."

A loud exhalation of pent breaths sighed through the room. Norman Ritter was in an ear-to-ear grin. "Well you bluffed the hell out of *those* guys, didn't you," he exclaimed happily.

Then the grin faded and he asked, "You *were* bluffing, weren't you?"

Winston sank wearily onto the desk and drew a leg over the edge to massage the ankle. How long and how short a time ago it had been since he'd bruised that ankle, fighting

his way free of Tom Fairchild. And suppose he hadn't . . .
suppose he'd meekly allowed them to put him away? What
course would history have taken?

"I honestly don't know, Norm, if I was bluffing or not,"
he told Ritter. He pulled an empty cigarette package from
his pocket, crumpled it, dropped it into the wastebasket,
ran a hand across his eyes and pinched his lips in his palm.
"Hell. Out of cigarettes. Out of gas. Out of everything. I
suggest we all retire, gentlemen. It appears that the ship of
state will float, even with the likes of us at the helm."

Winston walked out of the room without a backward
look.

Norman Ritter announced to no one in particular, "That
guy *still* scares the hell out of me."

General Bogan moved slowly to the door. He turned to
gaze back upon Ritter. "With good reason," he said
simply, then went on out.

"A principled man is a scare-some thing, Mr. Ritter,"
Silverman intoned soberly. Then his eyes lit on Ritter and
he winked at him and added, "And a *thoroughly* principled
man, like our Mr. Winston, scares the hell out of me too,
my friend."

EPILOGUE

It is a matter of historical record that Michael Andrew Winston became the first President of the re-constituted United States in the year 2000. Historians write with warmth and pride of that eight-year tenure following the day when America jogged around a dangerous corner of world history.

Awakening from a quarter-century of drug-like slumber, the United States reasserted itself as a leading world power early in the twenty-first century, and proceeded unfalteringly to her present position of greatness and prestige among the world commonwealth of nations. To the quiet but insistent pressure of the national attitude of "do it *because* it hurts," a phrase attributed to President Winston, America led the way to the restoration of human values throughout the world, and to a balancing of planetary resources for the well being of all peoples.

Boundaries of geography, race, religion, politics, and of basic human personality still exist—but, *thank heaven for our differences*, as President Winston often remarked.

Senator Abraham Lincoln Williams had a rather dramatic way of expressing that same idea, as he so effectively did in his now famous senate speech of 2005: "It is our unity of differences that make us unique. It is our harmony in discord that makes us great. It is the mutual respect and esteem with which individual Americans regard one another that establishs the framework of mortality and justice insuring us all a sane today, a sure tomorrow, and an America everlasting. May God respect us every one."

The End

the Executioner

The gutsiest, most exciting hero in years. Imagine a guy at war with the Godfather and all his Mafioso relatives! He's rough, he's deadly, he's a law unto himself — nothing and nobody stops him!

THE EXECUTIONER SERIES by DON PENDLETON

Order		Title	Book #	Price
————	# 1	WAR AGAINST THE MAFIA	P401	$1.25
————	# 2	DEATH SQUAD	P402	$1.25
————	# 3	BATTLE MASK	P403	$1.25
————	# 4	MIAMI MASSACRE	P404	$1.25
————	# 5	CONTINENTAL CONTRACT	P405	$1.25
————	# 6	ASSAULT ON SOHO	P406	$1.25
————	# 7	NIGHTMARE IN NEW YORK	P407	$1.25
————	# 8	CHICAGO WIPEOUT	P408	$1.25
————	# 9	VEGAS VENDETTA	P409	$1.25
————	#10	CARIBBEAN KILL	P410	$1.25
————	#11	CALIFORNIA HIT	P411	$1.25
————	#12	BOSTON BLITZ	P412	$1.25
————	#13	WASHINGTON I.O.U.	P413	$1.25
————	#14	SAN DIEGO SIEGE	P414	$1.25
————	#15	PANIC IN PHILLY	P415	$1.25
————	#16	SICILIAN SLAUGHTER	P552	$1.25
————	#17	JERSEY GUNS	P328	$1.25
————	#18	TEXAS STORM	P353	$1.25
————	#19	DETROIT DEATHWATCH	P419	$1.25
————	#20	NEW ORLEANS KNOCKOUT	P475	$1.25
————	#21	FIREBASE SEATTLE	P499	$1.25
————	#22	HAWAIIAN HELLGROUND	P625	$1.25
————	#23	ST. LOUIS SHOWDOWN	P687	$1.25

TO ORDER

Please check the space next to the book/s you want, send this order form together with your check or money order, include the price of the book/s and 25¢ for handling and mailing to:

PINNACLE BOOKS, INC. / P.O. Box 4347
Grand Central Station / New York, N.Y. 10017

☐ CHECK HERE IF YOU WANT A FREE CATALOG

I have enclosed $————— check—————or money order—————
as payment in full. No C.O.D.'s

Name——————————————————————————

Address————————————————————————

City————————— State————— Zip—————
(Please allow time for delivery)

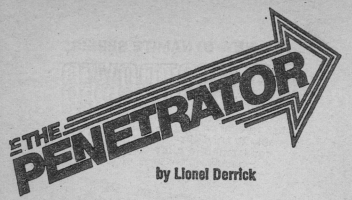

THE PENETRATOR

by Lionel Derrick

Mark Hardin. Discharged from the army, after service in Vietnam. His military career was over. But *his* war was just beginning. His reason for living and reason for dying become the same—to stamp out crime and corruption wherever he finds it. He is deadly; he is unpredictable; and he is dedicated. He is The Penetrator!

Read all of him in:

Order		Title	Book No.	Price
_____	#1	THE TARGET IS H	P236	.95
_____	#2	BLOOD ON THE STRIP	P237	.95
_____	#3	CAPITOL HELL	P318	.95
_____	#4	HIJACKING MANHATTAN	P338	.95
_____	#5	MARDI GRAS MASSACRE	P378	.95
_____	#6	TOKYO PURPLE	P434	$1.25
_____	#7	BAJA BANDIDOS	P502	$1.25
	#8	THE NORTHWEST CONTRACT	P540	$1.25
_____	#9	DODGE CITY BOMBERS	P627	$1.25
_____	#10	THE HELLBOMB FLIGHT	P690	$1.25

TO ORDER

Please check the space next to the book/s you want, send this order form together with your check or money order, include the price of the book/s and 25¢ for handling and mailing to:

PINNACLE BOOKS, INC. / P.O. Box 4347
Grand Central Station / New York, N.Y. 10017

☐ CHECK HERE IF YOU WANT A FREE CATALOG

I have enclosed $_____ check_____ or money order_____
as payment in full. No C.O.D.'s

Name_____

Address_____

City_____ State_____ Zip_____
(Please allow time for delivery)